"I slept very little last night, Silver," Nicholas said.

"Half the time I was cursing you, and the other half I was lying there remembering how you looked standing naked before me, taunting me. Did you think about that after I left you?"

She stiffened. She didn't want to think of either her gesture of defiance or the look on Nicholas's face as he'd sat there like some golden-haired god watching her disrobe. The memory made her ache deep inside and quickened the beat of her heart.

Nicholas dropped to his knees before her. "I think you wanted me to touch you as much I wanted to last night. I imagined running my hands over your body, caressing you until you moaned—"

"Stop!" Her voice was shaking and she had to take a deep breath to steady it. What was he doing to her? He hadn't touched her, yet her body felt aroused. Desperately, she said, "Go away. I don't want you here."

He sat back on his heels and smiled. "Yes, you do. You want me to carry you to that bed and love you again and again . . ."

"No, no. I don't." Her cheeks flushed with color. "You're nothing to me."

"Except a man who can please you. A man who can stop you from burning. Because you are burning, Silver. But don't worry. I won't let you burn for long. . . ."

THE DELANEYS, THE UNTAMED YEARS

Wild Silver

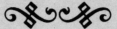

Iris Johansen

BANTAM BOOKS

TORONTO • NEW YORK • LONDON • SYDNEY • AUCKLAND

WILD SILVER

A Bantam Book / May 1988

ISBN 0-553-21898-0

Published simultaneously in the United States and Canada

Bantam Books are published by Bantam Books, a division of
Bantam Doubleday Dell Publishing Group, Inc. Its trademark,
consisting of the words "Bantam Books" and the portrayal of a
rooster, is Registered in U.S. Patent and Trademark Office and in
other countries. Marca Registrada. Bantam Books, 666 Fifth
Avenue, New York, New York 10103.

PRINTED IN THE UNITED STATES OF AMERICA

O   0 9 8 7 6 5 4 3 2 1

Wild Silver

Prologue: The Firebird

The Kuban, Russia
November 18, 1863

Nicholas first saw the bird when he crested the hill. The great bird hovered like a phantom against the sullen red glare of the winter sunset, seeming to hang between heaven and earth, belonging to neither, scornful of both.

Nicholas stopped at the summit of the hill, his breath coming in harsh gasps, his heart beating painfully in his breast. The wind was sharp, cutting through his ragged tunic and striking the open wounds on his back as viciously as Igor's knout had. He would rest for just a moment before descending to the steppe.

He eased the rawhide straps of the harness off his shoulders where they were cutting into his flesh. What difference did it make anyway? It would be a miracle if they didn't die before they reached the other side of the desolate steppe ahead. The lowering blue-gray clouds on the horizon could mean only snow and chilling cold within a matter of hours, and they had not even the protection of boots. It was insanity to keep trying to ward off the death Igor had decreed for them.

"Leave me."

Nicholas turned to look at the man on the makeshift stretcher he had fashioned of pine branches bound together with strips of rawhide. "No."

Mikhail slowly shook his head, his wild mop of hair shining bloodred under the rays of the setting sun. "You will die. I am too big for you to pull like this. Without me you might make it to shelter before the snows."

"I'm to walk away from you?" Nicholas asked savagely. "Simply to leave you lying here with two broken legs and a storm coming?"

Mikhail shrugged his massive shoulders. "The cold death is not so bad. I will just go to sleep and not wake up. You saved me from a much worse death. It is enough."

Suffocating darkness. Nicholas drew a deep breath and quickly suppressed the memory. He didn't want to remember those moments before Igor had granted them mercy. Mercy? The irony caused his lips to curve in a mirthless smile. Yet Igor had actually thought he was being merciful to set them out in the wilderness with no boots, no food or water, and a storm sweeping toward the steppes. Cossack mercy. Cossack justice. Survive and triumph or die. It was a lesson Nicholas had learned well in his years with Igor.

And he *would* survive. He would not give up the battle. He smiled down at Mikhail. "We won't die, my friend. We've gone through too much to let Igor kill us now." Again he tightened the leather straps of the harness across his shoulders. "We have only a little farther to go."

"You don't even know where we are. Our only chance is to reach the Sea of Azov and take shelter. If we go in any other direction, we will die in the hills or on the steppes." Mikhail paused, then said once more, softly, "Leave me, Nicholas."

Nicholas didn't look at him. "Don't be foolish. I may need the heat from that big body of yours to keep me warm if the storm does come. I'm only being selfish."

"Nicholas—"

Nicholas shook his head. "No, Mikhail, we go together." A sudden reckless smile appeared on his face. "As for which direction, suppose we leave it up to the firebird." He pointed to the bird still silhouetted against the horizon. "We'll let her lead us to the Sea of Azov."

"That is not a firebird; it is a hawk."

"How can you tell from this distance? It could be a firebird sent to lead us to a land of milk and honey."

"You are mad, Nicholas," Mikhail murmured, his voice full of affection.

"Why?" For an instant, bitterness, pain, and sadness turned the boy's expression bleak. "It's as reasonable as anything else in our lives at the moment. We'll watch our pretty firebird to see which direction she flies and follow her benign guidance."

"It is a hawk, Nicholas." Still, Mikhail's gaze

compulsively followed Nicholas's to the horizon. "Only a hawk."

The bird suddenly spread its great dark wings and soared proudly, gracefully, a wild monarch of the heavens it ruled. Against the crimson sky the silhouette took on the aura of the sunset itself, and for a moment its wings looked as though they were outlined in tongues of flame. The two men watched in fascination as the bird swooped and tumbled on the air currents in an ecstasy of flight and then turned and swooped off toward the east.

Nicholas laughed softly. "You're wrong, my friend. We go east."

He lurched forward, dragging the heavy stretcher behind him, the lacerated flesh of his back throbbing as the muscles beneath it strained with his herculean effort to save himself and Mikhail . . . and to follow the firebird.

1

New Orleans
May 5, 1874

"I'd like to see his highness, Prince Nicholas Savron." Simon Bentsen strode up the gangplank of the *Mississippi Rose,* his gaze fixed distastefully on the sandy-haired young man in rumpled denim trousers and shirt-sleeves who was half sitting, half leaning on the wooden rail of the boiler deck. A coarse stubble darkened the riverman's lean cheeks and the scent of perfume and brandy emanated from his unkempt clothing. "I was told at the Hotel Royal that his highness had left there four days ago and taken up residence here."

"Four days," the young man repeated dazedly. "Lordy, has it really been four days?"

The fellow was obviously tipsy and Bentsen's disapproval deepened. If a man in his employ were in this condition in the middle of the day, he would reprimand him severely at the least; more likely, he would dismiss him. "I'm Simon Bentsen of the Randall Investigative Agency. I have a report for his highness. If you'll tell me where to find him, I won't trouble you further."

"No trouble." The young man straightened away from the rail, swaying unsteadily for a moment before giving Bentsen a half bow. "My name's Robert Danfold, pilot of the *Mississippi Rose*. Glad to make your acquaintance. I think Nicky is in his cabin."

"Nicky?" Bentsen inquired. "You're a friend of his highness?"

"I guess so," Danfold said vaguely as he carefully negotiated the wide staircase leading to the next deck. "I never met him until he took me over four days ago."

"Took you over?"

"When he won the *Rose* from Mr. Bassinger." Danfold gazed blearily but proudly around the deck.

It was a craft worthy of pride, Bentsen thought. Indeed, he'd admired it from the riverbank: it was long and white and impressive; two tall plumed smokestacks towered over its three decks and a flag on the jackstaff whipped lazily in the breeze. An ornate golden rose was emblazoned on the huge white paddlebox above the name of the riverboat.

"Where the *Rose* goes, I go," Danfold declared.

"I doubt his highness will entrust this boat to you if you continue to overindulge in this fashion."

Danfold glanced at him over his shoulder, his hazel eyes no longer vague but sharp with annoyance. "We're docked, dammit. I don't touch a drop when I'm on the job. I not only just got my captain's papers, but I'm the best damn pilot on the river and don't you forget it."

"It's none of my concern," Bentsen said. He wouldn't have wasted time talking to this fellow if his nerves hadn't been frayed by worry over his client's reaction to the report he was about to give. The information his agents had acquired was flimsy at best; still, he probably could bluff his way through the interview, for any man who would permit drunkenness in his employees couldn't be too difficult to handle. "And I'll hardly bother to remember anything that concerns either the *Mississippi Rose* or yourself. I merely thought it best to issue a warning. Prince Savron is a very rich and powerful man and accustomed to instant obedience and decorum from his employees."

"Decorum?" Danfold blinked. "Nicky?"

"And I'm sure he'd prefer you to be more formal in your address. Russian nobility is very finicky about etiquette."

"Formal." Danfold nodded solemnly, his lids veiling his eyes. "Yessiree, Mr. Bentsen. I'll try to remember that." He opened a handsome mahogany door. "This leads to the saloon. The master stateroom can be reached by either the saloon or the hurricane deck, but this is quicker. By the way, when did you meet Prince Nicholas?"

"We've communicated only by letter but—" Bentsen broke off as he stepped through the entrance of a saloon stretching an astounding three hundred feet in length, its wall ringing with the music of a lively waltz. "Good Lord, what's going on?"

"A party," Danfold said blandly as he closed the door of the saloon behind him. "To celebrate his

highness's acquisition of the *Mississippi Rose*. Nicky—
I mean, his highness—likes parties."

Party? Orgy more accurately described the goings-
on in the saloon, Bentsen thought sourly. A four-piece
orchestra was playing with enthusiasm at the far end
of the long room, and the scent of cigar smoke,
perfume, and alcohol permeated the air. The saloon
was crowded with a motley collection of well-dressed
New Orleans bucks, rivermen in denim trousers and
coarse cotton shirts, and pretty ladies in satin gowns
in all the hues of the rainbow. Then, as he saw one of
the gentlemen who was dancing with a particularly
buxom beauty pull down her bodice and bare her
naked breasts, he mentally substituted the term
women for *ladies*. Orgy, indeed!

He averted his gaze from the man who was now
nuzzling the blond woman's nipple. "A party at one
o'clock in the afternoon?"

"Well, it started at night." Danfold crossed the
saloon to the door of a stateroom with a beautifully
executed painting of a peaceful river scene. "Four
nights ago when Nicky won the *Rose* in a poker game
in the cardroom at Madam LaRue's place, he invited
all the customers and Madam's girls to come down for
a celebration." He nodded at the man who was occupied with the mammary attractions of the blonde.
"Even Mr. Bassinger." He knocked on the door. "I
guess he thought Mr. Bassinger needed a little cheer-
ing up after losing the *Rose*. It's a damn fine boat."

Fine was an understatement, Bentsen thought,
looking around the enormous saloon. The high white

and gold ceiling was divided into large diamond
shapes by the crossing of Gothic arches. Above were
large stained-glass skylights through which streamed
a rainbow of colored light that ignited a fiery glitter
on the sparkling crystal of the twelve large chandeliers. A plush crimson carpet ran the entire length
of the saloon, and the doors of the innumerable
staterooms lining the main cabin on either side were
embellished with beautifully painted landscapes similar to the one on the door in front of him.

The door abruptly swung open in answer to Danfold's knock.

Immense. The word immediately struck Bentsen as
he gazed at the huge man who had opened the door.
He was dressed in a white tunic, black trousers, and
polished knee-length boots, and was at least seven
feet tall. With blazing red hair crowning his head like
scarlet snow cresting a mountain, and his features as
rough as the crags of a rocky summit, he was a
breathtaking figure.

"Mikhail Kuzdief, this is Mr. Bentsen of the Randall
Investigative Agency," Danfold said. "He wants to see
Nicky." He snapped his fingers. "Damn, I keep forget-
ting. He wants to see his highness, Prince Nicholas
Savron."

A low, sobbing moan, undeniably feminine, drifted
from the interior of the stateroom beyond Mikhail's
broad shoulders.

"Unless he's busy," Danfold added hurriedly.

"He is busy." Mikhail's impassive brown gaze
rested on Bentsen's face. "But he is almost finished

and he will not mind if you both come in." He threw open the door and stepped aside. "Sit down. Would you like a glass of wine while you wait?"

"What?" Shocked, Bentsen stared at the wide bed across the room on which two naked bodies were engaged in an activity best suited for that piece of furniture. The woman moaned again and the man paused to glance down at her and chuckle. Bentsen jerked his gaze back to the big Russian. "Perhaps I'd better wait outside."

"Nonsense, sit down and watch."

Bentsen hastily looked around. An overstuffed brocade chair to the left of the door was occupied by a slender, young man who was elegantly garbed. One leg, encased in tight fawn-colored gabardine trousers, was thrown casually over the arm of the chair and swung indolently. "Allow me to introduce myself. I am Valentin Marinov." He gestured with the crystal goblet in his hand toward the man on the bed. "And that's Nicky. I'm afraid he's too busy at the moment to stand up and make his bow."

"I see. Suppose I wait on deck until he's less . . . occupied."

"Why?" Marinov's brow rose. "It's damnably hot up there. The heat in your city of New Orleans is almost unbearable in the afternoon." He gestured to the chair beside him. "You'll be much more comfortable here. I assure you Nicky will not object."

Bentsen hesitated. "The lady . . ."

"The 'lady' likes an audience," Marinov murmured. "Five nights ago at Madam LaRue's she satisfied three gentlemen simultaneously at one of Madam's little staged presentations. Liza tells us that being watched adds immeasurably to her excitement." He lifted the goblet to his lips. "Which is the reason Mikhail and I are here. Nicky always tries to please his ladies."

"She does seem to be enjoying herself." Danfold grinned. "And it tends to make a man's juices rise, doesn't it?" He turned to leave. "I thought I was too tired to enjoy myself anymore in that fashion, but I suddenly feel refreshed. I believe I'll go back to the party. Good day, gentlemen."

The door swung shut behind him.

Bentsen hesitated and then moved to seat himself in the chair Marinov had indicated, trying to keep from looking at the writhing figures on the bed. "This is most . . . unusual." He accepted the glass of wine Mikhail Kuzdief handed him. "I have a report to make and—" The woman gave a low, keening cry and his gaze flew to the bed before he could stop himself. Good Lord, he was actually becoming aroused. He had never been present at any of the bordello presentations of the type Marinov had mentioned, but they couldn't have been more erotic than the scene he was witnessing now.

Sheer white draperies were drawn around the canopy bed, but the veiling concealed very little from view. Sunlight poured into the room from the long window across the stateroom, piercing the filmy curtains, touching Nicholas Savron's hair with a nimbus of gold and highlighting the powerful muscles of his naked bronzed body as he moved over the woman beneath him.

He could see very little of the woman, but the prince was really quite beautiful, Bentsen thought. He was immediately as embarrassed by the adjective that had occurred to him as he was by watching this intimate display. Yet, if he suppressed his discomfort, it was rather like observing a fine statue come to life. Savron was boldly masculine, his muscles developed to sleek perfection, his shoulders broad, his waist slim, his buttocks tight as they rippled with movement.

The prince was moving faster and Bentsen felt his own desire mounting. It was impossible not to imagine oneself in Savron's place held tight within the woman's body. He forced his gaze away and glanced around the room, trying desperately to distract himself. A thick plush beige carpet embossed with cream roses, fine mahogany furniture, peach-colored velvet draperies at the windows, and the canopy bed. A tufted velvet cushioned bench at the foot of the bed matched the olive green chair across the room. Murals painted on the polished pine walls . . .

Murals! Bentsen's eyes widened as he stared transfixed by the pictures painted on the walls.

"Quite decadent, aren't they?" Marinov chuckled. "Bassinger evidently enjoys several rather interesting perversions and decided to have them given a certain immortality. Nicky was very amused when he saw this cabin."

The murals were both lewd and explicit. "His highness appears to be easily amused."

"Sometimes," Marinov drawled. "He finds most things hard to take seriously these days." He smiled faintly as his gaze narrowed on Bentsen's flushed face. "Are you experiencing . . . difficulty? I'm sure Nicky would understand if you joined the party."

"Certainly not." Bentsen casually put his hat on his lap. "I'll wait."

Marinov shrugged. "As you like." He downed the last of the wine in his glass. "I was only being courteous. Nicky wouldn't want—"

The woman Marinov had referred to as Liza gave a guttural scream and Bentsen's hand tightened on the stem of his goblet. He kept his gaze fixed desperately on Marinov's face.

"I believe it's over." Marinov said. "More wine?"

"No, I have sufficient." Bentsen looked down into the clear depths of his glass. He heard a rustle, a low masculine laugh, and then the squeak of the bed. Mikhail moved past him toward the bed, his stride incredibly graceful for one so large. Bentsen took another sip of wine. When he finally looked back at the bed, a dark-haired woman was buttoning the bodice of a loose yellow silk robe and Nicholas Savron was slipping his arms into a long robe of emerald velvet held by Mikhail. The prince was a tall man, over six feet in height, but he looked slight compared to the bearlike Kuzdief.

Nicholas didn't bother to button the robe before he turned to the woman, a radiant smile illuminating his face and lending it a beguiling charm. It was the first time Bentsen had beheld his face and he received a small shock. The man had the indescribable beauty of a fallen angel, features nearly perfect except for those broad Slavic cheekbones and the sensual curve to his lower lip. The small imperfection was overshadowed by eyes that were midnight-dark, full of mystery and complexity. The man came closer to the ideal of human beauty than anyone Bentsen had ever seen. My God, no wonder the woman was gazing up at him with her lips parted, as if sunning herself in his radiance. The prince took her hand and kissed it lingeringly. "You were enchanting. I look forward to the next time, Liza."

"Yes . . . when?" the dark-haired woman asked bemusedly.

"Soon." He kissed her hand again before releasing it and stepping back. "Mikhail will escort you to your stateroom. I'll see you later in the saloon. *Au revoir, ma chère.*"

She blinked as if suddenly coming awake. "Uh, right." She drifted toward the door. "*Au rev*—whatever you said."

Mikhail ushered her out and closed the door.

"Well?" Marinov rose to his feet.

Nicholas Savron made a face. "You win." He reached into the pocket of his velvet robe and tossed Marinov a coin. "It's much more exciting watching such an exhibition than performing in one. Not only did it disturb my concentration, but I became so bored I could barely finish."

"You never become that bored. Little Liza evidently found it quite exciting."

"Unless she was just pretending." The prince's lips twisted cynically. "The fair sex is miles beyond us poor males in the practice of deceit."

"I wouldn't say that," Marinov drawled. "You treated that pretty whore as if she were a princess. Isn't that deceit?"

The prince laughed, his black eyes sparkling with amusement. "*Touché.* But remember, I sometimes treat princesses as if they were whores. It all evens out." He shrugged. "And besides, she had given me gifts. She asked nothing from me this time, and a woman who asks nothing is rare indeed. No doubt she will make up for it the next time." His glance shifted to Bentsen inquiringly. "And you are . . . ?"

Bentsen stood up hurriedly. "Simon Bentsen. We've had correspondence in regard to your investigation of your cousin's death."

Nicholas Savron nodded, his smile fading. "I trust you've come with more information than your previous emissaries," he said softly. "I'm becoming very impatient with your company's incompetence in this matter. It's been over a year since I received that letter from Durbin."

"Arizona Territory is still wild country, and the Delaneys are a powerful family," Bentsen said defensively. "We had to move slowly."

"At a snail's pace. If I had been able to obtain the Pinkerton Agency's services, I doubt if they would have been as inefficient."

The words were biting, and Bentsen felt a chill ripple down his spine. He considered himself a fair judge of men and he knew he had never met one more dangerous than this velvet-clad individual before him.

"That's why I left St. Petersburg and came to New Orleans. I decided it was necessary to hurry you along."

Bentsen moistened his lips with his tongue. "I believe I have the information you need."

"That's fortunate." Nicholas coolly examined Bentsen's face. "I sincerely hope so, Mr. Bentsen." Without waiting for an answer he turned and crossed the stateroom toward the washstand against the far wall. "Take Mr. Bentsen on deck, will you, Valentin? I think I need some fresh air. I'll join you shortly."

Marinov nodded lazily. "Delighted." He gestured to the door leading to the deck. "Mr. Bentsen."

Bentsen felt the need for air, too, and took several deep breaths as soon as the door closed behind them. He felt as if he'd been caged with a stalking lion. Strange, before the prince had faced and spoken to him he'd felt contemptuous of the man with his exhibitionism, his fine velvets, and his exquisite manners. Then, before his eyes, Savron had changed, deepened, taken on a gleaming cutting edge.

He walked to the rail and his hands closed tightly on the ornate wooden barrier. "His highness is an unusual man."

Marinov's gaze was shrewd as he strolled over to stand beside him. "You thought Nicky was a fool?" He shook his head. "Only when he wants to be. You might remember that fact. He can be quite deadly with either a sword or a pistol." He looked out at the still and muddy river. "Nicky's seldom intense about anything anymore, but he was fond of André. I think you'll find him a trifle explosive regarding the boy's death. I hope you don't disappoint him this time."

"Are you threatening me?" Bentsen asked, astounded.

Marinov shook his head. "Warning you." He smiled faintly. "I have a distaste for your hot, muggy weather here in New Orleans. It's been an interesting trip, but I want to go home to St. Petersburg. Tell Nicky what he needs to know and we can get this business over with."

"I agree." Savron's voice behind them caused both men to turn to face him. He was dressed now in polished black boots, a fine white linen shirt of faultless purity, and pale gray trousers whose sleek lines over his thighs and buttocks could be the work of only a master tailor. "Tell me what I want to know, Bentsen." He moved forward, his expression as grim as his tone was soft. "Was Dominic Delaney responsible for my cousin's hanging?"

"He was definitely involved in his death."

"That isn't what I asked you."

Bentsen drew a deep breath. "You don't understand. In towns like Hell's Bluff, people don't talk to strangers. Our agents had great difficulty finding out even the simplest facts."

"I'm interested in only one fact. Did Delaney goad

that crowd into hanging André as Durbin's letter states?"

"Possibly. He was there at the hanging and he paid for the funeral."

"Guilt?"

"Dominic Delaney doesn't have a reputation that would lead one to believe he has a conscience," Bentsen said dryly. "He was an outlaw for almost ten years before his family managed to buy him a pardon."

"A criminal," Savron said slowly. "Then Durbin's letter probably was true. What did you find out about Durbin?"

Bentsen looked surprised, then uncertain. "Why . . . nothing. You didn't ask us to investigate anything but the circumstances surrounding André Marzonoff's death."

A flicker of impatience touched Savron's features. "*Merde!* Do I have to spell out everything for you? Durbin must have had his reasons for writing that letter beyond being a 'friend of justice' as he called himself." He smiled crookedly. "A man seldom bestirs himself for the sake of justice. It was more likely for Durbin's sake. Is that all you know?"

"Dominic Delaney's wife-to-be and his fifteen-year-old niece, Silver, were present at the lynching."

"A cozy evening of family entertainment." Savron's lips curled with distaste. "Bloodthirsty bitches. I would have thought watching a man die by hanging would be a little too much even for the most hardened woman. I wonder what they would think of the guillotine." He frowned. "You're giving me damn little solid evidence on which to make a decision."

"Decision?"

"Whether or not to kill Dominic Delaney." The prince's reply was almost casual. "I suppose I'll have to seek the bastard out and make my own determination. Where can I find him?"

Bentsen shifted his shoulders uncomfortably. "We're not sure."

"What?" Savron's voice once again held a dangerous softness. "What do you mean, you're not sure? I told you that locating Delaney was of primary importance."

"We tried," Bentsen said hurriedly. "He and his wife, Elspeth, were participating in an archeological dig in Cahokia, Illinois, up until a few months ago. Then the excavation was completed and the members of the party scattered. No one seems to know where the Delaneys went from there." Savron's face was darkening more with each word, and Bentsen rushed on quickly. "We know he didn't return to the home ranch, Killara, in the Arizona Territory. No one there knows of his whereabouts."

"We seem to know where he isn't," Savron said caustically. "What a rare pleasure it would be to know where the man is."

"There's one person who might know: Silver Delaney, Dominic's niece. She's enrolled in a school for young ladies in St. Louis."

"Ah, the sweet young maiden who enjoys attending

hangings," Savron murmured. "I can see how he might confide in such a sympathetic relative."

Bentsen nodded eagerly. "Delaney and his wife visited her regularly, and the girl spent several vacations at the dig. If anyone would know where Dominic Delaney went, it would be Silver Delaney."

"Then may I ask why you didn't send an agent to the school to ask the young lady?"

Bentsen's glance slid away. "We did."

"And?"

"She told him to go to hell."

Marinov burst out laughing. "Obviously a lady of exquisite taste and delicacy of speech. Nicky, I believe I'd like to meet this fair flower."

Savron smiled grimly. "I'm beginning to think you may get your wish. The Randall Agency's men appear to be pitifully ineffectual."

"Now, see here." Bentsen bristled indignantly. "We're not entirely at fault. We did find out quite a bit about the girl."

Nicholas leaned back against the rail and folded his arms across his chest. "Indeed? I wait with baited breath."

"She's been at Mrs. Alford's academy for two years and has been expelled twice. Both times the fees were doubled to get the school to accept her back."

"I'm hardly interested in a schoolgirl's pranks," Savron said in a bored tone. "Tell me something that will lead me to Dominic Delaney."

"She has a lover," Bentsen said triumphantly. "Perhaps several lovers. Luke Carey, our agent, has been watching her day and night since she refused to tell him anything. He was hoping she'd lead him to her uncle, but every night she sneaks out and goes to the circus."

"Maybe she has a fondness for menageries and side-shows," Marinov said lazily. "I enjoy the circus myself."

"She has a hired carriage waiting for her two blocks from the school shortly after dark. She doesn't come back until three or four o'clock in the morning." Bentsen paused. "Carey has seen her with several men on the circus grounds, but he thinks it is Sebastien, the knife thrower, she goes to see."

"You think this is of interest to me?" Nicholas asked coldly. "Why are you telling me this drivel?"

"It's not drivel," Bentsen protested. "It might be a way to make her tell you where her uncle is now. No lady wants her reputation ruined by scandal."

"Lady?" The prince's soft voice stung like a velvet lash. "A bloodthirsty viper at fifteen who has developed into an accomplished harlot at the ripe age of nineteen years? She would laugh at a threat such as that."

"Why don't you let my man approach her and—"

"No!" Savron met his gaze with sudden fierceness. "Do nothing else. Your firm has blundered this business from start to finish. I'll handle the affair myself from now on."

"But if you'll give us the opportunity to—"

Savron made a slicing movement with the edge of his hand. "No, it's finished. Good day, Mr. Bentsen."

At that moment Nicholas Savron was more imperial tsar than landed prince, and Bentsen found himself bowing as he backed away. "Good day, your highness, I'm sorry we—" He stopped. What the hell was he doing? He was an American, dammit, and he didn't bow to anyone. He straightened and jammed on his hat. "We'll expect your payment for services rendered." He turned and walked away, his back straight and the faintest hint of a swagger in his gait.

Marinov gave a low whistle. "I do believe you've been subjected to lèse-majesté, Nicky."

"So it appears." A sudden reckless smile banished the sternness from Nicholas's expression. "These Americans have no respect for a fellow's consequence. Give a man a taste of equality and he tries to march like a king over the face of the earth."

Marinov's expression sobered. "You're safe enough here, but a remark like that will get you sent into exile once we're home again. God knows I may have complained about this heat, but I won't promise to follow you to Siberia if the tsar decides to curb that wild tongue of yours."

Nicholas's smile deepened. "It might be worth it. Siberia could be a welcome change. St. Petersburg has been abysmally boring of late. I used to be able to bear it when I knew I could go back to the Kuban, but not . . ." He trailed off, his dark eyes gazing broodingly down at the waters below him. "Maybe I'll pay a visit to court when this is all over."

"Good God, why?" Marinov asked, startled. "You hate life at court."

"I don't know. It's as good a place as any other in which to be bored. Perhaps . . ." He shrugged impatiently. "But that's in the future. Now we have to find Dominic Delaney."

"You think he's to blame for André's death?"

"Who knows?" Nicholas said wearily. "But I'm here to find out and I won't go home until I do." His hand clenched violently on the wooden rail. "Why the hell did he go to a primitive place like Hell's Bluff? What a fool he was."

"But you loved him," Marinov said quietly.

"He was my cousin." Nicholas was silent a moment. "Damn, he was as clumsy as a big puppy and I can't remember how many scrapes I had to get him out of, but he had a good heart. He didn't deserve to be hanged in a land so far from home."

"I take it we go to this St. Louis to question the young woman? She doesn't sound as if she would willingly tell you anything." Valentin's eyes twinkled. "Except the same advice she gave Mr. Bentsen's agent."

"She'll tell me." Nicholas turned away from the rail. "Come along. Let's go find Robert and inform him that he's going to get the opportunity to beat the *Robert E. Lee*'s record to St. Louis. You recall how enthusiastic he was in the telling of that tale. How long did he say it took? Four days?"

"A little less, I think." Valentin fell into step with him. "Our celebration is over, I assume."

"Why? I'm sure we'll need amusement on the trip. We'll ask our guests to go along." Nicholas's ebony eyes were suddenly gleaming. "Don't you think that's a fine idea?"

"Lee Bassinger too?"

"You object? He's not exactly charming, but he may improve upon acquaintance."

"You know damn well he's a dangerous man. He's a vicious bastard, and he didn't like losing this pleasure barge to you. It was the pride of his fleet of riverboats."

"All the more reason to invite him. It will make the journey more interesting."

Valentin slowly shook his head, but said nothing. There was no use remonstrating with Nicholas when he was in such a mood. The streak of wildness that had always been a part of him had been growing steadily of late, and arguing only triggered more extravagant behavior. "You realize the journey could all be for nothing? What if Delaney's niece refuses to tell you where her uncle has gone?"

"There are always ways of handling vipers." Nicholas suddenly threw back his head and laughed. He clapped Valentin on the shoulder. "Stop frowning, my friend. She's young, a schoolgirl. It will take no time at all to get the information from her. Silver Delaney will pose no problem for me."

2

Where in hell had the blasted girl gone?

Luke Carey carefully moved from the shadows of the high stone wall to a beech tree closer to the three-story building that housed Mrs. Alford's Select Academy for Young Ladies, his gaze searching the darkness.

She had to be somewhere on the grounds. He had caught a fleeting glimpse of the Delaney girl as she had slipped from the sill of her third-floor chamber to the branch of an oak tree and begun her usual agile descent to the garden below. Then, somehow, he had lost sight of her after she had reached the ground. One moment she had been there, and the next she had faded into the shadows. Maybe he should—

A strong arm encircled him from the rear and jerked his neck back sharply. The sharp point of a dagger pricked his throat.

"Don't move!" The voice behind him was low and fierce. "Or I'll slice your gullet like a chicken for Sunday dinner."

Carey froze, his heart pounding so hard he could

almost hear it in the darkness. "I'm not moving," he said hoarsely. He swallowed. "Will you shift that knife an inch or so? I'm scared to breathe."

"Soon." The knife remained pressed against the hollow of his throat. "When you tell me what I want to know."

It was the Delaney girl, he realized with amazement. Though the tone was fierce, her voice held the same melodious, bell-like womanliness as that of the schoolgirl who had damned him to perdition three weeks ago in Mrs. Alford's prim parlor.

He found himself unconsciously relaxing. "Now, Miss Delaney, you're being a little hasty. You don't want to—" A fresh ripple of fear surged through him as the dagger drew blood.

"How do you know what I want to do? You know nothing about me except what you've discovered by spying on me. Did you think I didn't realize you were following me?" Her tone was edged with scorn. "An elephant couldn't have been more clumsy about hiding his sign. You wouldn't last two days on the trail. The only reason I put up with it was to see how long you'd keep at it when you saw I wouldn't lead you to Dominic."

Carey muttered a low curse beneath his breath. "You could have stopped me at any time. It's your uncle we want. We have no interest in your activities."

"But I'm interested in yours. Who is this client who wants so much to learn Dominic's whereabouts?"

Carey nervously licked his lips. "I told you the day we met in the parlor that I don't know."

"Charles Durbin?"

Carey started to shake his head and then stopped. Lord, he'd be spitting himself on that damn little dagger in another minute. "I wasn't told. My orders were to find out Delaney's location and report to our man in New Orleans."

Silver felt a swift, sinking disappointment. The man truly didn't know. Carey's voice was shaking with fear and his muscles were taut with terror. She had hoped he had been lying to her when she had first asked him who was pursuing Dominic, but a man seldom lied with a blade biting into his throat. She reluctantly lowered the knife, her arm dropping from around his neck. She stepped back. "Then send word to your man in New Orleans that Dominic doesn't want to be found." She drew her dark blue cloak more closely around her. "And tell him that questioning his kin can be very dangerous. Don't follow me again, Mr. Carey. It annoys me."

There was no sound of a footfall, nor even a whisper of movement in the grass, and it was not until he heard the soft clang of the garden gate that Carey realized the girl was no longer behind him. He whirled around, too late to catch anything but a brief glimpse of Silver Delaney before she was gone, hurrying down the sidewalk toward the hired carriage waiting in the next block.

A few moments later Silver settled back against the leather cushions of the carriage and closed her eyes, attempting to relax her taut nerves. It was unusual for her to be this nervous, and she must not let emotion sap her strength. Fear wouldn't help Dominic. Those men still didn't know where Dominic and Elspeth had gone and, with luck, would not find out. She only wished she could contact Dominic and tell him he was in danger once again. It was frustration that was causing her distress and exasperation to grow more desperate with every passing day. Dom had promised to contact her when they had found a villa to Elspeth's liking, but that might be months. Blast it, she should have gone with them.

Then her lips curved in a wry smile. She had not been invited to go along, and she probably wouldn't have gone if the invitation had been issued. Even after four years of marriage Dominic and Elspeth had no need for anyone else. Silver had realized early on that it was sometimes lonelier to see the love that bonded them together and shut her out than to stay at the academy, where the rejection was deliberate. She could armor herself against the cruelty of strangers, she could fight contempt and stupidity, but it was virtually impossible to stem the poignant, wistful feelings evoked by watching Elspeth and Dominic together. How would it feel to be loved as Elspeth was loved?

She was being foolish. She deliberately straightened on the seat and squared her shoulders. There was no reason to grow weak and tearful over something no one could change. She had been lonely all her life and could not expect anything else in the future. Perhaps some people were meant to be lonely. She had to accept the loneliness and go on with her life. There were many rewards she could wrest from the world once she had left this blasted school.

She smothered a chuckle as she imagined Mrs. Alford's expression of profound relief when Silver finally walked out her front door. She had made sure that the last two years had been as difficult for those around her as they were difficult for her. Well, it had been their own fault, she thought defiantly. No one could expect her to meekly let Mrs. Alford and her mawkish pupils treat her with contempt. If she couldn't have friendship, she would have respect.

She glanced out the window of the carriage. She could see the bright lights in the distance and the cheerful, alluring music of the calliope drifted faintly to her ears. She was almost there. She felt the anticipation begin to rise within her. The circus. Here she had acceptance. Circus people were also outcasts, yet proud, even splendid, in their isolation. They had brought her into their world without thought or hesitation. Soon, for a little while, she could forget loneliness and pretend she belonged to the brilliant, shoddy world of Monteith's Circus.

"You're late." Sebastien threw open the door of the carriage, his voice hoarse with strain. "Hurry!"

Fear clutched painfully at Silver's throat. "Etaine?"

Sebastien nodded jerkily. "She had an attack this afternoon." He tossed a coin to the coachman and easily lifted Silver out of the vehicle. "We did everything you told us, but she's not much better." His handsome face was anguished. "That son of a bitch made her go into the cage tonight. She could scarcely breathe and he still made her perform with the cats."

Anger flared white-hot within Silver. Damn Monteith. She'd like to cut his heart out. "She's in her tent?".

Sebastien nodded and hurried ahead, elbowing a path through the crowd for her.

"How is she, Sebastien?" a ticket taker called as they passed the entrance of the big tent.

"Not good," Sebastien said curtly, scarcely looking at the man. He hurried Silver past the big tent, the animal cages, and on to a small tent at the back of the field. "Khadil is with her now, but she'll have to leave before Monteith discovers her absence from the side-show." He lifted the flap of the tent and waves of moist heat struck them in the face. Then they were in the tent, stepping around the small banked fire on which a kettle of bubbling hot water was sending mists of steam into the air, to hurry toward the woolen pallet on the far side of the tent where Khadil was kneeling.

The albino turned to look at them, her strange eyes wide with anxiety. "She's scared, Silver," she whispered. "I've been holding her hand like you said, but she's so scared."

"It's all right, Khadil." Silver shrugged off her cloak and threw it on the brassbound trunk beside the pallet. "You've done very well. All you could do."

She looked down at the tiny figure on the pallet, a

sharp pang of sympathy wrenching through her. Etaine's eyes were closed and her mouth was wide open as she struggled desperately for breath. The child was still wearing her pink tutu and tights, her fair skin shining with a mist of perspiration that had darkened her white-gold curls to pale brown. She had lost weight in the last few weeks and appeared even younger than ten years of age.

Etaine's lids fluttered open and she saw Silver. Hope flared in the blue depths of her eyes. She smiled shakily. "I've . . . been . . . trying." Each word was torn from her as she struggled painfully for air. "It doesn't—"

"Shh." Silver dropped swiftly to her knees beside Khadil. "Save your breath. I know you've been trying. You just needed someone to help you try a little harder." She glanced over her shoulder at Sebastien. "I'll need someone to keep that kettle steaming."

He nodded. "Many of us will take turns coming in to tend it."

Silver turned back to Etaine and smiled. "Why don't we undress you and wrap you in a blanket the way we did the last time? That will make you feel much freer." She quickly began to take off the child's spangled pink finery. She experienced another ripple of rage as she had a sudden mental picture of how Etaine must have looked facing the lions tonight. Monteith always deliberately tried to accentuate his daughter's youth and childish vulnerability when she performed. He must have been very pleased tonight,

Silver thought savagely. Etaine's illness gave her an air of fragility, almost a transparency that was unbearably touching. "Sebastien!"

Sebastien paused at the entrance of the tent.

"Keep Monteith away from here tonight."

He hesitated and for an instant she saw the fear that was always present at any mention of defiance of Monteith. Then Sebastien nodded with determination. "We'll find a way."

Khadil helped Silver undress and wrap Etaine in the blanket and then sat back on her heels. "I have to leave now. Monteith always checks the sideshow and my friends won't be able to fool him for much longer."

"That's fine, I won't need you any more tonight," Silver said. "Etaine is going to be fine."

Khadil frowned, her eyes with their pink irises and red pupils fixed worriedly on Etaine. "I'll try to come back later if you—"

"No." Silver tried to smother the exasperation she was feeling. They all meant well, but their love for Etaine was so deep that these attacks frightened them as much as they did the child, and fear fed upon fear. "Leave us alone."

Khadil nodded uncertainly, her wild mane of pure white hair shining in the firelight. "Good night, Etaine."

Etaine's thin face was suddenly lit by a loving smile as she gazed at the albino. "It's . . . all right, Khadil. Don't be . . . afraid."

"Hush." Silver motioned for Khadil to leave and settled down beside Etaine, gathering the child into her arms. She began to stroke the silky crop of fair curls slowly and rhythmically. They were silent for a long time, and Silver gradually felt the tension that locked Etaine's muscles begin to ease and her breathing grow more steady.

"It's getting better," Etaine said, nestling closer. "I was afraid I . . ."

"It's bad for you to be afraid. It makes the breathing much worse. Now relax and think of pleasant things."

"Heaven?" Etaine tried to laugh. "I was wondering . . . before you came . . . about heaven. I thought this time . . ."

"Not heaven," Silver said firmly. "You're not going to see heaven for a long, long time. You've had these attacks before, and this is just another one. Maybe a little worse."

Etaine nodded. "Worse. Why?"

Silver was silent a moment. "I don't know, Etaine. I don't know why you have to suffer. Perhaps it won't always be this way. I have heard that some children grow out of lung afflictions." If they lived long enough. The thought brought panic in its wake, and she quickly blocked the emotion. She mustn't be afraid or Etaine would sense it and grow tense again. She could often talk the child through attacks like these if she could get her to relax. "A dry climate seems to help. Doctors send many people to heal in the land where I was born. Living here beside the river can't be good for you."

"We'll move on . . . soon. My father says the pickings are getting poor here."

Silver experienced a swift thrust of pain. She had known the circus would not remain here forever, but the news still came as a shock. She would miss them all so much. Sebastien, Khadil, Bruno the Strong Man, Etaine. No, not Etaine. She had plans for Etaine.

"Tell me about Killara, Silver." Etaine's lids had closed again and her breathing was becoming less harsh with every passing moment. "Tell me about your cousins . . . Patrick and Brianne and about . . . Rising Star. Am I really like Rising Star?"

"Yes." Silver gently stroked the blue-veined delicacy of Etaine's temples. "Not in appearance. My aunt was Apache, like me, but you remind me of her." Strength and fragility, gentleness and a joyous love of life that touched everyone around her. "I miss her very much. She loved me."

"Of course," Etaine said simply. "Everyone loves you, Silver."

Silver burst out laughing. "You're mistaken, Etaine. I'm not at all lovable."

Etaine's lids opened. "Then why do I love you?"

Silver gave the child a quick hug. "Because you love everyone. Someday you'll wake up and see me as I am."

"I don't love . . . everyone. Sometimes I feel very wicked."

Silver knew to whom the child was referring. How the hell could even a daughter love a monster like Paul Monteith? "You're not wicked. Some people aren't worth loving." She smiled down at her. "Do you think you can go to sleep now?"

"Pretty soon." Etaine's breathing was almost normal now, and her words were slightly slurred. "You won't leave right away? I always feel safe with you. I was so frightened before when I couldn't breathe."

Silver swallowed to ease the tightness of her throat. "I know, Etaine. I don't have to leave for a long, long time. Now, close your eyes."

In a few moments the child was asleep and Silver let out a deep sigh of relief. The attack was over. Tomorrow Etaine would be weak and exhausted, but in a few days she would be well again.

Until the next attack.

Silver knew a chill of terror that was quickly superseded by determination. Etaine mustn't be here when the next attack occurred. She must be at Killara, where she could be cared for. There had to be some way to get Monteith to relinquish custody of Etaine. He had no affection for her. Hell, he had no affection for anyone. She shivered as she remembered the last confrontation she'd had with the man. There was something terribly evil about Monteith, something not at all as it should be. . . . She would wire Patrick and ask him for help. Monteith appeared to be a greedy enough bastard; perhaps if Patrick offered him a great deal of money . . .

She sighed wearily and tried to relax. Yes, perhaps Patrick could help. Etaine would be happy at Killara, as Silver had never been. She was a golden child and she would be accepted by the family as one of them.

Her cousin, Patrick, had done everything he could to make his grandfather and grandmother treat Silver as a true Delaney, but he could not make them give her affection.

She had already resolved not to return to Killara, but the ties that bound her to the ranch were too strong to sever entirely. There were too many years, too many memories, too many dreams invested in Killara to walk away from it and not look back. Maybe she could settle somewhere close by and see Etaine now and then, it would be sweet to watch her grow strong and healthy and free of fear.

She was growing drowsy but she mustn't sleep. The carriage would return for her in a few hours to take her back to the academy, and she had promised Patrick the last time she had been expelled that she would try to avoid another scene with Mrs. Alford. It was all very stupid. There were so many foolish rules. How could any woman live smothered under so many rules and with as many simpered platitudes ringing in her ears? Still, she *had* promised. She wrinkled her nose in distaste as she thought about having to sneak out each night. Oh, well, three months more and it would be over. She would be free.

She looked down at the child's sleeping face and a wave of tenderness swept over her. Now she must find a way of freeing Etaine.

"Please, do be seated." Elisabeth Alford cast a flustered glance at Mikhail Kuzdief towering behind Nicholas Savron and moistened her lips with her tongue. "Perhaps your servant could wait outside, your highness? My young ladies are shy and easily frightened by the masculine gender and he is very . . . large, isn't he?"

Nicholas seated himself on the horsehair couch Mrs. Alford had indicated. "Mikhail isn't my servant, he's my aide. He's Cossack and a Cossack is servant to no man." He smiled easily. "And we have no intention of encountering any of your young ladies except Miss Delaney. I'm sure neither my aide nor myself could be considered a threat to the virtue of your charges."

The headmistress had distinct doubts on that score. Nicholas Savron possessed a beguiling masculine beauty that posed a danger far in excess of the attractions of an ordinary young man—and he was a prince to boot. Any young girl was bound to be dazzled by such a potent combination. From the supple leather of his black boots to his black frock coat and discreetly striped gray silk cravat, he was a picture of worldly elegance. How had that savage been lucky enough to manage to make the acquaintance of such a man? "Well, perhaps it would do no harm for him to stay." Her fingers fluttered up to fondle the cameo brooch at her throat. "I've sent for Silver. I believe she's in the garden this afternoon. The sweet girl is such a lover of nature. You say you have a message for her? Perhaps you're acquainted with her guardian, Patrick Delaney?"

Nicholas shook his head. "I have a connection with her uncle Dominic."

"A family connection?"

"Not exactly." The prince leaned forward and lowered his voice. "I have a message for her concerning her uncle. A very personal message. Naturally, you'll be understanding enough to give us the privacy needed for such a delicate matter."

Mrs. Alford frowned. "Leave you alone with Silver? That's not possible. It would be frightfully improper."

"But you're obviously a lady of great discernment." Nicholas's words flowed over her with honey-sweet persuasion. "And a woman of such intelligence is allowed to take risks when a lesser woman must cling diligently to the rules." He smiled, his dark eyes twinkling. "I promise I'll be alone with her for only five minutes. What possible harm could come to her in that short time?"

There was a sound from Mikhail that was suspiciously like a snort of derision.

"Five minutes?" The headmistress wavered. Those eyes were mesmerizing and that wicked smile capable of melting stone. She really shouldn't permit him to— She abruptly stood up as she made up her mind. Why not? That young demon could certainly protect herself and she, Elisabeth Alford, was not about to offend a prince. "Very well." She moved toward the door. "But not a minute more. Ah, here is Silver. Silver, this is his highness, Prince Nicholas Savron, and his aide, Mikhail Kuzdief. My dear, his highness has a message for you." She strutted from the room, her bustle swaying on her ample posterior.

"What sort of message?" Silver Delaney asked warily, moving a few paces into the parlor.

Nicholas felt a tingle of emotion that was curiously like shock. The girl before him was a dark flame burning in the fussy drabness of the parlor. Ebony hair, straight and silky, was left unbound to fall to the middle of her back. Golden skin glowed with a satin luminence that was irresistibly tempting to touch, and her eyes . . . wide-set, framed by long, curving black lashes, those clear silver eyes should have been cool but they were not. They were flashing, alive, and as passionate as those beautifully shaped lips.

Passion. Sensuality. She radiated those qualities like a shimmering beacon that would draw men to her as surely as his own body was responding right now. She was clothed in a dark blue school uniform consisting of a long-sleeved waist-length Zouave jacket, full shapeless skirt, and prim, high-necked white shirtwaist blouse obviously meant to convince all men that there was nothing worthy of their interest beneath. On Silver Delaney the attempt at subterfuge was completely useless. She held her slim body arrow-straight, her full breasts pressing against the prim shirtwaist and jacket as if boldly flaunting their presence. Yet there was an air of indifference to her appearance that was as intriguing as the sensuality she radiated with every breath.

"Well?" She strode forward, her gaze meeting his with impatience. "Speak up. Who sent you?"

Nicholas felt a touch of amusement. He couldn't remember ever having been spoken to like a dim-witted lackey even as a child at the tsar's court. He stood up and bowed mockingly. "Forgive me for not answering you at once. I fear your beauty held me speechless."

"Bullshit." She stopped before him, planting her hands on her hips. "I'm not even pretty. You were just taking my measure as I was taking yours."

Nicholas's laugh rang out. He had never encountered such honesty in a woman before. "Quite true. But may I say taking your measure was a very pleasurable experience? I hope you found me equally pleasing."

He knew she would find him pleasing, Silver thought. There was not a woman in the world who would not look at him and want to keep on looking. A golden sun god—bold, sensuous, lusty as any mythical Apollo. A sudden flush brushed her cheeks as she realized her heart was pounding painfully hard against her ribs. "You're handsome enough, I suppose. I have a fondness for dark men myself."

Nicholas felt a sudden sharp annoyance. Was her circus knife-thrower dark, then? Lord, what difference did it make what were the preferences of a promiscuous little schoolgirl? "Is your uncle Dominic dark?"

Her wariness immediately returned. "Yes."

"And you're very fond of him?"

"Yes." Her eyes suddenly narrowed. "Why are you asking questions about Dom?"

"I need to see him. Will you tell me where to find him?"

"Why should I? What do you want with him?" Her voice became fierce. "How do I know you're really who you say you are? You could be another one of those idiot detectives who came here looking for him."

His lips twitched. "Who you consigned to the devil?"

"You *are* one of them." She took a step back, her hands clenching at her sides. "I should have known that fool I frightened away two days ago would send for someone else to take his place. Why do you think I'd tell you anything about Dom?"

His amusement faded. "Because I intend that you will tell me."

She looked at him incredulously. "Can you promise me that you mean no harm to Dom?"

He hesitated before meeting her gaze. Should he lie to her? The clear fearlessness of her regard decided him. In a world of women who played with the truth as if it were a pretty toy, it was refreshing to find one who appeared to have no guile. "No, I can't promise you that."

"Then you're loco to think I'd ever tell you anything." Her eyes blazed. "I won't tell you. Not ever."

"You will, you know," he said softly. "Perhaps not now, but you will tell me, Miss Delaney. It's necessary that I find your uncle."

"Why?"

He smiled faintly. "I don't believe it would be wise to discuss my purpose with you. I think we've reached an impasse. I can't say that I'm sorry. Our situation promises to become much more interesting this way. The quest may become an adventure more satisfying than the discovery." His voice lowered to velvet sensuality. "I've always been quite fond of 'adventures,' haven't you, Miss Delaney?"

His dark eyes held mysteries, sensual secrets she knew he wanted to share with her. Yet his words were a mystery in themselves. Silver tore her gaze away from him. "I don't know what you mean."

Nicholas experienced a thrust of disappointment that surprised him. What had he expected, he wondered cynically. Just because the girl seemed more honest than most was no reason she would admit to her lustful indiscretions. The woman who occupied a man's bed one night was seldom the woman he met in the ballroom the next. "I'll endeavor to make my meaning clear . . . later. I'll make sure you understand every nuance and shading." His dark eyes glinted through half-lowered lids. "Unless you'd care to change your mind?"

"I don't understand what you're saying." She shrugged impatiently. "It makes no difference. I won't change my mind, so you may as well leave. Good afternoon, your highness. That is, if you really are a prince. It wouldn't surprise me if you were one of those detectives and only pretending."

He was dismissed, Nicholas realized with amusement, and with a royal indifference that would have done justice to an empress. "And it wouldn't surprise me if you were a princess."

Her gray eyes glinted with anger. "You're laughing at me. I'm no princess, nor would I want to be. I am what I am. Silver Dove Delaney. Apache. White. Half-breed."

Nicholas inhaled sharply, feeling heat flow through him and his stomach knot painfully. Christ, she was magnificent. Burning. Flaming with life. Her breasts were lifting and falling with every breath, and he felt a sudden desire to reach out and cover one of those breasts with his palm, to feel the fire, the softness. He pulled his gaze away from her and tried to remember what she had just said. "Apache? That's an Indian tribe of your American Southwest, isn't it?"

Her lips curved in a crooked smile. "Your fine detectives didn't tell you I was a half-breed? Well I am and I'm also illegitimate. My father thought my mother was good enough only to bed and forget. Not that it matters to me. I had no need of the Delaneys."

"Yet you're doing your best to protect one Delaney." He was scarcely aware of the words he was speaking. He just wanted to keep her talking, watch the play of expression on her face. Passion. He could feel the passion in her reach out and touch him like a stroking hand. My God, he wanted her. She had him achingly full, ready as he had never been before. *Merde,* and he hadn't even touched her yet.

But he would soon. He had never been more certain of anything in his entire life than that he must have Silver Delaney in his bed.

"I said I had no need. I didn't say I wouldn't choose to give." Two bright spots of color blazed beneath the golden smoothness of her cheeks. "I do what I please. And it pleases me to help Dominic."

And, Nicholas thought angrily, it pleased her to offer her body to this Sebastien and no doubt to any other man who caught her eye. He experienced a hot thrust of emotion that was totally new to him. "You appear to be exceptionally generous in your giving. That could be very dangerous for a woman. Some men prefer that such generosity be confined solely to themselves." His lips twisted. "I'm beginning to believe I may be included in that group. I find it quite a surprising discovery."

A bewildered frown wrinkled her brow. "Half the time I don't understand what you're talking about. Do all Russians say one thing and mean something else?"

"Probably, though it's a trait not confined entirely to my countrymen."

"What a waste of time and effort. It's far more sensible to say exactly what one means."

He threw back his head and laughed. "You like honesty?" His ebony eyes were suddenly dancing roguishly. He took a step closer to her. "All right, I'll stop being Russian and adopt your American ways."

"Nicholas," Mikhail said warningly. It was the first time he had spoken since she had entered the room and Silver's gaze flew to the face of the huge Russian. The Cossack's gaze was fastened on the prince with apprehension and rueful resignation.

"She wants honesty, Mikhail," Nicholas said in a reckless tone of voice. "Why not give it to her?" His gaze held Silver's. "Shall I tell you what I want? One, I want Dominic Delaney. Two, I want to take off all your clothes and carry you to a bed, even one in this nunnery. Not necessarily in that order. At the moment the urgency is definitely for the latter."

Her eyes were wide and wondering as a child's. "You wish to fornicate with me?"

He chuckled. "Good Lord, I'd wager you didn't learn that word at the staid Mrs. Alford's academy." He nodded. "That's exactly what I want to do and shall do at the earliest opportunity."

She gazed at him for a moment, her cheeks scarlet. Then she shook her head, hard. "No."

"Are you afraid I can't please you?" His tone was only a level above a seductive whisper. "I promise you won't be disappointed. Come with me now. I have a carriage waiting and we'll go back to my boat. You don't belong here among all these prim young misses."

A pained expression appeared on her face but quickly veiled. "No, I don't belong here. No one knows that better than I do." Her chin rose. "But I don't belong in your bed either."

"You're wrong; that's exactly where you do belong." He bowed mockingly once more. "But I can wait. It may even whet my appetite." Something hot and wild flickered in the darkness of his eyes. "Though I doubt it, because I'm already very hungry indeed." He glanced over his shoulder at Mikhail. "You see, my friend, I was very good. I didn't throw her down on the rug as you thought I might. Now we can go."

"A good idea," Mikhail said dryly. "This is no place for you either."

Nicholas made a face. "You're right. It's difficult to breathe in here." He turned back to Silver. "Good afternoon, sweet, I'll be looking forward to our next meeting."

"I'm not sweet, and we won't be meeting again."

He tilted his golden head and regarded her appraisingly. "I was mistaken. You're quite right: there's nothing sweet about you. You're like the vodka made in the Kuban. Hot going down and explosive after. I've always had an insatiable thirst for that vodka." He turned to the arched doorway and then turned back as a thought occurred to him. "Silver *Dove?*" He burst out laughing. "Good Lord, what a misnomer. You're more like a firebird." He put on his black silk hat and strolled leisurely out the door.

Silver found herself staring after him, seething with a wild confusion of emotions. "He's mad," she muttered. "He couldn't have meant . . ."

"He meant it." Mikhail Kuzdief had paused beside her and was gazing down at her, his deep brown eyes oddly sympathetic. "And he is not mad, only a little wild. Still, it would be better if you ran away."

"Why?" She looked at him in surprise.

"Nicholas is used to getting what he wants," the big Cossack said simply. "But if you are not here . . ." He shrugged. "He saw you only once. Maybe—"

"Why are you warning me?" Silver asked curiously.

"Because I think Nicholas is right. You do not belong among the tame hens in this place." His gaze gravely searched her face. "But I am not sure you belong anywhere else either."

She flinched. "If I don't, I'll make my own place."

A faint smile touched Mikhail's lips. "Yes, that is what we must do."

"We?"

"I also belong nowhere." He put on his big black sheepskin hat and turned toward the door. "Except with Nicholas. I have warned you, but my loyalty is to him." The glance he gave her over his shoulder was sober. "Always." He strode out of the parlor.

Nicholas was waiting for him in the carriage and cast him an amused glance as he climbed into the carriage. "You warned her?"

"Yes." Mikhail closed the door of the carriage and settled himself across from Nicholas.

"Do you think she will heed your warning?"

"No."

The carriage started to move, the horses hooves echoing on the cobblestone street.

"Neither do I." Nicholas leaned back on the leather seat. "Thank God. I believe I would be ready to break your head if you'd made it difficult for me."

Mikhail looked at him in surprise. He had known Nicholas since they were children, and one woman had always been much the same as another to him. He had assumed it was the rebellious defiance of Silver Delaney that had caused him to react so explosively. Now, as Mikhail studied Nicholas more closely, he was conscious of something else. "You want her that much?"

"That much." Nicholas closed his eyes. "God, I'm so damn hard, my guts are twisting."

"We will be back at the levee soon. I'll fetch one of the women to your cabin. Which one do you want?"

None. He wanted none of them, Nicholas realized with amazement. He wanted Silver Delaney or no one. What kind of a spell had she woven over him? He didn't answer for a long time, his gaze on the neat little hedges that bordered the equally neat little houses lining the street. "We'll be leaving St. Louis tonight. Tell Robert to be ready to cast off by nine o'clock."

Mikhail nodded.

"I'm taking Silver Delaney with me." Nicholas's gaze shifted to Mikhail's face. "You don't have to help if you choose not to do so."

"I will help," Mikhail said quietly. "I will send her carriage away and be waiting for her when she leaves to go to the circus tonight." He paused. "But I want to do it alone. The more men there are, the more chance that she will be hurt. I . . . I like her, Nicholas. Do not hurt her."

"Rape?" Nicholas made a face. "My God, when have I ever raped a woman? I have no taste for using violence on any woman."

But Nicholas had never been placed in a position where force was necessary, Mikhail thought worriedly, he'd only had to smile or speak sweetly and women flocked to his bed. But Silver Delaney was not a woman who would yield without a struggle. She would be as fierce as the women of his own people. "I would like your promise."

Nicholas looked at him in surprise. "What the hell

is wrong with you? I told you what Bentsen reported on Silver Delaney. The girl is no blushing virgin. There have been men aplenty between her thighs." His expression hardened. "And she stood there and watched while they hung André."

Mikhail merely gazed at him, not speaking.

"Oh, very well," Nicholas said with exasperation. "You have my promise. I'll not force her no matter how much I'm provoked. Satisfied?"

Mikhail nodded.

Nicholas slowly shook his head. "Why are you so concerned?"

"I do not know. You are right, she is probably able to take care of herself, even with you, Nicholas."

"Exactly," Nicholas said. But would Silver Delaney want to protect herself? He had known a plethora of passionate women and had learned to recognize the signs when he saw them. Silver Delaney possessed a potential for fiery sensuality greater than any he had ever encountered before. If he wasn't mistaken, it would take very little to arouse her to the point where she would be pleading for him to come into her.

Just the thought of her lying in his bed, her arms outstretched with yearning, sent an aching heat to his groin. His heart was suddenly slamming hard and fast against the wall of his chest. Tonight. He drew a deep harsh breath and tried to relax. Damnation, he didn't know if he could wait until tonight.

Silver moved slowly, heavily, through the arch of the parlor entrance toward the curving staircase. She must get to her small room on the third floor, she must close the door, close out what had happened between her and Nicholas Savron.

"Silver." Mrs. Alford's dulcet tones rang through the hall. "I do hope nothing is amiss with your family. No one has suffered an illness?" The headmistress' pale blue eyes were bright with curiosity as she hurried forward. "His highness was most insistent on speaking to you alone or I would have been there to support you."

Silver gazed at her blankly. She had never heard that note of concerned sweetness in Mrs. Alford's voice in the two years she'd been under her roof. At least, not when the woman was addressing her. "No, there's been no illness."

"Then perhaps it would be proper to invite his highness to dinner. It would be a social coup of the first order to entertain Prince Nicholas. You have no idea how prestigious it would be for the academy. I've just been speaking to Miranda's mother and she says the entire city is in a tizzy about his arrival. Rumor has it that he's fabulously wealthy and his mother is a favorite at the court of the tsar."

So he hadn't been lying; Nicholas Savron was truly a prince. The thought sent an unexplainable rush of disappointment through her. Why should it matter? Nicholas was only an extraordinarily handsome young man who had spoken words of lust to her. Such words had been spoken before and been stopped by the little knife she always carried with her. The knife could stop Nicholas also, perhaps he would be even

easier to discourage. His exquisite attire and cultured
manners could reflect a will that was equally soft.

"Silver! You're not listening to me."

"What?" Silver glanced absently at Mrs. Alford's
displeased face. "Oh, no, I'm not." She started up the
stairs. "And no, I won't invite Nicholas Savron to
dinner."

"You won't invite his highness?" The woman's voice
was outraged.

"No," Silver said again, even more clearly. "I will
not see him again."

She heard the headmistress' indignant gasp and
then proceeded to ignore the woman as she climbed
the stairs.

He was gone. Why did she still see his face before
her? She had behaved so stupidly. Pray God he hadn't
noticed the effect he'd had on her. She had blushed
and trembled like one of the giggling ninnies who
were her classmates. He had smiled at her with that
wicked golden charm and she had felt a melting
somewhere deep within her. She had wanted to reach
out and touch him, run her fingers over the clean
outline of his upper lip and then up the broad plane of
his jaw and perhaps—What was she thinking? Of
course she did not want to touch him. She had always
found it difficult to touch any person with affection.

Yet, if she *had* wanted to touch Nicholas Savron, it
could mean only one thing. Lust. She was beset by the
same malady that was common to all young animals,
the same fever that had driven her mother to lie with
Boyd Delaney. Fear shivered through her as she

remembered how strong had been the response of her body as she stood before Nicholas. She had never dreamed how terribly strong that response could be. She must fight it. Who should know better than she how dangerous lust could be? She had lived all her days on the fringe of life as punishment for her mother's yielding to that siren call. But she was stronger than her mother; she'd had to fight to prevent herself being crushed by the contempt of both Apache and white. She could close her ears to that siren call even when sung by a golden warlock.

Good Lord, the man was actually a danger to Dominic. A Russian prince could not be Durbin's pawn as she had first assumed, but Dominic had made many enemies during his years on the run. It was entirely possible Savron could be one of them. He wanted to use her only for his body's pleasure and to get the information he wanted from her. She had no intention of letting him reach either goal.

No, under no circumstances would she ever see Prince Nicholas Savron again.

3

$\mathcal{L}$

"My word, what have we here?" Lee Bassinger straightened away from the rail, his pale green eyes avid with curiosity as he watched Mikhail Kuzdief stride up the gangplank. The blanket-wrapped burden slung over the Cossack's broad shoulder was squirming and kicking vigorously, and a swath of long, silky dark hair suddenly became visible as the blanket loosened. "What, or should I say who, have you brought for our friend Nicholas? I would have thought he'd have enough feminine companions to choose from without importing more." His thin lips curved in an empty smile. "I suppose it could be that he prefers unwilling women occasionally. Well, so do I. Perhaps we could share her."

Mikhail did not answer, and his glance brushed Bassinger as if he didn't exist when he strode past him down the deck and then up the wide staircase toward the staterooms.

Bassinger's gaze followed him, the smile on his face never wavering until Mikhail disappeared from view. Then he turned back to look at the gleaming lights of the city. Interesting. He knew very well that Savron did not force his bed partners. All the bastard had to do was smile at a woman and she would perform acts Bassinger had to use a whip to persuade the little pullets to do for him. Why, then, had he sent that huge bull to bring this woman to him against her will?

A flicker of excitement touched him and his hands tightened on the rail. A weapon at last? He wasn't a patient man, and having to smile and be civil to Savron and his coterie had caused the hatred to fester within him until it almost choked him. Yet he had learned a long time ago that deceit was a quality that must be fostered if a man was to have everything he wanted in life.

And he would have everything. He may have been born dirt poor but he had fought his way this far and he wasn't about to let a fop like Savron take anything from him. He would have the *Mississippi Rose* again, and his highness would be punished for humbling him.

He consciously relaxed his grip on the rail and straightened, the smile returning to his face. There was always a key to be found to bring a man to his knees, and his instincts told him that Mikhail had carried that key on board the *Rose* tonight. It was only for him to wait and watch until he had the opportunity to use that key.

Mikhail threw open the door to Nicholas's cabin and strode into the stateroom. Nicholas rose easily to his feet, his gaze on the bundle over the Cossack's shoulder. "Good, God, Mikhail, did you have to use two blankets? She must be smothering under there."

"I should have used ten," Mikhail muttered as he strode across the room and dropped his burden on the bed. "And I should have let you come with me. I should have let an army come with me." He unwrapped the blankets with two quick jerks and Silver tumbled free, rolling over to the opposite side of the bed. Her wrists were tied behind her back and a handkerchief gagged her mouth, but her eyes blazed up at them as she continued to struggle to free herself. Mikhail tossed the blankets on the floor and reached over to pull the gag from Silver's mouth, quickly jerking his hand away as her strong white teeth snapped at him. "She is a wild animal." There was a curious note of pride in his expression as he gazed down at Silver's face. "If I had not taken her by surprise, I do not think I would have been able to overpower her. She is a fine, strong warrior." He carefully brushed a strand of hair from Silver's eyes, his expression gentle. "It is all right now. No one is going to hurt you."

"But *I* will hurt you." Silver glared up at him fiercely, still struggling desperately against her bonds. "You can't do this."

"It appears that he can because he has." Nicholas strode forward to stand over her. Her long hair was lying in wild silken disarray against the peach-colored velvet of the spread and he felt a sudden thrust of desire tighten his groin. He had been sitting there imagining how she would look lying on his bed, and the reality was even more erotic than his vision. "Though not without some effort."

"You!" Her light eyes were glittering with rage as she began to curse him with venom and amazing proficiency.

He lifted a brow. "My, my, she's quite talented isn't she, Mikhail? The last time I heard a vocabulary so explicit was from my groom at the estate on Crystal Island. Should we release her, do you think?"

"Only if you wish to relieve yourself of a few fistfuls of excess hair," Mikhail said dryly, gingerly touching his own tousled red mop. "Before I got her hands tied I was sure she would strip me bald. Best wait until you have talked reason to her."

"Reason?" Silver struggled to a sitting position. "There is no reason connected with this outrage. It's madness, as I'll soon show you."

"I'm sure you'll try." Nicholas smiled. "And it will be fascinating to watch your attempts. I may even be sorry to see you depart after you tell me where your uncle has disappeared to."

"You'll be sorrier to see me stay," Silver hissed. "Do you think I'll let myself be trussed up and served to you like a turkey for Christmas dinner?"

"The trussing is only temporary. I'll untie you as soon as we get far enough away for it to be safe." He tilted his head, listening. "Hear the paddles? Since I gave orders to cast off as soon as Mikhail came aboard, that should be very soon. I have no liking for bondage of any kind."

"You lie! And my presence here is proof of it."

A flicker of anger crossed his face. "I believe you're beginning to annoy me. So far you've cursed like a sailor, threatened me, and called me a liar."

"Let me loose and I'll do more than that to you. I'll stick my knife in you as I did your friend."

Nicholas stiffened. "Knife?" His gaze flew to Mikhail. "She *stabbed* you?" His attention had been so absorbed with the girl, he had scarcely glanced at Mikhail. Now he saw that the Cossack's tunic was torn and a rivulet of blood stained the whiteness of the left sleeve.

Mikhail shrugged depreciatingly. "A pinprick." He bent down and pulled a small dagger out of his boot and tossed it to Nicholas. "Yet it might be wise to remember she is not without fangs."

"Like all vipers." Nicholas looked down at the dagger, his beautifully molded features hard as the marble of a tombstone. "She could have killed you. I should have gone myself, my friend."

A touch of anxiety clouded Mikhail's features. "A pinprick," he repeated. "She was only defending herself. The wound will be gone by tomorrow."

Bewilderment pierced the seething fury Silver was experiencing. It was clear the big Russian was defending her from Nicholas Savron's anger. Why would he help the prince abduct her and then rush to her defense?

"Do you need a doctor?" Nicholas asked gently. "I'll have Robert dock again and send someone for help."

"The woman—"

"The woman is not worth one drop of your blood."

Nicholas gave Silver a glance as cold as winter sleet. "I will deal with her later."

Mikhail shook his head. "I have no need for a doctor. She did not hurt me."

"Only because you—" Silver broke off as Mikhail shook his head warningly at her. "I *will* speak. Do you think I'm afraid of either of you?"

"You obviously have no need to fear Mikhail. It seems he's been foolish enough to take a liking to you," Nicholas said softly. "But you'd do well to be afraid of me. I value Mikhail, and I don't think I've ever been quite so angry with anyone in my entire life."

"Liking? He *abducted* me."

"On my orders. And he insisted on going alone because he felt it would be safer for you."

"Or because you were too cowardly to go with him," Silver said contemptuously.

Mikhail inhaled sharply and took an impulsive step forward as if to place himself between Silver and Nicholas. "Nicholas, she is only a woman. She did not—"

"Only a woman," Silver repeated indignantly. "A woman can do anything a man can do. She can do more. Why do—"

"*Shut up!*" Nicholas enunciated with great precision.

"I should not have taken the gag off her." Mikhail sighed morosely. "I should have known her tongue would be as sharp as her dagger."

"Go take care of your wound." Nicholas's gaze was

narrowed on Silver's face. "I have a fancy to prove myself to the lady."

Mikhail gazed at him helplessly. Nicholas was dangerously infuriated, and it was evident that Silver Delaney was not about to try to placate him. "You gave your word."

Nicholas gave him an incredulous glance. "Good Lord, she stabbed you and you're still defending her?"

Mikhail's jaw squared stubbornly. "You promised me."

Nicholas muttered something fierce and obscene beneath his breath. "And I'll keep it, dammit."

Mikhail turned toward the door and then glanced over his shoulder at Silver, a gentle smile lighting his craggy features. "I will be back soon. Do not be afraid."

Silver glared at him. "I'm not afraid and I need no protection."

Mikhail slowly shook his head and shut the door quietly behind him.

Silver immediately turned to Nicholas and opened her mouth to speak. Nicholas raised his hand. "Not one word or I'll put the gag back on you." She hesitated and then pressed her lips together. "Very wise. I'm holding on to my temper by a very precarious margin, Silver." He sat down on the bed beside her, not touching her, but close enough so that she could feel the heat emanating from his body. The faint scent of musk, brandy, and tobacco drifted to her nostrils. "I'm about to give you the rules that will govern your stay while you're on the *Rose*. Are you listening?"

She gazed up at him mutinously.

"I see you are." He smiled faintly. "First, let's discuss why you're here."

"You want Dominic."

"Exactly. I suppose I should give you the option of telling me where he is."

"Would you let me go if I did?"

"I'm afraid I'd be forced to do so. Do you wish to oblige?"

Silver drew a deep breath. Lord, she hated lies. Still, if it would give Dominic a little more time. "He and Elspeth went back to Killara in the Arizona Territory."

Nicholas's expression hardened. "I see you're as prone to falsehood as the rest of your sex is. Randall's investigators ascertained that your uncle was most definitely not at Killara. It's obvious asking you for the truth will accomplish nothing, and I admit I'm a trifle disappointed. I thought you more honest than most."

A flush stung Silver's cheeks. "I'm honest with those I respect. You deserve only lies from me. I'll tell you nothing about Dominic."

"But when he finds you're gone from Mrs. Alford's nunnery, I'd say there's an excellent chance of him coming after you," he said softly. "I posted a letter to your former headmistress telling her you'd decided to accompany me on a little pleasure cruise. If he's as loyal to you as you are to him, he should be waiting at the levee when we return to St. Louis."

"He won't even hear that I'm gone. There wouldn't be—" She stopped. "You'll be disappointed if you think you can use me to draw Dominic to you."

His gaze narrowed on her face. "You seem very certain." He shrugged. "No matter. Then you'll remain on the *Rose* until you tell me where he is."

"You can't keep me here."

"Oh, but I can. Shall I tell you how?" Nicholas's long, shapely hand reached out and smoothed her hair back from one temple, his touch as delicate as the brush of the wings of a butterfly. "There is no one to help you here. This boat belongs to me and you'll find no one interested in any plea for aid. Mikhail and my friend, Valentin, are completely loyal to me. I have a party of acquaintances on board, but I assure you their only interest is to have an amusing time. They include fifteen or so strumpets from a New Orleans brothel and a number of gentlemen whose idea of pleasure would cause even you to blush." His gaze ran over her, touching on the primness of her dark blue school uniform. "I've told Valentin to inform them you're the resident of a similar baudy house in St. Louis and that you specialize in a pretense of little-girl purity. A certain kind of man finds that pretense very exciting, you know."

She hadn't known, but she brushed the knowledge aside as unimportant. "There is still the crew."

He nodded. "Who would lose very lucrative positions if they displeased me. I think they, too, would prefer to believe my story."

So she would be alone in her struggle with Savron. For a moment she felt a tiny frisson of apprehension before she dismissed it impatiently. Her struggles had always been alone, except when Rising Star had been there to support her. This was no different. "I don't need help. I'll still get away from you."

A flicker of admiration crossed his face. "No tears? No pleas? I can almost see why Mikhail has developed a fondness for you."

"I never cry." She met his gaze. "And you will never hear me plead."

"Oh, but I will." Passion flared in the darkness of his eyes. "And it will be my very great pleasure to grant those pleas."

Silver felt a breathless twisting sensation in the pit of her stomach. Lust. But it could not be lust when she felt only fury at this golden-haired man. Was her body's response so mindless that it took no note of her mind's bidding? She tore her gaze away. "You will see."

He was now looking at her with curiosity as well as sensuality. "Why are you not threatening me with the wrath of the Delaneys? I was told they're a very powerful family."

"I do not belong to them," she said haltingly. "I have friends among them. My cousins Brianne and Patrick, Elspeth and Dominic, but the others—" She stopped and raised her chin proudly. "I would not ask them for help. I told you I had no need of the Delaneys."

Nicholas experienced a strange aching tenderness that took him by surprise. Pride, isolation, and courage were all there in her face, and there was something beneath that armor that stirred him to pity. He understood armor. He had worn it himself since he was a small child and he knew what hid behind it: loneliness, hurt, and wariness. He felt a sudden impulse to reach out and draw her to him, cradle her in his arms as he had never been held himself in that time so long ago. His hand moved from her temple to her cheek. "Silver, I—" He broke off. My God, what was he thinking? This was the tiger cat who had just sunk her fangs into Mikhail, who had watched André die a horrible death, who had taken lovers as casually as any court demimondaine. Surprisingly, it was this last thought that brought the welcome anger that burned away any hint of softness. "Good, then I needn't worry about being punished for my sins."

"Worry. *I* will punish you."

He suddenly chuckled. "If I give you the opportunity, which I have no intention of doing. You will be confined in this cabin unless I give you permission to leave, and I promise you that if you bash me over the head while I'm sleeping or steal your little knife back and stick it in my heart, Valentin and Mikhail will be very displeased with you. I know you won't believe this, but they're both quite fond of me."

"I don't believe it," she said flatly.

"Pity. I'm a very charming fellow." He smiled wickedly. "I'll be glad to demonstrate how agreeable I can be."

She stared back at him unsmilingly.

"No? Well, then I suppose I'd better show you how impossible it would be to escape even if I were no longer an obstacle in your path." He leaned forward and quickly sliced through the ropes binding her wrists. He stood up and strolled toward the door facing the bed, pausing with his hand on the knob to gesture to the other door to the left of bed. "That door leads to the grand saloon, where you would encounter any number of gentlemen eager to drag you into the nearest stateroom and have their way with you. Please refrain from using that door under any circumstance. I intend to be the only one who's going to have his way with you on the *Rose*." He opened the door and inclined his head mockingly. "And this door leads to the deck."

Silver swung her legs to the floor and stood up. She crossed the room, her gaze fixed warily on his face. He stood aside to let her precede him.

Cool, moist air touched her cheeks and a lazy breeze ruffled through her hair as she walked out onto the deck. She heard the door close behind her as she moved over to the rail and looked down at the churning waters below. It had seemed as if only a short time had passed, yet the lights of the city had almost disappeared from view. Now there were only dark forests, high bluffs, and the river.

"I understand the Mississippi is over a mile wide in many places," Nicholas said softly in her ear. "An impossible swim for a woman. And I hardly think you're stupid enough to risk drowning yourself."

"No, I'm not stupid." Silver did not look at him as she deliberately fought down the flare of anger she felt at her own helplessness. Anger would blur her thinking and put her at a disadvantage, and she already felt more uncertain in Nicholas Savron's presence than she ever had before in her life. She needed all her wits about her to find a way to escape this boat and get back to Etaine. What if the child suffered another attack and she weren't there to help her? She had gotten better and Silver had been filled with hope, but what if the recovery did not last? Fear edged her voice. "You'll not hold me. I'll find a way." She glanced sideways at him and drew in her breath sharply. The moonlight frosted his golden hair with a silver sheen, and he was as beautiful as any ancient god. It was almost an irresistible temptation to let her gaze linger, but she forced herself to look back at the river. That angel-devil beauty was a snare, a weapon he no doubt knew well how to wield. She must not let herself become entangled in his web.

She had to think, to seek out a weakness in Savron. She was silent, her mind leaping from one possibility to another. "What promise did you give Mikhail Kuzdief?"

She felt him stiffen beside her. "Do you actually expect me to tell you?"

"Why not? I'm only a woman."

He chuckled. "That bit of irony would have done justice to Marc Antony at Caesar's funeral."

"Well?"

His gaze searched her face. It would be unwise to

tell her, yet he knew abruptly that he was going to do so. She was as valiant as the warrior Mikhail had called her and they had stripped her of every weapon. Giving her back one small assurance would surely do no harm. "I promised him I would never take you against your will."

"I see." She tried to keep her voice emotionless, to hide the tingle of excitement his words had ignited within her. "It was very kind of him to care. I owe him a debt."

"Mikhail has a gentle heart." His lips twisted. "He's completely unlike myself in that respect."

"I agree." She turned briskly toward the stateroom. "Can you summon him from your cabin?"

He nodded. "There's a bell pull beside the bed."

"Then send for him. I'm very good with healing. Sometimes a minor cut can be very dangerous if a bit of cloth or dirt gets into the wound."

"You're suddenly very solicitous," Nicholas said dryly. "It couldn't be that you think you can persuade him to help you?"

She looked at him in surprise. "No, he told me he was loyal to you. I know he would not betray you."

"Then why do you want to bind up his wounds and soothe his fevered brow?"

"He is a good man," she said simply. "And I owe him a debt. I always pay my debts. Besides, it was not his fault he felt bound to help you any more than it was mine that I had to defend myself. Until there is reason for us to fight again, we can be friends."

He gazed at her blankly. There was no doubt of her

sincerity. At that moment she had the clear simplicity of a small child. "You hold no grudge?"

"Not against him." She strode past him toward the stateroom. "Only against you, your highness." Her tone was coolly mocking. "I most definitely hold a grudge against you."

"Don't you think formality is rather absurd considering the intimacy of our circumstances? My name is Nicholas."

She glanced at him over her shoulder. "I think perhaps you're right. In one way or another we shall be more intimate than you dream, Nicholas."

She opened the door and entered the stateroom without another backward glance.

"You must change the bandage morning and night until the wound forms a scab." Silver's brow furrowed in concentration. "It seems clean, but I've seen lesser wounds than this fester and cause a fever."

Mikhail nodded as he stood up, his brawny muscles rippling in the lamplight as he reached for his tunic on the table beside him. "I, too." He pulled the tunic over his head. "Remember Boris Kravitz, Nicholas? One week hale and hearty with a tiny cut on his thumb." He drew his index finger across his throat. "The next week we were measuring him for a coffin."

"I remember." Nicholas's tone was abstracted, his gaze fastened on Silver. "You were telling the truth; you do know a great deal about caring for wounds."

"I should. Except for four months a year, when Rising Star insisted I come to Killara for schooling, I spent my entire childhood in an Apache village." Her lips twisted. "There was much opportunity to learn about healing battle wounds."

"Rising Star?"

"My aunt who married Joshua Delaney." Her lashes suddenly lowered to veil her eyes. "She died in childbirth four years ago." She turned back to Mikhail. "I have no salve to give you for the cut. If you'd allowed me to pack a portmanteau instead of snatching me away with nothing but a cloak, I could have brought my medicine and herb box."

He shook his head, his eyes twinkling. "You gave me enough trouble without stopping to fetch luggage. Perhaps next time—"

Silver's smile lit her face with warmth as she held up her hand to stop the flow of words. "Next time I'll do the snatching, Mikhail Kuzdief."

Mikhail burst out laughing. "Only if you put on two hundred pounds and grow two feet taller, little one."

Jealousy. My God, I am actually jealous of Mikhail, Nicholas thought with amazement as he gazed at Silver Delaney's glowing face. She had not smiled for him. It was Mikhail who had caused that sudden sunburst of radiance that made him realize yet again what a magnificently beautiful woman Silver Delaney was. Before, he had been conscious only of her stormy sensuality, now he knew she possessed an attraction infinitely more complex. He found his nails digging into the palms of his hands as his fists clenched, and he consciously forced himself to relax.

But it should have been him, dammit. She should have smiled first at him.

"My aunt was fond of telling me a tale from the Bible about a giant named Goliath and a boy named David." Silver's eyes danced. "I immediately went out and began practicing with a slingshot. I became very good at it."

Mikhail chuckled. "Better than with your little knife?"

She tilted her head as if to consider. "Well, the—"

"If you've finished, perhaps Mikhail should go to bed," Nicholas interrupted. "We wouldn't want him to become overtired."

Mikhail looked at him in surprise. "I am not—" He stopped and then nodded in comprehension. "I will go to bed." He glanced at Silver. "Thank you for bandaging my wound, little one. Do not worry. No harm will come to you."

"I know," Silver said calmly. "Sleep well, Mikhail."

When the door closed behind the Cossack, Silver turned to Nicholas. "I'm tired. I also wish to go to bed. Where do you want me to sleep?"

There was no smile, no hint of provocation; her expression was coolly matter-of-fact. He gestured toward the bed. "Did you expect any other answer?"

"No." She took off the waist-length jacket and began unbuttoning her high-necked white blouse. "It doesn't matter to me where I sleep, though perhaps it will to you."

His gaze clung compulsively to her rapidly moving fingers unfastening her shirtwaist. "No perhaps about it." He sat down in the chair Mikhail had just vacated and stretched out his legs before him, crossing them at the ankles. "It's of the utmost importance to me. I've thought of little else since I left you this afternoon."

"That seems a long time ago." She took off the rumpled white blouse and tossed it carelessly on the padded velvet bench at the foot of the bed. She heard a soft sound as if Nicholas had drawn a deep breath, but she didn't look at him. She had not thought this would be so difficult. Her hands must not tremble, she must show no signs of the turbulence she was feeling or she would be lost. Nicholas was a man accustomed to reading women and would leap on any hint of weakness. If she was to defeat him, she must show him nothing but indifference. She sat down and briskly unbuttoned her ankle-high boots and pulled them off.

"Would you like any help?"

He had asked his question in a voice that was hoarse, she noticed with satisfaction. He was hurting. "No." She set the shoes neatly together beneath the bench and stood up to begin untying the white silk ribbons of her camisole. "I am not a child who cannot unbutton her shoes. Why should you help?"

"Because I want my hands on you."

"Are you disturbed?" she asked coolly, still not looking at him. "I wonder why?"

"My God, you're bold. How many other men have you undressed in front of like this?"

She didn't answer as she slipped the strap of her camisole off one golden shoulder.

"How *many*, dammit?"

"I don't see what difference it makes. How many do you suppose?"

She heard a muttered curse as she pushed the other strap off her shoulder. The thin muslin slipped down until it barely crested her upper breasts, only their roundness keeping the garment from falling to fully reveal the lush bounty outlined beneath the material. Her fingers mustn't shake. It merely took strength of will, she reminded herself. She glanced around the room to avoid looking at him. Her eyes widened as they encountered the murals on the walls and her gaze swung back to Nicholas in surprise. She immediately regretted the lapse.

Nicholas's broad cheeks were flushed, his lips thickly sensual, his dark eyes fastened on her with an intensity that caused an odd current of heat to flow through her. She hurriedly looked away. "What . . . interesting murals you have. Exactly what I would have expected of you."

"You're not shocked?" His voice was suddenly rough. "One would almost think you're accustomed to the accoutrements of a bordello."

She shook her head as she unfastened her skirt. "I've only been in one bordello, and there were no pictures like this."

"Only one?" He laughed harshly. "At the advanced age of nineteen? Pray, what have you been doing with your time? May I ask whether you were purchasing or selling?"

It seemed she had struck pay dirt. Something she had said was evidently annoying him exceedingly. "Neither. Though Rina did once ask me if I wanted a job."

"Rina?"

"Rina Bradshaw." She took off her blue skirt, draped it over the bench, and stood garbed only in the camisole and her petticoats. "She runs a whorehouse in Hell's Bluff."

"You must have impressed her. Will you take off that goddam camisole?"

"You wish to see my breasts?" She shrugged. "Very well. I don't understand why white men become so excited when a woman takes off her clothes. Indians are much more sensible. They accept a naked body as a part of nature."

She took off the camisole, revealing a glimpse of full, heavy breasts crowned by pink areolas for only a tenth of a second before she turned her back on him to lay the camisole with the other garments on the bench. "Indian children run naked unless the weather becomes cold." She quickly finished disrobing. "Yet white children and even women are forced to wear layers and layers of clothing and become smothered with—"

"Turn around."

She could feel the muscles of her spine stiffen with tension and she forced herself to relax. Now she must face him and he must see no weakness. She slowly turned and unconsciously lifted her chin. "Yes?"

Nicholas hadn't thought he could become more aroused, but he now realized how mistaken he had been. The muscles of his stomach twisted and he could feel his manhood thrust against the material of his trousers as his gaze moved over her. Why had he sat there in a torment of lust while she teased him to this unbearable pitch? She had challenged him with her body and those damn cool words that incited anger and desire and jealousy until he thought he would go mad.

"Enough?" she asked, lifting one winged brow. "I'm getting chilly."

"No, not enough." He wasn't sure at that moment that he'd ever get enough of looking at her. Lord, she was beautiful. Golden rose-tipped breasts flowing to a narrow waist and then to sweetly curving hips and firm buttocks. Shining ebony hair streamed straight and silky to the middle of her back, and her eyes were brilliantly alive, challenging his mind almost as much as his body.

His gaze traveled down to linger on the soft thatch of hair protecting her womanhood. The palms of his hands on the arms of the chair began to tingle as he thought of rubbing them against that soft nest and then parting her thighs and— "Come here."

"Why?"

He looked up impatiently. "My dear Silver, the reason couldn't be more obvious." He glanced down at his lower body and made a face. "Oh, yes, very obvious."

"Why?" she repeated.

A muscle jerked in his cheek. "To consummate the fire you've built so skillfully. I want to *touch* you."

"But you can't touch me." Her gray eyes met his with absolutely no expression. "That wasn't what I intended at all."

His gaze narrowed on her face. "And just what did you intend?"

"I wanted you to hurt." Her voice was suddenly fierce. "I wanted you to want me as men always want women and not be able to touch me."

"The hell I won't!" His eyes were blazing with fury. "I'm going to—" He stopped. His promise to Mikhail. Dammit to hell, his promise to Mikhail!

She nodded slowly, the faintest smile touching her lips. "You will not do it because you promised your friend you would not. You value your friend, and I think you're a man who also values your word. You were very foolish to tell me of your promise."

"You little she-cat," he said through clenched teeth. "I told you that to make you feel more secure. I didn't want you frightened of me."

"I wasn't frightened." Her eyes blazed back at him. "I was angry. You forced me to come here against my will. Did you care that I have my own life to live? There are things I must do. The circus is leaving soon and I—"

He stiffened. "How unfortunate that you'll have to live without the embrace of your lover."

"My lover?" She shrugged impatiently. "All you can think of is . . ." Her gaze moved significantly down his body and rested with satisfaction on the hard column outlined beneath his tight trousers. "But that's what I want you to think of tonight and every night we are together." She whirled on her heel, her hair flying wildly about her silken nudity, and crossed the few paces to the bed. She brushed the sheer batiste bed curtains aside, jerked the peach-colored spread down, and slipped into bed. She glared at him across the room. "I told you I would punish you."

He could feel the fury surging through him, blinding, hot, breathtaking. Anger almost as intense as the desire that was a jagged torment in his body. He slowly stood up and moved deliberately across the room. "What a vengeful little bitch you are," he said softly. "I thought I had learned all the wicked little tricks a woman could find to torture a man. I was wrong." He stood over her, his gaze meeting her own. "I supposed I should have expected that you would be especially well versed in such arts. I've heard that savages were skillful in the ways of torture."

She flinched. "We are, but we acquired most of our knowledge from the white man. We never flaunted killing until they taught us how to scalp and count coup. How many scalps have you hung at your belt, Nicholas?"

"I've never counted." His hand suddenly tangled in her hair and jerked her head back. "But I believe I'm about to start."

She stared back at him fearlessly. "No, you won't. You're like most men who have honor toward men and not toward women. You won't break your promise."

He gazed down at her for a long moment, his chest moving harshly with the force of his breathing. Then, slowly, finger by finger, he released her hair. He straightened, moving jerkily, as if his every muscle was atrophied by age. He closed his eyes. "No, I'll not break my promise, damn you!"

His hair was tousled gold in the lamplight, his nostrils flaring with each breath, his bronze skin pulled tight over the broad bones of his cheeks. She had a fleeting memory of the first moment she had seen him, when she had thought he looked like a sensual Apollo. that resemblance was even more pronounced now. He was a deity burning, Apollo in a fever of passion. A woman would have had to be made of ice not to be stirred by Nicholas Savron in that moment. Ice, Silver prayed desperately. She must be ice.

His eyes flicked open and he smiled down at her. Surprise rippled through her. His smile was almost . . . loving. "A challenge?" His voice was velvet soft.

"No!" she protested.

"I think you lie, Silver." One finger gently touched her cheek. "I think you're a woman who must always have a challenge. Well, I intend to accommodate you. I won't force you. I won't even touch you without your permission." His finger trailed lazily down her cheek to the corner of her mouth. "Until you ask me to sheath myself in you and give you what you want."

"I won't—"

"You will." His lids half veiled the gleaming darkness of his eyes. "Because you didn't count on one thing. Your body. That very lovely body that wants me just as much as I want it. I knew the first moment I saw you that you were a very sensual lady. If I'm in pain, then you'll be in pain too." His finger slid down to the hollow of her throat. His smile deepened as he felt the sudden leap of her heart. "You see?"

"I see nothing." In spite of her effort, the words held a slight quaver.

His hand dropped away from her throat. "And to think I believed you were an honest woman," he said mockingly. He turned and strolled to the door he had told her led to the grand saloon. He paused with a hand on the doorknob to look back at her. "And I have one other advantage not available to you. There are any number of women on this boat who will allow me the relief you deny me, and I have no intention of allowing you to receive a similiar satisfaction from any other man. If you burn, you must appeal to me for relief." He gazed at her a moment longer, his expression a mixture of desire, anger, and pain. Then he was gone and she heard the door lock behind him.

The room was suddenly larger, less threatening, yet . . . empty. Silver drew a deep, quivering breath, her taut muscles wilting like wildflowers at the first frost. She was shaking, she realized, surprised and indignant at her body's betrayal. There was no reason for her to respond in this fashion. Nicholas was only a man, and she had been the victor in this encounter. This sudden weakness must be due to the strain of the

evening. After she had rested she would be better able
to face the challenge Nicholas offered.

Challenge. It had been he, not she, who had issued
the challenge. It had been ridiculous of him to claim
anything else. She had wanted only to punish him for
doing this to her. No one should be allowed to
victimize another human being, and he had vic-
timized both Etaine and herself. It made no difference
that he knew nothing about the child. Nicholas
Savron's arrogance was intolerable and she *had* punished him. Why did it leave her feeling so lackluster
and drained?

She would think no more of him, she decided. She
would sleep and gain strength for the struggles to
come. She sat up, drew back the filmy bed curtain,
and blew out the flame in the oil lamp on the bedside
table. Darkness. Sudden, overpowering darkness that
smothered and took her breath. She was excruciating-
ly aware of the closeness of the room, of the locked
door holding her captive. She found herself panting,
her heart pounding wildly, she was smothering with
the sense of her own helplessness.

Etaine. Was this how Etaine felt when she was
attacked by that horrible breathlessness? Dear God,
how could the child bear it so patiently? Etaine was a
prisoner in so many ways, a prisoner of her illness, a
prisoner of the cage, a prisoner of her monster of a
father. In her place Silver would have gone mad or
broken herself fighting against the bars of her helplessness trying to escape. Yet how much longer could
Etaine withstand the kind of treatment she was

receiving? She must be freed, and to do that Silver must free herself.

She suddenly leaned forward, her hand fumbling in the darkness until the lamp was once again lit. That was better. At least the light banished the smothering sensation. She lay down again, drawing the muslin sheet up to her throat and turning on her side to gaze at the oil lamp on the nightstand a few feet away. Seen through the sheer batiste of the bed curtain, the flickering flame appeared like a golden chimera, she thought absently. Would Nicholas return tonight? Probably not. He had told her he would seek out another woman, so she doubted she would see him before morning.

She was glad, relieved, she told herself. This time alone would allow her to think of Etaine and recover her strength of purpose.

Silver was asleep.

Her golden cheek was cradled on the softness of the white muslin of the pillow, her dark lashes forming feathery shadows on the beautiful line of her high cheekbones. She slept deeply, like a child exhausted from a day at play.

Nicholas stood in the doorway, his hand clenched on the china doorknob, his gaze on the sleeping woman in bed. Dammit, it wasn't fair for her to look so innocently vulnerable. This was the woman who had stabbed Mikhail with her dagger, who had taunted him with her body, who had confessed to frequenting whorehouses. Why was there no sign of dissipation or corruption on her face?

He softly closed the door and crossed the room to stand beside the bed. The clean line of her cheek possessed an air of purity in the mellow pool of light radiating from the oil lamp on the nightstand. As he watched, her rose-pink lips parted and she sighed, her cheek moving restlessly on the pillow as if fierce wariness still held her in thrall. How deeply must that wariness be embedded to erect barriers even while she slept. God, no child should feel such a strong need to protect herself, he thought with a strange tightness constricting his chest.

Child. He had not thought of her as a child before this. In spite of her youth, she had seemed as totally adult and womanly as any Eve or Delilah. While she was awake he had seen only the strength and the fire of her. Hell and damnation, that was all he *wanted* to see. He didn't want to think of her as a child growing up torn between Indian and white and yet wanted by neither. He didn't want to remember how painful it was being uprooted from the land you loved and sent to live among strangers. All he wanted was to lie down beside her in this bed and lose himself in her body. It was passion not tenderness he wanted from Silver. Yet he couldn't deny it was tenderness he was feeling for her now. Aching poignant tenderness that was almost unbearable in its intensity. Unexplainable, frustrating tenderness. His hand impulsively reached out to touch the flowing richness of her hair.

Then he stopped, his hand dropping to his side. His

wish not to wake her was as unexplainable as the gentleness coursing through his veins. He had come here tonight to begin the first foray in the battle to which she had challenged him. In the past hours he had indulged himself with two bottles of wine and the cloying attention of several voluptuous women. The wine had only made him morose and the women had no effect upon him whatever. It was Silver Delaney he wanted and Silver Delaney he would have.

But he knew now he would not have Silver Delaney tonight.

He turned down the wick of the crystal-prismed oil lamp, blew out the small lingering flame, and moved toward the door in darkness. His Cossack training told him he was a fool to let an enemy rest and gain strength, and his body told him he was worse than a fool not to appease the lust besetting it. He smiled crookedly as his hand closed on the knob of the door. Oh, well, it was said that the angels had a special blessing for fools and madmen, and God knew, he had need of all the help he could get from that elite circle. He would search out an empty stateroom and lie chastely in its bed, planning his campaign against the dubious virtue of Silver Delaney.

The thought of chastity in connection with himself caused his smile to become a chuckle of genuine amusement as he quietly slipped out of the stateroom and locked the door behind him.

4

"Awaken, sweet damsel." A knock had sounded on the door and the deep masculine voice that immediately followed was definitely not that of Nicholas Savron. "I've brought you a breakfast fit for the gods. Well, perhaps not the gods, they were noted for very peculiar tastes at times, but certainly fit for anyone who inhabits this mortal plane."

Silver sat up hurriedly, pushing an unruly strand of hair behind her ear and automatically pulling the sheet and velvet spread up to her throat. She was just in time, for the door was unlocked and a handsome young man strode into the stateroom carrying a tray, kicking the door shut behind him with one elegantly shod foot. "I hope you're hungry. Mikhail insisted you must have everything from eggs to fried fish." His bright blue eyes gleamed with both amusement and curiosity. "I told him it was very foolish of him to give you added nourishment, considering what you did to him on only schoolroom fare, but Mikhail seldom listens to me. He considers Nicky the only person who deserves his attention." He set the tray on the bedside table, his gaze appraising her with frank interest. "You don't appear lethal. I find it difficult to believe you stabbed Mikhail and put Nicky to flight."

"Who are you?" Silver asked bluntly.

"My apologies." The young man nodded formally. "I'm Count Valentin Marinov, and I'm delighted to make your acquaintance. Of course, I'd be more delighted if you'd tell Nicky what he wants to know so that we can return to Russia." His gaze wandered to her smooth, naked shoulders only half concealed by the velvet spread she was clutching. "You may find it difficult to eat unless you release your fierce grip on that coverlet. Are you, by any fortunate chance, naked beneath that spread?"

Her eyes flickered warily. "Yes."

"And still Nicky left you? How interesting." He walked the few paces that separated him from the large mahogany armoire. "And unprecedented. Tell me, do all young American ladies sleep unclothed?"

"I don't believe so."

"Pity. I thought for a moment I'd found a reason to stay here in spite of the abominable climate." He opened the armoire, took out a dark green velvet robe, and tossed it onto the foot of the bed. "This is Nicky's, but I'm sure it will look far better on you." He turned his back to her, folding his arms across his chest. "Do you notice what a gentleman I'm being? That's because Mikhail warned me he'd squash my head like a walnut if I insulted you in any way. What magic did you work on the poor fellow?"

"None." Silver threw the covers aside, stood up,

and reached for the robe. She slipped it on and found it was far too big. Still, the material did feel like a soft, sensuous caress on her flesh, and the scent . . . She curiously lifted her arm and sniffed at the velvet sleeve. Tobacco, soap, and the faint hint of musk she already identified with Nicholas Savron. It was like being sheathed in the man himself, she mused. Then she felt the hot color stain her cheeks at the thought.

"May I turn around?" Valentin asked politely.

"Yes." She finished buttoning the robe and hurriedly combed her fingers through her hair as he turned to look at her. She did not care how she appeared to Nicholas or any of these men, she assured herself. It was only that it was vaguely unpleasant to feel so disheveled and untidy in front of anyone.

"Lovely," Valentin said softly. "That color is ravishing with your complexion. Nicky tells me you're half Indian."

"Are you sure he didn't say savage?" Silver asked dryly.

Marinov's eyes twinkled. "I don't believe that word was used, though perhaps the implication was there. He was quite savage himself last night when he joined our party after he left you. I don't suppose you'd care to divulge what happened to make him so bad-tempered?"

Silver smiled ironically. "Perhaps his highness felt insulted by a rejection from one so far beneath him."

Marinov's amusement faded. "Not Nicky. He's had to battle too many insults and snubs himself to knowingly offer one to someone else for reasons of birth."

"Why would a prince suffer insult?" she asked in disbelief.

"His father was a prince, one of the most powerful boyars in all Russia, but his mother is the daughter of Igor Dabol, a Cossack leader of the Kuban who raised himself from serfdom by becoming the most superb fighter in the steppes." Valentin's lips twisted in a sardonic smile. "A boyar does *not* wed the daughter of a serf, and, if he does, the child of such a marriage is not accepted warmly by the nobility."

"And by the Cossacks?" Silver aked slowly.

"Among the Cossacks any man is allowed to prove himself, and Nicky was leading one of Igor's bands when he was only sixteen. He was chosen as Igor's successor and would have become—" He broke off and slowly shook his head. "You're too curious. Nicky wouldn't approve of me discussing this with you. Why don't you sit down and eat that breakfast Mikhail ordered for you?"

She sat down and rolled up the wide sleeves of the robe. "You're of the nobility and yet you're evidently his friend." Her gaze lifted to meet his. "Why?"

"You know, you have truly magnificent eyes," he said absently. Then he shrugged. "Why does any friendship begin? We were in the army together. God knows, we're nothing alike. He's rich and I'm poor. He's reckless and I'm cautious. He has the soul of a poet and I have the soul of a sybarite."

She simply looked at him, waiting.

He suddenly laughed. "Very well, he's the best friend I've ever had. We've fought together, gotten drunk together, even cried together. He's never failed me. Is that what you wanted to know?"

"Yes." It was as she had thought. Nicholas Savron was not a man to let down a friend or break a promise. If he could inspire loyalty in men like Kuzdief and Marinov, then his promise was even more binding than she had first believed and the weapon in her hands far more powerful. "That's exactly what I wanted to know. Why did you bring me my breakfast? I would hardly expect a count to lower himself to act as a servant." She picked up the fork beside the plate. "Though I've never met a count before. Perhaps you all—"

"You've never met a count before?" Marinov interrupted. "But what about . . ."

She glanced up. "What?"

He studied her thoughtfully. "Nothing. How's the fish?"

"Very good." She began to eat swiftly and with enthusiasm. "You didn't answer me."

"Oh, I was curious." He stood watching her, a slight frown wrinkling his brow. "It's the only flaw in my otherwise perfect character. Actually, Mikhail was going to bring your breakfast, but I persuaded him to let me do it instead. Nicky is giving permission only to Mikhail and myself to come into the cabin."

"I see." She finished the fish and eggs and began eating a large fluffy biscuit. "Am I to be allowed out of the cabin?"

He lifted a brow at the almost empty plate in front of her. "There's certainly nothing finicky about your appetite. I thought abducted ladies were prone to languish and swoon."

"I don't know how to languish and swoon." She finished the biscuit. "Perhaps you'd be kind enough to show me."

His delighted laughter rang out and was so contagious that Silver found herself smiling in return. "No?"

Marinov shook his head, a smile still lingering on his lips. "I believe I can see why Nicky was thrown into a tumult. I'm afraid swoons are not acceptable in dashing young men of impeccable lineage. You'll have to be tutored elsewhere."

"Too much trouble. I'll just have to get along as I have been."

He chuckled again. "You don't seem overly worried about your situation."

Her gaze was direct. "My situation will change soon. I will not let myself be kept here. In the meantime, there's no need for me to starve myself."

He glanced at the crumbs on the tray. "Very sensible. May I add to your comfort in any other way?"

"A bath," she said promptly. "And my clothes cleaned and pressed."

"Anything else?"

"I want to go for a walk."

He frowned. "I don't know. Nicky—"

"Is not here."

"True. But when he does make his appearance, he'll

probably have a head as big as a paddle wheel." He grimaced. "He was drinking wine as if it were water last night."

"Then he deserves to suffer."

"But I don't, and he has a tongue that can sting like frostbite when he's displeased." He bent to gather her discarded clothing from the padded bench at the foot of the bed. "I'll take these and give them to a servant to clean, and arrange for a hip bath to be brought to you, but we'll have to see about your little promenade."

"There's no reason—"

"No," he said with surprising firmness. "My dear Miss Delaney, you will please quit pushing me where I don't wish to go. I get more than enough of that from Nicky."

She studied him with amusement and the beginning of respect. Marinov was stronger than she had first thought. Then the amusement vanished as she realized that this meant Nicholas must also be stronger to merit Marinov's loyalty. "My name is Silver. May I call you Valentin?"

"I am honored," he said warily. "I think. You aren't, by any chance, attempting to seduce me, are you?"

"No," she said, looking at him in surprise. "I don't know how to do that either."

"No? I understood that—" He broke off. She was gazing at him with clear-eyed honesty that was as guileless as it was bewildering. There was something wrong here. The girl before him was like no other he had ever met, and he did not understand her. Bold-

ness and innocence did not usually walk hand in hand
in his experience, but he had seen both qualities in
Silver Delaney. "Perhaps a *small* walk would do no
harm."

"Where is she?" Nicholas asked tersely as he strode
down the deck toward Valentin. "For God's sake, I
didn't tell you to give her the run of the boat."

"She wanted to take a walk," Valentin protested
innocently. "And as you weren't stirring, I decided
someone should escort her."

"And then you promptly let her wander off by
herself."

"You malign me." Valentin shook his head mourn-
fully. "She isn't by herself and I know exactly where
she is."

Nicholas gritted his teeth and immediately regretted it as the aching throb in his head tripled its
tempo. "Valentin . . ." He spaced each word carefully. "Where is she?"

"The last I saw of her she was up in the pilot house
steering the *Rose*."

"What!"

"Not by herself," Valentin said soothingly. "Robert
is with her, of course. He appears to be quite proud of
her progress. He told her she'd make a fine pilot given
a year or two on the Mississippi."

"I didn't bring her aboard the *Rose* for her to
apprentice as a riverboat pilot." Nicholas looked up
at the pilot house perched like a tiny gingerbread
cottage on the Texas deck. "And how the hell did she

get Robert to let her invade his sacred domain? He doesn't let anyone up there."

"I'm aware you have another apprenticeship in mind for her," Valentin murmured, his gaze following Nicholas's to the pilot house. "And I'm sure that any of Madam LaRue's ladies would be a fitting tutor for the occupation you've chosen for her."

There was an edge to Valentin's voice that caused Nicholas to look at him sharply. "What is that supposed to mean?"

Valentin's gaze remained on the pilot house. "It means I think you should limit your vengeance to Dominic Delaney. Silver told me a few things about herself, and her life hasn't been easy. Did you know she was left on the Delaneys' doorstep at Killara and they rejected her and sent her back to her mother's tribe? Isn't it possible to let her go?"

"No."

Valentin's expression was troubled. "There's something wrong, Nicky. She's not . . ." He shrugged helplessly as he searched for words. "What I expected."

"She's not what I expected either," Nicholas said tightly. "But that doesn't mean—" His fist suddenly crashed down on the wooden rail. "What is there about her that's making all of you turn soft as bonbons? First Mikhail, then you, and now—"

"You?" Valentin eyed him shrewdly.

"I assure you I'm feeling not at all soft toward Silver Delaney."

"No assurance necessary." Valentin chuckled. "Your 'hardness' toward her is more than obvious."

Nicholas cast him a quelling glance. "I was referring to Robert. How did she mesmerize our young river pilot?"

"Why don't you go see for yourself?" Valentin asked softly. He straightened away from the rail. "In fact, I believe I'll go with you. I told Silver I'd be back in an hour anyway."

"I'm sure you wouldn't want to renege on your promise," Nicholas said caustically as he turned toward the stairs leading to the Texas deck. "She seems to inspire an amazing degree of devotion."

"Perhaps because she doesn't try to be anything but what she is," Valentin said. "I find that very refreshing."

When Nicholas opened the door of the pilot house it was quickly obvious that Robert Danfold found Silver equally refreshing. The two were so absorbed that neither realized Nicholas and Valentin had arrived.

Robert's face was alight with enthusiasm as he stood behind Silver at the wheel, watching with razor-sharp eyes every move she made. "That's right, now a little to the starboard. See those lines and circles on that slick water? That means it's shoaling up and that's a danger."

"What about that slanting mark on the water down-river?" Silver asked, her brow wrinkled in concentration.

Danfold grinned. "You have a good eye. There's a

bluff reef under the surface there that could wreck any riverboat that comes too near."

"So many dangers." Silver shook her head. "The river looks lazy and peaceful and yet every mile poses another threat."

"Not only the river," Robert Danfold said. "Half the boats on the river are miserable scows manned by pilots who don't know a sandbar from a clear channel. Before I got the job on the *Rose* I was a pilot on another of Mr. Bassinger's boats, the *Mary L.*" He shook his head. "Her boilers should have been re-placed five years ago. Someday they're going to blow the *Mary L* clear to Hades, just like the *Sultana*."

"The *Sultana*?" Silver asked.

"Watch that floating log," Robert warned crisply. "The *Sultana* was carrying Yankee soldiers up north back in April of sixty-five. After midnight one night the boilers blew. Over fifteen hundred men, women, and children died from fire and drowning before dawn."

"How terrible," Silver whispered, her gaze flying to Robert's face.

He nodded. "I told Mr. Bassinger it could happen to the *Mary L*, but he wouldn't listen to me." He smiled comfortingly at Silver. "Don't you worry though. The boilers on the *Rose* are sound as a dollar. She's the best boat on the river."

Silver nodded. "Yes, and she's beautiful, too, Robert. I can see why you're so proud of her."

They exchanged a companionable smile that was full of mutual respect.

Nicholas felt a surge of hot irritation that was beginning to be uncomfortably familiar. He took a step forward. "She won't stay the best boat on the river if you continue to leave her fate in the hands of novices."

Robert and Silver both looked over their shoulders and Robert grinned. "Oh, hello, Nicky. Don't worry about the *Rose*. Silver is doing a fine job. Better than me when I was a cub pilot."

"I'm sure that's true." Nicholas looked squarely at Silver. "She's already demonstrated a talent for negotiating through very dangerous waters. However, even the best pilot can run aground. Don't you agree, Robert?"

"Maybe." Robert shifted uneasily. The emotions vibrating between Silver and Nicholas were charging the air of the pilot house with unrest and he didn't like it one bit. The river was enough of a challenge for a man, and no decent river pilot could concentrate on anything else when he was at the wheel. "You'd better run along, Silver."

She smiled warmly at him. "Thank you for teaching me, Robert. It was very interesting. May I come back?"

Robert glanced at Nicholas's taut face and then shook his head. "I reckon you'd better not." He turned back to the river with a feeling of relief. He'd a hell of a lot rather face a hidden reef than Nicholas Savron at this moment.

"We're disturbing Robert," Nicholas said. "I think it's time you went back to the stateroom."

Silver released the steering wheel and strolled across the room, smiling at Valentin, who stood a pace behind Nicholas. "It was very exciting, Valentin. You should have stayed and watched. The river is like a book if you know how to read her." She laughed as she glanced back over her shoulder at Robert. "Listen to me, Robert. I sound just like you."

She was ignoring him, Nicholas realized, feeling a quick wave of fury wash through him. She had smiles and words for every other man on the boat, but she completely ignored him.

Robert nodded. "River talk."

Valentin was looking apprehensively from Nicholas's face to Silver's. It was the first time he had seen them together and he was beginning to understand much that had eluded him. Sweet Jesus, the atmosphere between them was near explosive and Silver was making it no better by deliberately ignoring Nicholas.

"I'm sure it's fascinating." Valentin feigned a yawn. "But it's hot as the devil up here. Why don't we go back to the stateroom and have a glass of wine?"

"If you like." Silver brushed by Nicholas and fell into step with Valentin. "Though I have no likeness for wine." She laughed, tossing back her shining mane of dark hair as she started down the stairs to the hurricane deck. "Perhaps you haven't heard that we Indians have to be careful of firewater. Whites have taken too much from us when our heads weren't clear."

"It's understandable," Nicholas said silkily. "I'm

sure they felt they needed every advantage against the heathen horde."

Silver's smile faded. "You bet they did." She had avoided looking at Nicholas since that first breathless moment in the pilot house, but she forced herself to meet his gaze now. "Apaches know how to make war."

"But you're only half Apache."

"But the other half is Delaney, and I'd wager they could teach your fine Cossacks a thing or two about fighting."

"We shall see," Nicholas said. He turned to Valentin. "Silver and I have something to discuss. I'm sure you can amuse yourself elsewhere."

Valentin's eyes flickered. "How rude you're being, Nicky. I'm sure Silver would not be unwilling to tolerate my presence."

Nicholas drew an impatient breath. "But it's not Silver's choice." His hand was suddenly beneath Silver's elbow, propelling her along the deck toward his stateroom. "I believe it's time that both she and the rest of you remember that fact."

Valentin gazed after them for a moment, an anxious frown darkening his face. Then he gave a resigned sigh, turned, and headed for the door leading to the saloon.

Nicholas leaned against the stateroom door, his gaze following Silver as she crossed the room and plopped down on the olive velvet wing chair beside the bed.

She stretched her legs before her with the coltish

carelessness of a young boy and gazed at him coolly.
"Well, we're here. What do you want with me?"

"I think you know the answer to that question." His
gaze traveled slowly over her, lingering on the soft
fullness of her breasts. "I've certainly done my best to
be very clear on the subject."

She gestured impatiently. "I don't understand why
you're so determined to fornicate with me. Surely one
woman is as good as another as far as men are
concerned. Women's bodies are all much the same."

He looked at her in surprise. Then a smile lit his
face. "You either have very little vanity or you grossly
underestimate my discrimination. I assure you there
are vast differences in women." He hadn't realized
how different a woman could be until he had encountered Silver Delaney. His smile faded when he re-
called he was not the only man who had found the girl
unique. She had deftly wound Mikhail and Valentin
around her little finger and even Robert had proved
he wasn't immune. "What were you doing up in the
pilot house?"

She looked at him innocently. "Learning to steer
the boat. It was very boring cooped up in this room.
What else should I have been doing?"

"Perhaps trying to persuade Robert to help you
escape? He seemed quite taken with you."

"Because you think of nothing but lust, you believe
all men are like you. Robert would never be tempted
to give up his beautiful river for a woman."

"I'm glad you realize that. Then you don't have any

reason to go back there. You seem to forget you're a prisoner."

"I'm trying to forget." Her eyes were suddenly blazing. "Because when I remember, I feel like cutting off your balls."

My God, every word she spoke was a shock and most of the time totally outrageous. He threw back his head and laughed.

She glared at him. "You wouldn't think it so funny if I still had my knife."

"I'm sure that's true." He continued to laugh. "I fancy I would be taking your every word very seriously." He straightened away from the door and began to move toward her, his dark eyes still sparkling with humor. "Just as I intend you to take mine seriously." He stopped before her and his voice lowered to a level above a whisper. "I had a very bad night last night."

"It was your own fault. Valentin told me you drank too much wine."

"It wasn't the wine."

"It was me? Good, you deserved it. Perhaps next time you will think a second time before you abduct a woman."

"I'll certainly ascertain whether she carries a knife and has an Apache code of vengeance." He shook his head, a smile still lingering on his lips. "Half the night I was cursing you and the other half I was lying in that bed down the hall remembering how you looked standing naked before me, taunting me. Did you think about that moment after I left you too?"

She stiffened. She didn't want to think of either her gesture of defiance or the look on Nicholas Savron's face as he had sat there like some golden-haired diety watching her disrobe. The memory brought a hot aching between her thighs and caused the beat of her heart to quicken. "No." She unconsciously moistened her lips with her tongue. "I told you, Indians have a more sensible attitude toward their bodies than whites. It meant nothing to me."

He suddenly dropped to his knees before her, his gaze searching her face. "I think you're not telling me the truth," he said softly. "I think you wanted me to touch you as much as I wanted to touch you last night. Would you like me to tell you what I was thinking as I watched you? I was thinking I'd never seen a more magnificent woman in all my life. I was thinking your breasts were like perfectly shaped golden melons, firm, solid, generous—just meant for a man's hands. I was thinking I'd like to lift your breasts to my mouth and suck until those pink nipples were flame-red and hard." His eyes were riveted to her rounded fullness beneath the prim white bodice. "As hard as I was."

"You're talking foolishness." Her voice sounded choked even to her own ears. She wanted to look away but she couldn't seem to pull her gaze from his face. "I wouldn't have let you—"

"And I was thinking how I'd like to run my hand down your body." His gaze dropped to her lap, demurely draped in the gabardine skirt. "I want to tangle my fingers in those soft curls and tug and tease until you open your thighs and welcome me. Then I'd press my thumb on your—"

"Stop!" Her voice was shaking and she had to take a deep breath to steady it. What was he doing to her? He hadn't touched her, yet her body felt heavy with an aching sensuality, her breasts swollen and sensitive. She suddenly wanted to tear open her shirtwaist and free her breasts. She wanted his hands lifting and fondling her, his mouth— No, she must not, she thought desperately. "Go away. I don't want you here."

He sat back on his heels and smiled. "Oh, yes, you want me here. And you want me to carry you to that bed and drive into you again and again and—"

"No. No, I don't." She pressed back against the tufted cushions of the chair, her cheeks singeing with color. "Why should I? You're nothing to me."

"Except a man who can please you." His gaze narrowed on her face. "A man who can stop you from burning. Because you are burning, Silver."

Her breasts were lifting and falling with every breath as she tried to force air into her lungs. Move away, she thought dizzily. Though not touching her, he was still too close. She could feel the heat of his strong male body and caught the scent of soap and musk she was learning to recognize as his own.

"I'm not burning," she protested.

"Yes, you are." His face lit with a strange tenderness as he smiled at her. "But don't worry, I'm not going to let you burn for long." His smile deepened to ruefulness. "I couldn't. I thought I wanted to punish you, but I decided last night it would only be punishing myself. I'm much too selfish to do anything so idiotic." He rose lithely to his feet and looked down at her. "I also decided that next time I would act as a lady's maid when you chose to disrobe in front of me. You shouldn't mind my assistance." His dark eyes were suddenly dancing with mischief. "After all, nudity is nothing to you, and I've promised to restrain my lustful nature." He paused. "Unless you issue an invitation."

She tilted her head back to look up at him. She didn't dare speak, for she knew her voice would tremble, but she refused to lower her eyes or avoid his glance.

He nodded and for a moment there was a flicker of both admiration and pride in his expression. "Later." He turned and walked toward the door. "It will be all the better if we both think about it for a while. I just wanted you to know what I would be thinking when I looked at you this evening." He opened the door and glanced back at her. "I've decided that since you seem to have such a distaste for being confined, there's no reason why you shouldn't have dinner with our guests. They may be a trifle disreputable, but a woman of your background shouldn't be uncomfortable in their presence. Dinner is at eight. Valentin will escort you to the table."

Silver breathed a sigh of relief as the door closed softly behind him. She was tingling, trembling, and her heart was pounding crazily. And he had been aware of his effect on her, dammit. She should have

known she wouldn't be able to hide her emotions from
him. She had never been good at subterfuge even as a
child. When she had tried to hide her loneliness and
fear behind a wall of defiance, Rising Star had always
been able to see right through the deceit to the
terrified child. Now this golden-haired satyr was
reading her just as easily as her aunt had.

No, that was not true. He was aware only of her
body's response, not the responses of her heart and
soul. Even if her body betrayed her, she could still
keep from yielding him anything else. He would never
know the curious aching tenderness she had experienced when he had thrown back his head and
laughed so joyously, nor her wistfulness when she had
watched him with Mikhail and Valentin. Those reactions had both been madness and she would not
acknowledge that they had existed for more than a
fleeting moment.

She rose from the chair and wandered over to the
window to gaze out at the bluffs bordering the banks
of the river. According to what Robert had revealed to
her, she might not have long to worry about Nicholas
or her reactions to him. The *Mississippi Rose* would
proceed down a channel almost in the middle of the
river for the next twenty-four hours. Then the boat
would have to bear toward the western shore to avoid
a chain of sandbars. Even a strong swimmer would
have difficulty making it to shore now, but the
distance would be cut in half tomorrow evening when
the *Rose* veered around the sandbars. She must only
make sure she was not locked in the stateroom or

surrounded by Nicholas's guests when that time came. Her hand clenched on the peach-colored velvet of the heavy curtains. It shouldn't be too difficult, much easier and less dangerous than spending another day with Nicholas.

Oh, yes, far less dangerous than staying with Nicholas Savron.

5

V alentin stood in the doorway, his gaze traveling over Silver from the top of her dark head to the tips of her sensible patent leather boots. He bowed gracefully. "You look as fresh as a spring daffodil."

"I look no different than I did this afternoon." Silver touched the bodice of her white shirtwaist. "I have nothing else to wear. Not that I would have changed for dinner anyway. Why should I care what you all think of me?" She came toward him, her back very straight, her carriage majestic. "I didn't choose to come here."

Valentin grimaced as he looked down at his own elegant attire. "Ah, such confidence. I'm afraid I've always relied upon my tailor to lend me boldness when facing a social evening."

Silver smiled. It was difficult to believe Valentin could be anything but confident in any situation. "I have a confession to make."

"Wonderful, I love to hear lovely women's confessions. I do hope it's shocking."

She lowered her voice to a whisper. "I did scrub my face and brush my hair."

Valentin's laugh rang out. "A touch of vanity at last." He offered her his arm. "Since we're obviously kindred spirits, may I escort you to the grand saloon, Miss Delaney?"

She slipped her arm in his. "I'm not nervous, you understand."

"No, of course not," he said gently. "But I am. So perhaps you'll be persuaded to bear me company this evening. A man always feels more confident with a pretty woman at his side."

She tried to hide the relief that cascaded through her. "I don't see why not." She didn't look at him as she permitted him to escort her from the stateroom. "You've been very kind to me."

She was glad for his polite chatter as well as his silent support as they traversed the long, glittering expanse of the saloon. The chandeliers shimmered with color, borrowing brilliance from the stained-glass skylights and casting a festive glow on the scene at the opposite end of the saloon. The long dinner table was covered with a rich lace cloth and set with fine china and tall white candles in silver holders. Four musicians played on a raised circular platform a few yards away from the dinner table. They were quite skilled but no one was paying any attention to their music, Silver noticed. The men and women seated at the table were too involved with one another, their laughter and conversation so loud the music could scarcely be heard. Dinner was already in progress and four white-coated servants were bustling around the table filling wineglasses and serving roast chicken from a silver tray.

Her gaze flew to the head of the table. Nicholas was dressed entirely in stunning black and white, his golden hair shining with light as he bent to speak to the lovely red-haired woman sitting on his left. He seemed very amused by the woman, she noticed with a pang that she permitted to last only until the instant she identified its nature. She swiftly shifted her glance to Valentin. "I don't see Mikhail."

"Mikhail feels uncomfortable at most social functions and Nicky seldom insists he attend."

No one appeared to notice their arrival, and Valentin was unobtrusively seating her near the foot of the table when Nicholas's voice rang out over the hubbub of conversation. "Not there, Valentin." He casually gestured to a chair farther up the table. "Seat her beside our good friend Bassinger, and then come and sit by me. We want our newcomer to get acquainted with our other guests, don't we?"

"Do we?" Valentin murmured. He shrugged resignedly, but whispered in Silver's ear as he escorted her to the chair Nicholas had indicated, "Be careful, Bassinger is . . ." He trailed off. "I'll see you after dinner."

Silver nodded as she seated herself between a plump, pretty woman in a violet taffeta gown and a slim elegant gentleman with pale green eyes. "Thank you, Valentin."

Valentin hesitated and then muttered something

beneath his breath before stalking toward the head of the table. He threw himself into the chair at Nicholas's right and immediately reached for the wine goblet beside his plate.

"Count Marinov appears to be disturbed at being forced to share you with the rest of us." The man at Silver's left leaned toward her and smiled intimately. "Who could blame him? You're very lovely, Miss . . . ?"

"Silver Delaney." She glanced at him briefly. She judged him to be middle-aged; his features were nondescript and gray threaded his dark hair like winter frost. His light green eyes reminded her also of frost. Even though his lips were smiling, his eyes were cold. "And there's no reason why Count Marinov should be disturbed."

"I'm Lee Bassinger." The man's smiled remained intact. "I've heard a number of very interesting things about you. I understand you're Savron's property, but tonight you appear with Marinov. Is Nicholas sharing you?"

"I'm no man's property." Silver watched as a servant placed a chicken breast on her plate with silver tongs. "I've heard of you too, Mr. Bassinger."

Bassinger's lips tightened. "Really? His highness has spoken of me?"

She shook her head as she picked up her knife and fork and cut into her chicken with exquisite precision. "Robert Danfold. He said you were a very rich man with many riverboats in your shipping company and offices in St. Louis, Memphis, and New Orleans."

His smile deepened. "That's true. I'm as rich as you could wish, and I can be very generous if a woman pleases me."

She took a bite of her chicken. It was delicious, delicately flavored with herbs. "He also said you were stupid enough to lose this fine riverboat to Nicholas in a poker game."

He stiffened, a flare of anger twisting his nondescript features to ugliness. "Stupid? I don't like being called stupid by a whore."

"I'm not a whore." She didn't look at him as she began eating in earnest. "But you most certainly are stupid, if what Robert says is true."

His hand suddenly fastened on her wrist with painful force. "I'm not—"

"Let me go." She glanced at his now livid face with eyes as cold as his own. "Or I'll skewer you instead of the chicken with this fork."

He glared at her with a venom greater than any she had ever encountered. Then his hand slowly released her and he smiled again. "You have spirit and I admire that in a woman."

He was lying, Silver thought. He was an easy man to read and was obviously one who liked only fear and respect to surround him.

"I'm sure we'll get along very well." Bassinger patted the wrist he had so recently grasped with such cruelty. "You can always count on me for any assistance you may require."

Silver began to eat again. "I need no assistance."

She proceeded to ignore him as the servant brought another course and set it before her.

"Why did you do it?" Valentin lifted his brooding gaze from his wineglass to Nicholas's face. "It would have done no harm to let me sit beside her. I would have—"

"Protected her," Nicholas finished for him. He smiled and shook his head. "But I don't want her protected."

"I know," Valentin said sourly. "But why Bassinger?"

"She appears to think I'm Satan incarnate. I wanted her to see there are a *few* men more degenerate than I." Nicholas lifted his wineglass to his lips, his dark eyes dancing over the rim. "Besides, she's obviously come to no harm. She seems more interested in her dinner than anything going on around her. The lady has a hearty appetite."

"I've noticed." Valentin's tone was abstracted as his gaze followed Nicholas's to rest on Silver. "She was nervous about coming here tonight."

Nicholas paused in the act of setting his glass back on the table. "Really? I find that difficult to believe. She appears quite composed."

"She has courage." Valentin's hand tightened on the stem of his glass. "Dammit, Nicky, I tell you there's something wrong. She told me she'd never met a count before. How could that be, if she knew André in Hell's Bluff?"

"I have no idea. Perhaps André was hesitant about

confiding his title to the citizens of such a democratic society."

"André?" Valentin's tone was unbelieving.

Nicholas shrugged. "Perhaps he had changed from what we knew of him. Men do change."

Valentin nodded and then was silent for a moment before bursting out, "But just *look* at her, Nicky. She doesn't belong here."

Nicholas had been avoiding looking at Silver all evening and he had no intention of changing that now. He was well aware of the contrast she presented to the rouged and besatined strumpets surrounding her. It had taken only one glance to permanently engrave it on his memory. In spite of the fiery sensuality that was so much a part of her, there was also a simplicity, a pristine quality about Silver that set her worlds apart from the company at the table. "It's that hideous schoolgirl uniform. I'll have one of the women send her a gown to wear tomorrow night."

"It's not the—"

"*Stop it!*" Silver's voice rang out with bell-like clarity, instantly capturing the attention of everyone at the table.

"What the devil," Nicholas muttered, already halfway out of his seat.

Silver was standing, glaring down at Bassinger. She reached for a cooled bottle of wine from a copper bucket carried by a passing servant. "You don't listen well. I told you to stop." She held the bottle over the man's head. "Now!"

The rich red wine poured over Bassinger's head,

streaming in rivulets down his cheeks, matting his dark hair, and turning the gray streaks threading it to pale pink. He sat frozen in disbelief.

Laughter exploded from the other guests at the table, soaring around Bassinger with a stinging mockery that caused his pale cheeks to flush with color.

Silver set the empty bottle down on the table. "Now, don't do it again."

Bassinger was pop-eyed with rage and seemed to have trouble forcing the words from his throat. *"You . . . you . . ."*

Valentin started to his feet. "He'll kill her."

"The hell he will." Nicholas pushed back his chair and was striding around the table. In three paces he was beside Silver, jerking her chair out of the way and grasping her by the elbow. "I believe it's time we retired for the evening, my dear. What a pity. Such a pleasant dinner, don't you agree, Bassinger?"

He began to propel Silver firmly away from the table and down the long, carpeted expanse of the saloon. "Don't fight me," he said in a fierce undertone. "I'm in no mood to kill Bassinger at the moment. I had something else entirely planned for tonight."

"I don't intend to fight you. Why should I? I don't mind leaving the table. I'd already finished dinner."

He blinked. "You'd already finished . . ." He suddenly began to laugh. He slowly shook his head, his eyes still sparkling with humor. "Do you usually finish your meals by anointing a gentleman's head with fine wine?"

"He wasn't a nice man," she said simply. "He was

afraid to vent his anger on me so he was being cruel to that poor woman on the other side of him."

"Cruel?"

"He was pinching her thigh beneath the table."

His gaze searched her face. "Men often fondle women. Perhaps she enjoyed it."

She shook her head. "He was hurting her, but she was too frightened to stop him. I could see it in her face." She shrugged impatiently. "Stupid woman. *She* should have been the one to pour the wine on his head."

Nicholas opened the door to the stateroom and stood aside to let her precede him. "You call her stupid, yet you drew Bassinger's anger against yourself to protect her."

Silver entered the cabin. "She was afraid. Sometimes it's not easy for women to stand up to men." She whirled to face him. "But he *hurt* her. Why would he want to hurt her?"

"Some men find it gratifying." Nicholas closed the door and locked it behind him. "I don't understand it either." He turned to look at her. "Beautiful things should be treated gently, with the most exquisite care."

Silver felt suddenly breathless. "Women are not things."

He bowed slightly. "I stand corrected."

"But you don't believe it. You think women are weak and puny. You think we're nothing."

"I'm not such a fool. I believe some women have great strength." He smiled crookedly. "Perhaps the reason men try to keep women weak is that we know their strength is often used to subordinate and destroy us."

"Destroy?" She shook her head. "I don't wish to destroy anyone. I want only to be left alone to go my own way."

"Impossible." His voice was velvet soft. "You're not a woman any man would be willing to leave alone. Haven't you realized that yet?"

The air in the stateroom was too close, and she couldn't breathe. No, the fault was with her, her chest was so tight. She abruptly turned away. "Sweet words, but you don't mean them. You just wish to lure me into fornicating with you."

"I mean them," he said gravely. "But the other is also true. I've never denied my intentions. And I've never lied to you."

No, he had always told her the truth, she thought, even when a lie would have served him better. It was a realization that disconcerted her. Honesty was the virtue she admired above all others, and she didn't want to admit even to herself that Nicholas possessed that quality. "Go away. I'm tired. Good night."

He chuckled. "You're nothing if not direct." His smile held an entrancing sweetness. "Aren't you going to undress for me again?"

"No."

He lifted a brow. "Why not? Don't you want to see me suffer? Are you softening by any chance, Silver?"

Her gaze rose swiftly to meet his. "I'm not softening. I just want you to leave."

"And I will leave." He moved across the room and stood before her. "As soon as I tuck you into bed." He reached up and began to slowly unbutton her shirt-waist. "I told you I intended to act as lady's maid, remember? Surely you're not afraid?"

"I'm not afraid." Silver lowered her gaze to his swift, clever fingers unfastening her blouse. His knuckles were lightly grazing her breast with every move, and that light touch was causing a most peculiar sensation. Her breasts felt as if they were swelling, tautening more with each passing second. She moistened her lips with her tongue. "I don't fear anything you can do to me, but I don't need your help."

"I think you *are* afraid," he taunted softly, pausing to look at her. "Or you'd be willing to let me have my way in this."

She drew a deep breath and then lifted one shoulder in a half shrug. "Go ahead. It means nothing." She tried to keep all expression from her voice. "Be quick about it. I wish to go to bed."

"Very quick." His fingers left the half-unbuttoned shirtwaist and with two swift movements stripped away her waist-length jacket and tossed it aside. "You see, I obey your every command." He finished unbuttoning her shirtwaist and pushed it down over her shoulders and then slipped it off entirely. "Much faster than you would do it yourself." His fingers deftly untied the satin ribbons of her bodice and pushed the straps of her camisole from her shoulders. "Let me see, this was the way you did it last night, wasn't it?" His gaze was fastened on the thin muslin clinging to the tips of her breasts. "But there's something different, isn't there?"

She could feel the furnace heat of his body reaching out to touch her like a burning brand. She took a deep breath and the male scent of him surrounded her in a sensual haze. "I see nothing . . . different."

"Perhaps I'm mistaken." He slid the camisole down, down, with painful slowness until the white ribbons contrasted with the pink of her nipples. "No, I believe you're considerably more . . . ripe, Silver." Then her breasts were bare, full golden mounds spilling saucily over the lacing of her camisole. His eyes were midnight soft as he looked down at her. "I can make them even more ripe. Would you like me to do that?"

She was burning, heavy, her nipples hardening under his gaze as she struggled against the tightness constricting her lungs. "You said . . . you would hurry."

"Ah, yes, I did say that." He slowly pulled the camisole over her head, letting the soft material brush her swollen breasts like a caress. "I'll go faster after this, but you're so . . . I don't want to hurt you." The material tugged teasingly and then released her breasts. Then the camisole was over her head. "There, it's gone." He threw the camisole aside and stepped around behind her.

"What are you doing?" She looked over her shoulder, startled.

"Nothing." He took a step closer, his arms going around her, his hands moving deftly to unfasten her skirt. "My looking at you seems to have an odd effect on you." He smiled. "I thought you'd be more comfortable if I finished the task in this fashion."

"How kind," she said warily. The skirt had dropped in a pool at her feet and she slowly turned her head to face forward. Comfortable? She had forgotten what the word comfort meant. Her heart was pounding, slamming against her chest, and she could feel every breath he drew against her naked back. He was unfastening her petticoats, his lips so close to her ear that each word was a warm, sensual explosion. "Do you see that picture on the wall? The one right in front of you?"

"I'm not interested in your pictures." She tried to keep her gaze from the mural he'd indicated but found herself staring at it in compulsive fascination.

"Not my pictures. They were commissioned by the gentleman you christened with that bottle of wine tonight." Nicholas chuckled. "One way or another Bassinger seems to like to bring ladies to their knees, doesn't he? That woman in the picture has a lovely mouth but not as lovely as yours. Would you like to do that to me?"

"Certainly not."

His hand slowly pushed down her petticoats, his palms skimming the naked flesh on her belly. She inhaled sharply and flinched back. But that brought her into direct contact with the hard muscles of his body. Very hard, she realized breathlessly. As hard as she was melting soft, as taut as she was pliant.

"Then would you like me to do that to you?" he

asked thickly. "I will, you know." His palm was rubbing back and forth on the softness of her belly, every touch causing an aching clenching between her thighs. "I'd like to do it." His fingers tightened suddenly in the hair surrounding her womanhood, and he tugged gently. She made a low sound in the back of her throat as a tiny explosion of heat tore through her every vein. Her back arched, her shoulders pressing back against him. "That's right, let it come, Silver." His palm covered her and he began to rub. "You like it so much." His teeth gently bit at the lobe of her ear. "Let me do that to you." His warm tongue darted in her ear, sending another hot shiver through her. "Let me do everything to you. This was what you were meant for. . . ."

"No!" Her cry held the violence of desperation as Silver wrenched out of his grasp and whirled away from him. She turned to face him, clutching her loosened petticoats to keep them from falling. "I will not." She backed away from him, her naked breasts lifting and falling. "Go away!"

His black eyes were brilliant in his taut face, his nostrils flaring with the harshness of his breathing. "Come back. You know you want to let me touch you." His voice was as softly seductive as the song of a nightingale. "You know I can please you."

For a moment she could feel the words pulling her with the force of a riptide. Dear God, he was right, she thought desperately. He *could* please her body. He could do more than please her, he could drive her to the brink of sensual madness. Even knowing how close she had come to submitting to that allure, she still wanted to fling herself in his arms, run her hands over his body, beg him to do whatever he wished with her.

Beg. The repugnant thought brought her immediately to her senses. She did not beg. Not ever. She drew herself up and faced him. "Go away. I don't want you here."

He took a step forward. "Liar."

She lifted her chin. "No, it's lust. My body may want you, but I am not my body." She touched her breast, glaring at him fiercely. "I'm more than that. I am Silver Delaney. I don't lie down and spread my legs because a man tells me I must." A patch of color burned in each of her cheeks and her voice was shaking with feeling. "I am not a toy. I am not my mother!"

"I never said—" He stopped, his dark eyes blazing. "Dammit, you know you're going to let me take you to bed. It's only a question of time. Why not . . ." He trailed off as he read the rejection in her face. His breath released in an impatient explosion of sound as his hands clenched into fists at his sides. "You're sending me away?"

Silver made no answer.

He stood very still, looking at her, then he turned and strode toward the door and threw it open. His voice held a note of barely restrained savagery. "I have no liking for women who pretend to be what they are not." His glance over his shoulder was a burning sword thrust. "You're no prim schoolgirl, and the only reason you let me undress you was because you wanted my hands on you. You wanted *me*, dammit!" The door slammed behind him with a force that shook the crystal prisms on the rim of the lamp on the bedside table.

Silver gazed at the panels of the door for a long moment. He had been so angry. Why couldn't she summon a like anger to use against him? Her body still ached with hunger and emptiness. She closed her eyes, a shiver of yearning rippling through her. Nicholas could have filled her body and stopped the aching. Had he spoken the truth? Had she allowed him to undress her not because she wanted to meet his challenge but because she desired him? She must stop thinking of him. He cared nothing for her. He was the enemy. Tomorrow evening she would escape this boat and never see Nicholas again.

An unexplainable thrust of pain pierced through her. No, she thought in sudden panic. She would feel nothing for him. Not lust, certainly not love. Nothing.

It was a litany she repeated over and over to herself as if saying the rosary as she finished undressing and turned out the lamp. A litany she continued to murmur as she lay in the darkness for the many sleepless hours that followed.

Nothing. She must feel nothing for Nicholas.

6

A yellow satin gown was delivered to the state-room by Valentin shortly before six the next evening.

He stood in the doorway, the brilliantly colored garment draped over his arm, a pair of yellow satin slippers in his hand, and a faintly apologetic smile on his lips. "Nicky sent these. He thought you'd be a trifle more comfortable at the dinner table tonight wearing something more appropriate."

"I'm not surprised he feels a whore's gown more fitting for me." Silver's face was without expression as she took the items from Valentin and tossed them carelessly onto the padded velvet bench. "I'm to join all of you for dinner again? I'm amazed Nicholas wants to chance my presence. I've not seen anyone but Mikhail all day, and he vanished as soon as he delivered my breakfast and lunch."

Valentin made a face. "Nicky decided you needed time to ponder and told us we weren't to approach you."

And a very clever move it had been, Silver thought. She had nearly gone mad confined to this room all

119

day with nothing to do and nothing to think about besides Nicholas Savron and her response to him last night. She had paced the floor, trying to incite herself to an anger that would submerge the tumult of feeling she was experiencing. Anger had not come until now. She felt it sear through her in a furious tide as she gazed at the yellow gown. By all that was holy, now it was a silken gown! *Damn* Nicholas and his crystal chandeliers, soft velvets, and fine damask tablecloths. How easy life was for him. When she thought of the comparison between his life and Etaine's, she wanted to take a tomahawk to that arrogant golden head. Etaine struggling desperately for breath; Etaine forced every night into that hellish cage. And now Nicholas's actions were making life even harder for Etaine by preventing her, Silver, from being close enough to help when needed. "How kind of him to decide to permit the poor prisoner a brief respite."

Valentin was clearly troubled. "Tell him what he wants to know, Silver. Nicholas can be very difficult. You're going to get hurt."

"You think that if I tell him where Dominic can be found it will be over?" Silver shook her head. "You aren't such a fool. There is more between us than that."

"I suppose you're right. But don't be so—" He broke off and turned to go. "It's no use talking to you any more than it is to Nicky. I'll be back for you at eight." He looked over his shoulder. "Wear the gown, Silver. Nick was adamant about his wishes on that score. He said he was weary of gazing at a frumpy schoolgirl at his table; he prefers you to look more womanly."

The anger Silver was feeling suddenly flamed higher. The damnable arrogance of the man! "Oh, does he?"

Valentin sighed. "Hellfire! I knew . . ." He was still shaking his head as the door closed behind him.

Silver's gaze swung from the door to the gleaming heap of yellow satin on the bench. She was tempted to send word to Nicholas that she would not only not wear the gown, she would not join them for dinner. Yet she knew she couldn't do that if her attempt to escape was to be successful. She must be out of this cabin and on deck early this evening when the *Rose* veered toward shore.

She walked quickly to the window to look at the western bank. Surely it was already a little closer. Robert was beginning to change course to avoid the sandbars downriver. Excitement and anticipation warred with the anger surging through her. Soon she would no longer be a helpless prisoner.

She turned and glared fiercely at the gown again. She would *not* give Nicholas the satisfaction of meekly obeying his orders. This was the last time he would see her, and she was determined that their final encounter wouldn't be one he would remember with triumph.

But Nicholas was no fool and there was no way that she could think to do both. She quickly thought through the possibilities but came up with no answer. Surely there must be some weakness she could play on. Possessiveness? Valentin had said Nicholas was very possessive of her and she had noticed signs of that quality in him herself. Perhaps there would be some way to use that fault to accomplish her own ends.

Her gaze shifted abstractedly from the gown on the bench to the bed. There had to be something . . . She froze, her eyes widening, and then threw back her head and began to laugh in sheer delight.

That was it! She had it!

Valentin looked at her warily. "You won't need that cloak. The saloon is quite comfortable tonight."

"I felt chilled." Silver drew her dark blue cloak still closer about her. "I'm ready to go."

"Does the gown fit? Mikhail said you sent for a needle and thread."

"It does now." She held out her foot to reveal the dainty yellow slippers with matching ribbons criss-crossing at the ankle. "And the shoes fit well too."

"I see that they do." Valentin opened the door and then hesitated. Silver was glowing, blazing with vitality and an excitement that made him vaguely apprehensive. "I'm glad you took my advice."

Silver sailed through the doorway, smiling sweetly at him as she passed. "I think you'll agree that I've tried very hard to obey Nicholas's command. May I have your arm?" Her gaze went to the far end of the saloon. The scene was much the same as last night: Nicholas at the head of the table, the musicians, the hovering servants, and chatting guests. She glanced

Get one full-length Loveswept FREE every month!
Now you can be sure you'll never, ever miss a single Loveswept title by enrolling in our special reader's home delivery service. A service that will bring you all six new Loveswept romances each month for the price of five—and deliver them to you before they appear in the bookstores!

Examine 6 Loveswept Novels for

15 days FREE!

(SEE OTHER SIDE FOR DETAILS)

Postage will be paid by addressee

Loveswept

Bantam Books
P.O. Box 985
Hicksville, NY 11802

BUSINESS REPLY MAIL
FIRST-CLASS MAIL   PERMIT NO. 2456   HICKSVILLE, NY

NO POSTAGE
NECESSARY
IF MAILED
IN THE
UNITED STATES

America's most popular, most compelling romance novels...

Here, at last...love stories that really involve you! Fresh, finely crafted novels with story lines so believable you'll feel you're actually living them! Characters you can relate to...exciting places to visit...unexpected plot twists...all in all, exciting romances that satisfy your mind and delight your heart.

EXAMINE 6 LOVESWEPT NOVELS FOR

15 Days FREE!

To introduce you to this fabulous service, you'll get six brand-new Loveswept releases not yet in the bookstores. These six exciting new titles are yours to examine for 15 days without obligation to buy. Keep them if you wish for just $12.50 plus postage and handling and any applicable sales tax. Offer available in U.S.A. only.

▶ Detach and mail this postage-paid card today! ▶

at Valentin as she slipped her arm through his and started the long promenade to the far end of the saloon. "Do you suppose he'll seat me next to Mr. Bassinger again?"

"It's not likely," Valentin said dryly.

"Then why don't you take me to the head of the table at once so that Nicholas can make his decision about which of these gracious individuals he wishes me to get to know this evening?" Silver asked softly. "It will save time."

Valentin looked at her suspiciously. "Silver—"

"Hush, Valentin." Silver didn't look at him, her gaze on Nicholas. He had just caught sight of her and he straightened in his chair, his gaze raking over her slim form completely enveloped in the blue cloak. "It's too late now anyway. Take me to him."

"What the devil are you up to?" Valentin muttered.

She didn't bother to answer. They were only a few yards from Nicholas now and Valentin would find out soon enough.

She stopped beside Nicholas's chair and curtsied deeply. "Good evening, your highness."

The chatter of the guests suddenly dwindled and then ceased entirely as everyone's attention became centered at the head of the table.

Nicholas's gaze flicked over her once again, a smile of satisfaction touching his lips as he saw the yellow satin slippers peeping from beneath the hem of her cloak. "Take off your cloak, it's quite warm in here. I want to see how you look in something besides that uniform." He smiled lazily. "I thought yellow would quite wonderfully complement your hair."

She smiled back at him. "I've always been fond of yellow. We Indians adore bright colors, you know." She shook her head sadly. "Unfortunately, the gown didn't fit as well as I would have liked."

He stiffened. "You're not wearing it?"

"No, but I'm sure you won't be disappointed." She smiled brilliantly as her hand reached for the button at her throat. "I believe you told Valentin you wished me to look more womanly." With one swift gesture she slipped the cloak from her shoulders and let it fall to the floor. "Now, what could be more womanly than the woman herself."

"Oh, my God," Valentin murmured, closing his eyes. "It's the bed curtain." Then he yielded to temptation and looked again.

The sheer white batiste had been fashioned into a simple loose Grecian tunic, leaving one shoulder bare and falling straight to the floor. Silver's smooth golden skin, taut pink nipples, all the secret places of her body, were only lightly veiled and could be seen in all their ravishing loveliness. She looked as wildly beautiful and shockingly desirable as a high priestess in the temple of Aphrodite.

"Don't just stand there. Put that goddamn cloak around her!" Nicholas's harsh voice pulled Valentin's gaze from Silver to Nicholas's face.

He inhaled sharply and hurriedly picked up Silver's cloak from the floor. Christ, he'd never seen Nicky look like that. White-hot jealousy, anger, and desire blazed from him in waves that were nearly tangible. "I'll take her back to the stateroom, Nicky." He took a step toward Silver, intending to put the cloak around her.

She had no intention of letting him accomplish his aim. She backed away from the table, her gaze still holding Nicholas's with defiance. "You don't look pleased, Nicholas. Why is that? I certainly don't look like a frumpy schoolgirl."

"*Damn you*," Nicholas said with soft violence. "Put that cloak on!"

She shook her head, a reckless smile on her face as she continued to back away. "I'm not uncomfortable like this. I'm Apache, remember?"

Nicholas stood up so suddenly that his chair crashed to the floor behind him. "Then, by God, you'd better learn to behave like a white woman. I won't have you stripping yourself for every man to gape at like some—" He broke off, his chest rising and falling with the force of his breathing. "Put on that cloak or I swear you'll regret it, Silver."

She laughed, the sound rising to ring around the white and gold of the ceiling. "You cannot make me regret anything. You are nothing to me, your highness."

Then she was gone, flying down the length of the saloon toward the door leading to the deck, her straight dark hair streaming behind her in a wild, shining banner. She heard Nicholas call her name, but she ignored it. Fierce joy was surging through her veins. She had done it! She had bested Nicholas and now she would complete her plan.

Cool night air struck her hot cheeks as she rushed out on deck and ran toward the stairway leading to the boiler deck. She glanced over her shoulder. Nicholas and Valentin had just emerged from the saloon and were running after her.

She should take off the slippers, but there was no time. She glanced over the rail at the shore that was scarcely forty yards away. She had reached the boiler deck, but she couldn't jump here. It was too close to the paddle wheel. She streaked across the deck, climbed up on the rail, and then slipped onto the narrow ledge hanging over the water.

"Silver!" Nicholas shouted.

She glanced back over her shoulder. His face was pale in the moonlight. Strange, he didn't look angry now as he ran toward her. If she didn't know better, she would swear his expression reflected panic.

"Good-bye, Nicholas." She waved mockingly and then dove into the waters of the Mississippi.

The river was cold and for a moment she lost her breath and felt frightened. Then she struck out with swift strong strokes toward the shadowy bank.

"You're going after her?" Valentin asked as he watched Nicholas jerk off his boots and toss them aside.

"You're damn right I'm going after her." Nicholas flung off his coat and threw it on top of his boots. "If she makes it to shore, she'll disappear before we can launch a boat and get to the bank."

If. The qualifier caused an icy chill to chase through him. Silver appeared to be swimming with exceptional strength, but he had heard there were many dangers lurking in the river. Whirlpools, currents . . . He climbed over the rail, his gaze searching the water. Now that she had left the glowing perimeter of the riverboat's lanterns, he could no longer see her. Where the devil was she? Then he saw a gleam of moonlight shining on a seal-wet head and felt a relief so intense it made him dizzy.

He balanced on the ledge, keeping his gaze fixed desperately on Silver. "Tell Robert to wait until dawn to send a rescue party after us. We don't want any more people than necessary blundering around lost in that damn forest." He dove into the river and struck out after Silver, cleaving the water with powerful strokes. His heart was pounding with fear as his eyes strained in the darkness. Incredibly, he found himself muttering a prayer beneath his breath.

She was almost to the bank. Relief coursed through her, revitalizing her tired muscles. Another fifteen yards and she would be safe. She wanted to hurry, to strike out with greater speed, but she knew she must hoard her strength.

She swam steadily, drawing closer, closer still. Soon she would be there. Stroke, breathe deeply, another stroke, breathe deeply, str—

Blackness! A gnarled, scaly monster bearing down on her!

There were no river monsters, she thought wildly, no monsters here.

The monster struck! She gasped as an avalanche of pain tumbled through her head. Dizziness. Pain. Blackness. She must keep moving. But she couldn't remember what to do, how to move her arms. Panic ripped through her. She was going to die. She was going to be with Rising Star. Oh, God, she didn't want to die!

"No!" Her arms began to thrash wildly. She wanted to live. There was something wonderful waiting for her. Something that was meant to be . . . Someone . . .

The blackness returned and she fought against it. She wouldn't die. She was strong. She wouldn't be destroyed when that wonder was waiting for her.

Then the blackness deepened and the waters of the river closed over her head. She sank slowly downward, a silent scream of protest resounding through every cell of her being. *Nicholas!*

Nicholas's face was intent in the firelight, a slight frown knitting his brow. His golden hair was touseled and a little damp and he was wearing no shirt. That was strange, she thought vaguely. She had never seen Nicholas when he was not faultlessly dressed. "Where's your shirt?"

His eyes flew up to meet hers and relief flooded his face. "I'm sorry to appear with such a shocking lack of decorum, but I thought you needed it more than I did," he said lightly. "Your gown may have been eye-catching, but it gave you little protection from the elements."

She looked down at herself in surprise. She *was* wearing his shirt. The linen of his white shirt was no longer crisp, but wilted and slightly damp. She was barefoot and she could see the yellow slippers she had worn lying watersoaked and ruined on the bank a few yards away. "Why are we wet?"

His smile faded. "Don't you remember?"

She tried to think. Something wonderful waiting for her. Someone . . . She suddenly sat bolt upright. "The monster!"

"Lie back down," Nicholas said, trying to push her onto the bed of moss and leaves. "There was no monster."

"There was." She dazedly lifted her hand to her head. "I saw it. Black and scaly and—"

"It was a log being carried by the current," Nicholas said. "No monster. It struck you a glancing blow on the head and stunned you." His lips tightened grimly. "But it was enough to have drowned you if I hadn't been a few yards behind."

"I thought I was dying." She suddenly began to shiver. "I *was* dying. I was so afraid." Her voice held a note of wonder. "I don't think I've ever been afraid before. I thought my heart was bursting and I couldn't breathe and—"

"Hush." Nicholas's arms were suddenly around her,

rocking her as if she were a dearly loved child. "Don't think about it. It's over now."

"No." Her words were muffled in the warm flesh of his shoulder. "I thought I was strong enough to win over anything. But I wasn't." The shiver had evolved into shudders that racked her slim frame. "I was so frightened."

Nicholas suffered a poignant ache deep within him. God, she was young. How long ago it had been since he had believed he had the strength to win every battle, vanquish every foe, even one as powerful as death itself. "It's all right to be frightened. No one expects a wo—" He stopped. This was not a comfort Silver would be able to accept. His hand gently stroked the silky dark hair at her temple. "No one is strong every moment of every day. Everyone is afraid at some time in his life."

"You?"

"Oh, yes, many times."

She began to relax, the shivering gradually ebbing. "Truly?"

He chuckled. "Truly."

She lifted her head to look more directly at his face. "Why are you being so kind to me?" she asked haltingly. "You were very angry with me in the saloon tonight."

"I'm still angry with you." Something flickered in the depths of his eyes and then was gone. "But I've never enjoyed a battle against an unarmed opponent, and I believe it's safe to say you're amazingly defense-less at the moment."

She looked away. He was right. She had never felt weaker or less sure of herself. She moistened her lips with her tongue. "It won't last."

He laughed again. "I'm well aware of that, but for tonight, at least, we'll call a truce. I gave orders that a boat not be launched until dawn, so we must rely on ourselves until then. Lay down your weapons, Silver. I promise I'm no threat to you and I'll protect you from danger." His ebony eyes twinkled in the firelight. "Including river monsters."

How foolish she was being, clinging to him as if he were a life preserver thrown to save her from the river. She released him and edged backward. "I feel very stupid. I'll try not to be—"

He placed two fingers on her lips, silencing her. "Not stupid," he said softly. "Now, lie back down and rest while I see if I can find us something to eat. If you recall, we didn't have dinner."

"I can help," she said eagerly. "Apache girl children are taught exactly the same skills as boys until they reach the time for the rites of womanhood. I can travel forty miles a day through rough country. I can trap and hunt and fish and I was the best tracker in the village." She frowned. "Though some of the warriors wouldn't admit it. I told them—"

"I'm sure you did," Nicholas interrupted, his eyes dancing. "And I'm certain you're as competent as you claim, but let me be the provider this time. I may not have your qualifications, but I have a certain amount of experience in foraging."

"But you're—" She stopped.

He lifted a brow. "Yes?"

"You're a prince." She scowled. "And I think I'm hungry."

He burst out laughing as he rose to his feet. "I assure you, my entire existence hasn't been spent in marble palaces being pampered by armies of servants. I'll find you something to eat, Silver." He glanced down at his bare feet. "Though I have no intention of hunting or trapping tonight. I know what stones and brush can do to unprotected feet."

"But I still think—"

"No." He turned away.

She gasped, her gaze fastened in shock on the long line of his back. White scars crisscrossed his flesh from his shoulders to the base of his spine, scars that could only have been inflicted by the lash of a whip.

He turned to look over his shoulder. "What's the matter?" Then, as he saw her face, a crooked smile lit up his face. "As I said, palaces are not the full extent of my experience." Then he faded into the dense forest shrubbery with a silent grace that surprised her.

She sat frozen, staring after him in the darkness. She felt . . . strange. What kind of a man was Nicholas Savron? She couldn't really know, since their every encounter had been colored by anger, conflict, and lust. She had seen glimpses of the character of the man in his relationship with Mikhail and Valentin, but had been too wary to believe what she had seen. Now her defenses were down and she was forced to accept another Nicholas. A Nicholas who had held her and comforted her with a tenderness she had never known, who had laughed and teased her, who had made her aware he possessed a past that could hold the same pain and humiliation she had known. A Nicholas who had saved her life at the risk of his own.

He had saved her life! The realization came with the shocking force of a blow. "No!" She didn't wish to owe Nicholas Savron anything. He was the enemy.

But he had not been an enemy when he had held her in his arms and told her it was all right to be afraid. He had permitted her to lean on his strength and had taken nothing from her in return. How would it feel to be able to lean on someone else as Elspeth leaned on Dominic? Not that she needed support, she assured herself quickly. But it would be pleasant to know there was a hand to hold your own on a rough path. So pleasant . . .

Pleasant. It was not a word to describe Nicholas Savron. He dazzled and wooed, he struck with the glittering sharpness of a renaissance dagger and then danced away to watch with an entrancing smile as his opponent crumpled. Yet she had felt something else in him tonight, a strongly anchored rock to cling to in the darkness.

Oh, she just didn't know. She was confused and weakened, as much from that moment of tenderness from Nicholas as she was from the blow on the head. She would think about it when she was fully herself again. Tonight he had offered a truce that she would gladly accept.

The warm night breeze gently touched her cheeks and playfully tugged at her hair, bringing with it the pungent scent of moss, river, and burning wood. She had been imprisoned in cities too long. She glanced around her, curiously content with both this place and this moment. Two huge weeping willow trees showered veils of lacy fronds over the mossy bank, and the moonlight on the Mississippi was breathtakingly lovely. She could see the pale gleam of the riverboat hovering in the distance, but both the *Rose* and her captivity seemed far away.

She drew closer to the fire, her gaze on the brightly glowing flames. The night was warm and the fire was not really a necessity but it would serve to finish drying her clothes. She threaded her fingers through her hair, holding the long straight strands out to let the heat flow through them. Her hair was nearly dry. She must have been unconscious longer than she had believed, yet the blow had been really nothing. It was very puzzling.

Dear heaven, surely she hadn't *swooned*? Indignation surged through her at the thought. She couldn't have been such a ninny. She had been frightened but she did *not* swoon. It was ridiculous and she—

She suddenly began to chuckle. Perhaps she had swooned. What difference did it make? She didn't have to be strong all the time. As Nicholas had said, no one was strong every moment of every day. . . .

"You have juice on the corner of your mouth." Nicholas leaned forward to wipe away the errant drops with his index finger. "And you have raspberry lips."

"So do you," Silver said placidly, glancing at his well-shaped lips dyed red-purple by the same juice that stained her own. "And you have some on your chin too. You look as if you're wearing war paint."

Nicholas wiped the offending smudge away. "I'm surprised you're not complaining that I managed to grab a few handfuls of your berries to stave off starvation. Do you always eat so heartily?"

She nodded. "I like to eat. There are so many wonderful tastes." She sighed blissfully. "Do you know that some flowers have a lovely taste? When I was a little girl, there was a honeysuckle bush beside the front door of the homestead at Killara. I used to pull the blossoms and suck the sweetness. I love to taste delicious things and breathe the scents of the earth and the flowers." She inhaled deeply. "And woodsmoke. Is there anything more wonderful than the smell of woodsmoke? Tangy and rich."

Nicholas gazed at her thoughtfully. Sitting there across the fire, she was a wild, lovely pagan, completely at home in her surroundings. She radiated a natural sensuality that formed an aura of heat that reached out and touched like the warmth of the fire itself. If she was so responsive to taste and scent, how much more responsive would she be to touch?

But he didn't want to think about Silver's responses tonight. He promised her a truce that was already proving a difficult vow to keep. He asked abruptly, "Do you want any more berries? There are plenty of bushes in that patch downriver. I would have brought

more if I'd had a bucket. All I had was my handkerchief in which to carry them."

"Are you angry with me?" She suddenly looked like
a hurt child. "Did I truly eat more than my share?"
She jumped to her feet. "Stay here. I'll get you some
more raspberries. Why didn't you tell me you were
hungry?"

"Silver . . ." His frown vanished and he began to
laugh. "I'm not hungry and I'm not angry with you. I
was joking before."

She gazed at him uncertainly. "You're sure?"

"I'm sure," he said a trifle impatiently. "For God's
sake, can't you tell the difference?"

"No," she said simply. "Not always. I suppose I
don't really have a very good sense of humor. No one
has really joked with me much."

Poignant tenderness caused his throat to tighten
helplessly. Her answer caught him off guard and
touched him with unbearable intensity. Christ, why
did she have to say things like that? Wild child, lost
child, fighting for acceptance with every ounce of her
being and nothing left over for laughter. "I was
joking," he repeated. "Now, sit down and finish your
berries."

She dropped to the ground, her gaze fixed thoughtfully on the fire. "Of course, my cousin Patrick
sometimes joked with me. Patrick laughs a lot, but it's
never unkind."

"And was some of the laughter unkind?"

"At times." She lifted her gaze from the flames. "I
am a half-breed."

The simple words hurt. He couldn't stand it. He deliberately shuttered his emotions and smiled carelessly. "So am I. Serf and boyar." He continued lightly. "I never understood why a pure strain was considered more prestigious than a mixed. More is surely better."

"Valentin told me your mother was not of the nobility."

His lips twisted. "Much to her dismay." He shrugged. "When I was a small child I tried to comfort her by telling her about the firebird, but she dismissed it as foolishness."

"The firebird? You called me that once."

"Did I? I don't remember. I recall thinking you reminded me of a firebird the first time I saw you." His gaze gravely met hers. "The firehbird is a half-breed too, Silver. Half diety of the sun and half mortal bird."

She smiled tentatively. "A fairy story?"

He nodded. "A fable. There are many stories about the firebird in Russia." He turned away. "Lie down and try to sleep. This moss won't make too poor a bed."

She lay down, curling up and laying her cheek on her arm. "Tell me about the firebird."

He gazed into the flames. "I told you, there are many stories."

"Tell me your favorite."

He laughed softly. "My firebird isn't a god but a goddess."

"It would be," Silver said dryly.

"She was a creature so magnificent, no words could describe her. Her wings were like flames and her eyes pure crystal. She ate only golden apples and just one of her feathers could bring light to midnight darkness and banish the fears of the night."

"Beautiful," Silver murmured dreamily. "She must have been beautiful. . . ."

"Yes, she was beautiful, but she was more. She was magical." Silver's eyes were shining in the firelight like the shimmering crystal of the firebird, and for a moment he lost track of what he was saying. Then he pulled his gaze away and fastened it once again on the flames. "There was a mighty Cossack warrior who lived in a desolate, barren land. He was very ambitious and wanted to become a great leader. Then one day the firebird appeared before him and he climbed on her back and they soared away in a flare of flaming brilliance, locked together in a secret world of radiance. The warrior had never known such excitement and happiness, but in time he yearned for the victories and glories of the mortal world. So the firebird returned the warrior to his own land. She told the warrior she loved him but would not hold him with her magic. Instead, she gave him her magical blessing that insured he would receive all he desired, and she flew off toward the sun."

"Sad," Silver murmured sleepily.

"The warrior became a great leader and won riches and fame. Many maidens wished to mate with him as the years passed, but he found he couldn't bring himself to marry. He continued to prosper but gradually realized a great loneliness was devouring his soul. Fame and riches meant nothing if he couldn't have his firebird. He offered his palace and all his riches to any man who could lure the firebird back to earth and capture her. Many men tried to win the prize and capture the firebird, but to no avail. Finally, in great despair, the warrior left his fine palace and journeyed back to the canyon where he had last seen the firebird."

"Was she there?"

"No, but he found one shining feather that had dropped from her wing as she flew away from the earth toward the sun. He picked it up and felt it throb as if it were alive beneath his fingers. Then he heard the surging of her great wings and the clouds parted and she landed beside him. She had felt his need of her when he had grasped the feather and been summoned back to him."

"And they flew away together and lived happily ever after," Silver finished.

"Perhaps."

"What do you mean, perhaps?" Silver covered her lips with her hand as she yawned. "How else could it end?"

"This is a *Russian* fable." Nicholas's eyes twinkled. "Which makes it more complex. There are two endings. In one, the warrior mounted the back of the firebird and became her mate forever. In the other ending, the firebird had been so crazed by her grief that her heart now held only bitterness for the warrior and she rent him to death with her talons."

She scowled. "In this country we would never permit such an ending. I'm convinced Russians must be a very peculiar people." She closed her eyes and her voice, though drowsy, was very firm. "The first ending is correct. I'm sure of it."

"Then who am I to disagree?" He settled down a few yards from where she lay, his eyes dark with secrets as they narrowed on her face. He didn't speak for several minutes, and when he did, his voice was almost a whisper. "And who should know better . . . Firebird?"

Silver didn't answer, and Nicholas saw that she was asleep.

7

The monster rushed toward her, its dark scales shining, its red eyes staring at her with hungry malevolence. He opened his giant mouth and she could see his pointed yellow teeth and smell the foulness of his breath—

"No!" Silver sat bolt upright, her heart pounding wildly.

Nicholas was beside her, his arms enfolding her. Solid strength, the scent of tobacco and musk . . . She clung to him with desperation. "Nicholas, it was a monster with big yellow teeth."

"It was only a nightmare." His palm cupped the back of her head as he rocked her back and forth. "It wasn't real."

"I don't have nightmares," she said indignantly.

He laughed but made no rebuttal as he continued to rock her.

She should move away, she thought, but it was very pleasant being held like this with her cheek pressed against the warm bare smoothness of Nicholas's chest. "Elspeth used to have terrible dreams when she was ill."

"Did she? Then you know there's no shame in having them."

"I didn't say I was ashamed. I just never have them. I sleep very soundly."

Like a child, Nicholas thought tenderly, remembering those moments when he had watched her sleep that first night she had been brought to him.

But it wasn't a child he was holding in his arms, and he wasn't accustomed to playing nursemaid to young women who were wrapped only in diaphanous bed curtains covered by linen shirts. His body was responding with an alacrity that signaled an achingly uncomfortable night if he didn't move away from her.

Her cheek nestled and rubbed against his chest like a cat against a satin pillow. Heat surged to his groin and he inhaled sharply. He should move away. He had promised.

"Do you have nightmares?" she asked.

Her warm breath caressed his flesh with every word, and the muscles of his stomach began to knot. "Sometimes. Not lately. I used to have them frequently." Her hair was clinging to his fingers like tousled silk. She smelled of raspberries, moss, and something more elemental that caused his head to swim dizzily. One moment more and he'd move away from her.

"What about? Monsters?"

"No, about being buried alive." He was scarcely aware of what he was saying. She had nestled closer and he could feel the womanly fullness of her breasts pressing against him. "Darkness. Not being able to breathe."

"How terrible," she murmured. The thatch of dark golden hair on his chest looked invitingly springy, and Silver moved her cheek to rest against it. The texture was gently abrasive against the smoothness of her cheek. Her throat tightened and her heart suddenly began to pound. Such a tiny thing to ignite such excitement. His roughness against her softness, his maleness against her womanliness. How would her naked breasts feel pressed against that springy rough hair?

The thought brought a tingling emptiness between her thighs that shocked her. This was not a yearning for comfort, this was lust. How had her body's needs changed so quickly? She must slip out of his arms now, before he became aware of her weakness. Her breasts were swelling, the nipples hardening as they had last night when he had teased her. No, she mustn't think of those moments. Her heart was throbbing so hard, she thought it would leap from her breast.

His hand tangled in her hair. "Silver . . ." His voice was thick, soft, seductive. "I shouldn't . . ."

The heat of his body was enfolding her wherever flesh touched flesh, and she was aware of the changes taking place in his body. The tautening of the ridge of muscles beneath her cheek and the leaping drum of his heart that echoed her own. "What?"

He muttered a curse. For one instant he crushed her to him, letting her feel the scorching heat of his body and an arousal that caused her breath to stop in her lungs. Then he was gone, his hands dropping away from her hair as he edged back away from her to his former place by the fire. "Go to sleep," he said between his teeth. "For God's sake, go back to sleep."

He was hurting, hungry, so aroused that she could feel the vibrations of his desire like a great bell resonating, summoning, enticing. It seemed impossible that she had ever wanted him to hurt like this. Now she understood that pain because it was throbbing in her own body. Emptiness, heat, aching, a passionate urge to leave loneliness behind and join with Nicholas.

"Don't look at me like that." His dark eyes were blazing at her across the few yards separating them. "I'm trying to remember you were hurt tonight and have no defenses." He closed his eyes but he could still see her gazing at him, crystal-gray eyes shining with excitement and curiosity. The eyes of a firebird. "I'm not used to being self-sacrificing, dammit."

Even if he was unaccustomed to self-denial, he was still doing it, Silver thought. Another facet of this complex man revealed. The soul of a poet, Valentin had said, and she had seen that tonight herself. But it was not the poet in him that was flooding her body with heat. How beautiful he was lying there with his rumpled golden hair and the long clean lines of his body taut and rigid with desire. Not Apollo now, but a man, and a man more vulnerable than she had ever seen him. A strong wave of tenderness shimmered through her, blending with desire until she did not know where one ended and the other began.

"You're still looking at me." Nicholas didn't open his eyes.

"Yes." Excitement was building, the decision was forming. Madness. He would not force her, would not even try to seduce her. All she had to do was close her eyes and go to sleep. Yet, why should she do that? That very knowledge was a seduction in itself. She wanted this man. It would be she who took, not he. She could have what her body craved, and then be the one who walked away. As for the consequences, she would find a way to protect herself from the consequences of giving herself to Nicholas.

A sudden thrill of fear rained through her as she realized that one of those consequences might be that she'd be with child . . . as her mother had been. But she was far stronger than her mother, and coupling did not always result in a child. Rising Star had been married fourteen years before she had conceived, and Elspeth was still not with child though four years had passed since she had wed Dominic. There was a chance she would be fortunate and still take her pleasure without suffering for it.

Consequences? When had she ever worried about consequences? she wondered. She had always acted first and thought later and she knew suddenly that was exactly what she was going to do now. Soon she must leave Nicholas and go back to Etaine and her own life. She could not look forward to many pleasures in the future, why should she not satisfy this craving that racked her body with burning need? "I don't want to go to sleep." She got to her knees and quickly unbuttoned the shirt she was wearing and slipped it off. "What if I fell asleep and the monster devoured me?"

"It's not any monster you have to worry about tonight." His eyes remained tightly closed. "I assure you that I—" He broke off and his eyes flew open. Long strands of fragrant satin-dark hair were trailing across his chest as she leaned over him, veiled only by the sheer tunic. "My God," he whispered.

A faint flush colored her cheeks as she slipped the tunic to her waist and leaned closer. "I do not fear you." Her lips touched his shoulder. "Do you fear me?"

"God, yes. I'm scared as hell you're going to tie me in knots and then leave me. It's a game you're quite adept at playing."

"I will not leave you." Her mouth moved to the golden thatch of hair on his chest and she opened her lips to tug at a tuft like a playful puppy. His heart gave a great leap and then started pounding errratical- ly. "Not until you have what you want." Pressing her breasts to the thatch of hair, she rubbed back and forth, closing her eyes to enjoy the sensation more fully. It was even better than she had imagined. Each brush against her sensitive nipples caused a hot tingle to rush through her and the aching between her thighs to increase tenfold.

"You're hurt."

"No longer. It was nothing. I'm strong now."

"You're sure?"

"I'm sure." She took his hand and placed his palm on her left breast. "Touch me. I think it will give me pleasure."

His hand slowly closed on her breast, his eyes narrowing on her face. She was flaming. Glowing. Her excitement so intense she was trembling as he squeezed the rounded globe. He felt a sudden surge of power flood him. He could do this to her. He could make her flame and tremble. He reached out with the other hand and cupped her right breast and began to squeeze rhythmically, watching with pleasure the hardening of her nipples, the swelling of her breasts in the palms of his hands. "I think it does give you pleasure, love. Come here." He moved her up so that her full breasts hung over his mouth like ripe golden apples. He licked delicately at one rosy nipple. "And I think this gives you pleasure too, doesn't it?"

Pleasure. It was too tame a word for the emotion tearing through her. She was burning. She couldn't breathe. She bent closer, nudging at his mouth with her breast. "More. Please."

He opened his lips and enveloped her with his mouth, sucking strongly. She cried out, throwing back her head as the wild, unbearably exciting sensations tore through her. Her hands went to his cheeks, stroking, helping him take. . . .

The tears brimmed and then rolled down her cheeks. She was panting. "Nicholas, I want—"

He pulled away, his mouth releasing her. "Shhh. I know." His hands continued to squeeze her, watching the expressions on her face. "My God, your breasts are sensitive. I wonder . . ." He removed his hands and gently pushed her away. "Let me up, I have to get out of these clothes before I—" He was tearing at his clothes, his gaze still on her face. Her hunger was naked and so arousing to behold that when his manhood finally sprang free, it was with a power greater than he had ever experienced.

She was staring at him, her pink tongue absently moistening her berry-stained lips. He felt a thrust of heat so intense, he made a guttural sound deep in his throat.

"I want to touch you." Silver's gaze never left him. She got to her knees, her fingers running delicately, curiously, over the thatch of hair surrounding his manhood. "Your hair is golden all over your body. It's darker gold here but . . ." She forgot what she was going to say as her hand grasped him. He jerked, a great shudder racking his body. It was like holding a great stallion with only a satin hair ribbon, she thought. All that force and power held helpless by the pleasure of her hand.

She slowly raised herself so that her breasts were touching him and gently brushed against him, letting him feel her softness against his manhood. His chest was moving in and out with the harshness of his breathing as he looked down at her dark head. "Silver . . ." His voice was choked. "I can't bear much more. I'm . . ." He groaned through his teeth as her tongue touched him. His nostrils flared. "No! Not now!"

He jerked away from her and sank to his knees. His ebony eyes were glazed as he pushed her down on the moss and opened her thighs. He was wild, savage, as he tore the sheer veiling from her body. "I have to . . ." He trailed off, his hands searching.

She knew what he had to do, what she wanted him to do. The desire she felt was as wild and primitive as what he was feeling. Her palms slid up his chest, savoring the heat, the textures of him. She was making tiny frantic sounds as she felt his fingers probe and then enter her before beginning a gentle thrusting motion.

"More!" she gasped. "Nicholas, more!"

"Shh. Soon." He moved between her thighs, his manhood nudging against her. "It's just that you're so tight. I want to make sure I don't hurt you."

Her nails dug into his shoulders. "I don't care if you hurt me," she said fiercely. *"More."*

"Yes, yes!" A groan came with the same explosive power as his action as he suddenly plunged deep inside her.

Pain. Silver inhaled sharply as the expected wave of pain rolled over her. Then it was gone and there was only the hot, sweet fullness of joining.

"Silver." Nicholas was looking down at her, stunned.

"It was nothing," she said impatiently. "I expected much more pain. Go on. Is it always this good?"

"No." He was still frozen, gazing at her blankly. She was so damn hot, tight, enveloping him. He was quivering, flexing, his manhood fighting to take more. More! My God, hadn't he taken enough from her?

It appeared he hadn't, for she was glaring up at him. "Don't you dare stop. I won't be cheated after I've gone this far."

His laugh was a half sob in his throat. Only Silver would react to her deflowering in this fashion. Well, he would not cheat her or himself either. It was too late to stop now anyway.

He plunged again and began a wild rhythm that started the tension throbbing, rising, within them both.

Silver's head was thrashing back and forth, her eyes gleaming like crystals as she gazed up at him. She was panting, moaning, ablaze. A firebird rising, fiery wings outstretched, soaring toward the sun. He rode the firebird into the dazzling radiance waiting for them beyond the horizon. Burning away the wind, the earth, the stars. Then in a wild and shimmering burst of flame, they burned away the sun itself.

And were left only with the velvet darkness of eternity . . . and each other.

Silver lay in hazy contentment, lost in a dreamy lethargy of sensual pleasure she had never known before. Where was Nicholas? She had been vaguely conscious of him leaving her, but she had been too breathless and happy to protest.

Then he was beside her, kneeling and parting her thighs.

"What are you doing?" A cool dampness soothed her flesh. "Where did you get the cloth?" she asked lazily.

"That bed curtain is quite versatile in its uses." He didn't look at her as he threw the cloth aside. "It would have been of no use to you as a gown after I ripped it off you." He reached for his white shirt. "Sit up."

She obediently sat up and put her arms in the sleeves as he held his shirt for her. "Why do I have to put on clothes when you don't?"

"Because I don't pose the same temptation." He rapidly buttoned the shirt. "I haven't the slightest doubt I'll be taking this off you very soon, but there are a few questions I want to put to you first."

He was wrong, she thought dreamily, he posed a temptation that was almost irresistible now that she knew what pleasure he could give her. "I've made a decision."

"Indeed?"

"I've decided I like doing what we just did better than smelling woodsmoke or eating raspberries or tasting honeysuckle." She smiled. "Better than anything."

His lips tightened. "You seem to have no apprehensions about yielding your virginity."

"I didn't yield it. I gave it. I *chose* to do so, and you gave me much pleasure." She smiled. "Thank you."

He stared at her incredulously. "You're speaking as if I'd just given you a handful of those raspberries. I *deflowered* you, dammit!"

"I told you I liked it far better than raspberries," she

said, her eyes twinkling. "I regret I'm not duly dismayed."

"Why should I expect anything else?" he asked caustically. "Perhaps Apaches are as casual about discarding their virginity as they are their clothing."

"No, virginity is just as revered among the Apaches as it is among the whites. Why do you think my mother was forced to leave her tribe when she lay with Boyd Delaney? There was shame upon her head." She gazed at him curiously. "Why are you so angry? You told me this was what you wanted from me from the very first moment we met. Now you have what you want and you're still not content."

"Because you were a virgin, dammit." He grated the words out through set teeth. "You weren't supposed to be a virgin. The reports I received said you were lying with one of those damn circus performers. The knife thrower, I think."

"Sebastien? He is my friend; all the people of the circus are my friends. Except Monteith, the man who owns the circus. I would not have him for a friend."

"I don't give a damn about your friends at the moment. I want to know about your lovers. The Randall Investigative Agency told me—"

"They are obviously fools." She shrugged. "You should have hired Pinkerton."

"I agree. For some reason they wouldn't accept my retainer."

"If you told them you wanted to find Dominic, it's not surprising. Dominic pays them very well to protect Elspeth. They would not have wanted to lose his business."

"Protect Elspeth?" He sat back on his heels. "Why—" He stopped and drew a deep breath. "Later. I'm not interested in anything right now but why the Delaneys allow you to frequent brothels and run around unprotected when you are—" he stopped to change the word—"*were* as untouched as any of those schoolgirls at Mrs. Alford's nunnery. They should have guarded you from—"

"Men like you?" she finished calmly.

His dark eyes flashed. "I'm no thief. I don't rob virtuous women of their purity. How was I to know you were untouched? You talk of whorehouses and bare your body with a boldness I've seldom seen from any woman."

"You did not rob me. Why are you so upset?"

He stared at her in frustration. "Damnation, because you're not!"

She threw back her head and laughed. "You wish me to weep and wail? Why should I? I enjoyed what you did to me."

"I know you did," he muttered. "I've never known a woman so responsive. You were . . ." A firebird soaring, passionate, beautiful. "Why didn't you fight me? A woman's life can be ruined by letting herself be seduced."

"You didn't seduce me." She gazed at him with a touch of impatience. "Why do you keep saying that? It was my choice to lie with you tonight, and I will be the one who walks away."

"Walk away?" His eyes widened in shock. "What in hell are you talking about?"

"Men fornicate with women and leave them with no more thought than if they were flowers they had picked by the roadside. Why should women not do the same?"

"Because that's not the way of the world. Because women don't—" he broke off. Womenkind in general might not, but Silver was capable of anything. A sudden searing jealousy tore through him. "I find I don't like the idea of being discarded so summarily, and I most certainly won't permit you to go about picking other 'flowers' by the wayside."

"I didn't say I wished to fornicate with other men," Silver said. "You're the first man I've desired in that way. Perhaps I will not find another who pleases me."

"I don't believe I'll risk the chance of your discovering one." My God, the woman was talking about leaving him! Possessiveness, jealousy, outrage, and an odd hurt invaded him. "Now that I've shown you how much you enjoy it, I'm sure you'll want to indulge your appetite to the fullest. You're the most passionate woman I've ever had, and I have no intention of letting you permit any other man to satisfy you."

"Permit?" Silver asked with dangerous softness.

"You'll return with me to St. Petersburg. I'll take very good care of you. I'll buy you a fine house and jewels fit for an empress." He paused. "But you'll belong to no man but me."

"Or?" she asked curiously. "What if I took a lover?"

He smiled. "I would take great pleasure in emas-
culating him and then quite probably I would kill
him."

He meant it, Silver realized, gazing at him in bewilderment. There was no question that he would elimi-
nate any man she permitted in her bed. Yes, Nicholas
would be as possessive of his mistress as he would his
wife. Fierce pain, as intense as it was unexpected,
seared her. Why should she feel like this, when she
had known there was no question of Nicholas offering
her more than this arrangement? Men did not offer
half-breeds marriage. "I don't want your fine house or
your jewels. I won't be your mistress, Nicholas."

"Oh, but you will." His smile deepened. "You may
not want a house and jewels, but I can give you something you do want very much." He began to unbutton
the shirt he had so recently fastened. "Something you
like better than woodsmoke or honeysuckle." He
pushed aside the edges of the shirt to gaze at her. "Or
even raspberries."

Silver felt a flood of heat wash over her, igniting a
tingling between her thighs. His eyes were caressing
her, moving over her with possessiveness and desire,
lingering on her breasts and then moving down to the
soft hair guarding her womanhood. The muscles of
her stomach clenched and she suddenly couldn't
breathe.

His gaze didn't lift as he continued softly, "You have
a splendid appetite, Silver, and I'll keep you well fed
and purring. You want me right now, don't you?"

Silver moistened her lips with her tongue. "Yes."

"Then come here and let me pleasure you."

She moved the few inches to where he sat, her gaze on the magnificent rigidity of his manhood. Beautiful. Everything about him was beautiful, his face, his body, and most of all the radiantly sensual expression lighting his face.

His hand slowly began petting her. A shiver of excitement went through her as she felt the warm hardness of his palm. "There are many ways I can please your body. Do you like this?"

She nodded jerkily.

His fingers moved down and found what he sought. His thumb began a circular, pressing movement.

Her eyes widened. "Nicholas!" She arched toward him, her muscles contracting in agonizing pleasure. "It's—"

"You like it?"

Hot shudders were shaking her body and she gazed up at him almost blindly. "Yes. Oh, yes. So much."

"I can see you do." His gaze was narrowed on her flushed face. "It's such a little thing and so easy to do. I could do it in the carriage on the way to a ball or behind the bushes in a garden. All you would have to do is lift your skirts and part your legs and say 'Nicholas, pleasure me.'"

She was panting, her head thrown back, her throat arched as waves of pleasure cascaded over her.

"I would never say no," he whispered. "Because I love to see your face like this. Do you know how beautiful you are?"

She didn't answer; she couldn't answer.

"Of course, it might be dangerous to do it in too public a place because I'm quite sure this would follow." He suddenly lifted her onto his lap, sheathing his manhood within her in one swift plunge. Arranging her legs around his hips, he gazed into her face. "And you would let me. You couldn't help yourself." He flexed slowly, pressing her so close she could feel the gentle prickle of his hair against her womanhood. "Any more than I could stop myself from doing it." His hands cupped her buttocks and squeezed gently. His head bent and she felt his tongue on her nipples.

"Move, please!"

"Soon." He held her firmly against him, nibbling at her engorged breasts. "I'm trying to make you understand something, Silver." He bit gently. One hand reached between them and his thumb touched, pressed, rotated while his fingers teased her like hot fluttering butterflies.

She cried out. "It's . . . too . . . much."

He froze, his fingers stilling their excitation. "Yes, it is," he said thickly. With one quick movement he fell backward and then rolled over until he was astride her. He plunged wildly, almost brutally, in a fever of passion. The pace was unbearable. Silver was lost in heat and desire. Then it was over, exploding with the same fiery force as before.

His breath was coming in gasps as he looked down at her. "You see," he said, meeting her eyes. "This is what we'll have together, and you cannot deny you want it." He bent down and gently kissed her lips. "Can you, Silver? And this is only the beginning; it gets better and better until it's a fever in your blood. I intend to make sure you never recover from that fever."

But what of him? Silver thought with sudden jolt of pain. She had no doubt that he could enslave her senses with this physical pleasure, but would she have the same power over him? What if he tired of her? Men tired easily of women's bodies, but she had never known lust before meeting Nicholas. What if she were one of those foolish women who could not know lust without love? And if she became his mistress, she would almost certainly bear his illegitimate children. She would bring the same shame and hurt to her child as her mother had brought to her. The thought sent a wild thrill of panic through her.

He moved off her and then lay down beside her, pulling her into his arms. "You'll come with me to Russia." His voice was soft, coaxing. "Say it, Silver."

Perhaps she was already starting to love him, she thought frantically. The signs had been there, but she had refused to read them. No, she must *not* love him.

"Say it, Silver." His long, graceful hand gently stroked her hair.

She reached desperately for something, anything to break the spell. "Will you stop looking for Dominic if I go with you?"

He stiffened against her. "You're bargaining? No, Silver, that's not negotiable."

"Then there's no reason for me to go to Russia." She tried to keep her voice careless and unconcerned. "My life is here and I have things to do with it."

He was silent for a long moment. "It appears I must increase my efforts at persuading you." His lips brushed her temple. "It's fortunate that I have time and intimacy on my side, isn't it? And when at last we get back to St. Louis to see if Dominic has taken the bait, I think you may change your mind."

"You're still not going to let me go?"

His arms tightened around her. "No, did you expect me to?"

"No, I didn't expect this to make any difference. I know you regard the taking of a woman as unimportant."

Then why did he feel as if he had been lifted and torn from everything he had ever known? he wondered. Why was he experiencing anger, tenderness, and bewilderment now, when he had never felt these emotions toward any other woman?

"Very wise," he said. "Then you won't be disappointed to know you're still a prisoner."

"And you won't be disappointed to know that I have no intention of staying a prisoner." She nestled nearer, her eyes closing. "Nothing has really changed."

His hand stroked her hair with exquisite gentleness. "No, nothing has really changed."

She was nearly asleep when she remembered something. "Your scars . . . I dug my fingernails in your back. I didn't hurt you?"

"The scars are old. They no longer bring me pain."

No, she thought drowsily, it wasn't the scars on the outside that brought the lasting pain. . . .

* * *

"Wake up, Silver." Nicholas was kneeling beside her, pulling her into a sitting position. He slipped her arms into the sleeves of his shirt and rapidly buttoned it. "Lord, you spoke truth when you said you slept soundly."

"Why do I have to wake up?" she asked, yawning.

"It's dawn and a boat has been launched from the *Rose*. I believe we're about to be rescued." He stood up and began dressing quickly. "I realize you probably have no objections to being found nude, but I find I have a distinct aversion to the thought of any man except me seeing you unclothed." He frowned. "Though that shirt is scarcely modest. It doesn't even cover your knees."

She blinked sleepily. "Sorry."

He suddenly chuckled as he finished fastening his trousers. "I believe I may enjoy waking you from a sound sleep under other circumstances. You're amazingly docile on awakening."

She rubbed her eyes with the back of her hand and looked out at the river. A rowboat was drawing near to the shore and she was able to identify Valentin and Mikhail manning the oars of the craft.

She stood up and walked down to the bank. She waved and called cheerfully, "Good morning. Do you have a bucket in the boat?"

The prow of the boat bumped against the shore and Valentin jumped out on the moss-covered bank. "Just a bailing bucket."

"That will do." She turned to Nicholas. "Will you . . ."

He sighed. "I should have known you'd wake up hungry. Can't you wait until we get back to the *Rose*?"

"Of course, but this is for later."

Mikhail and Valentin gazed at Nicholas blankly as he crossed to the boat to fetch the bucket.

"What are you going to do?" Valentin asked.

"Raspberries," Nicholas answered succinctly. "Stay with her." He disappeared into the shrubbery.

"Raspberries?" Valentin repeated.

Silver nodded. "Huge, wonderful raspberries. We'll have them for lunch or dinner with cream. They should be even better that way."

Mikhail and Valentin exchanged glances and then suddenly broke into laughter.

"Why do you laugh?" Silver asked in puzzlement. "Truly, they're very, very good."

"I'm sure they are." Valentin said, trying to subdue his laughter. "Let's just say it wasn't what we were anticipating. When you jumped overboard last night and forced Nicholas to pursue you, we didn't think we'd find him meekly picking raspberries at your command."

"What did you expect?"

Valentin sobered. "To find Nicholas ready to strangle you."

Mikhail spoke gently, his gaze searching her face. "You are well?"

Sudden color rose to her cheeks. "Of course I'm well," she answered, not looking at him. "Nicholas was very kind." She turned away abruptly. "And he's not as meek at this moment as you may believe." She smiled over her shoulder. "He likes raspberries too."

Lee Bassinger moved back into the shadows of the boiler deck and watched with no expression as Mikhail Kuzdief leapt onto the deck from the rowboat and then leaned down to lift Silver Delaney up beside him. So Savron had caught his little captive, he thought as he observed Nicholas Savron and Marinov climb onto the deck. Perhaps she had spoken the truth and she wasn't a whore after all. Whatever she was, she was important to Nicholas Savron. No man jumped into a river to pursue a female unless she held value for him.

He felt a surge of savage satisfaction. The key. She was going to be the key just as he had thought when he had first seen her. His hands tightened on the rail until his knuckles turned white as he remembered his humiliation at that bitch's hands. Yes, he would use her to punish Savron and then he would break her and throw her away.

He could make no move while on the *Rose*, but in another day they should reach Memphis. They would have to stop to take on coal and it should be no problem to arrange to have Silver Delaney taken by his own men, particularly since she appeared more than eager to escape Savron.

Anticipation was a sharp pain within him as he turned away and began to stroll down the deck toward the saloon. Tomorrow. This goddamn charade was almost over. He had only to wait one more day.

8

"Why are we having dinner in the state-room?" Silver asked as she sat down opposite Nicholas at the damask-covered table. She spread her napkin on her lap and dropped her lashes to veil the hint of mischief in her eyes. "Have you decided I'm not presentable enough to mingle with your other guests?"

"I decided I didn't want every man at the table ogling you and remembering what you looked like with nothing but a wisp of cloth covering your privates," he said tersely. "I haven't forgiven you for that, Silver."

"I didn't ask for your forgiveness." She smiled at him. "I think you're just being selfish and don't want to share the raspberries with them."

His frown faded and a reluctant smile touched his lips. "That too." He looked down at his plate. "Talk to me."

"What?"

"Tell me about yourself."

She looked at him in puzzlement. "What do you

163

wish to know? I've already told you what is important."

"You've told me only that you're a half-breed," he said with barely leashed violence. "For God's sake, that's not the only thing you are. You have a mind and a soul."

"People aren't usually concerned with anything else," she said simply. "I know what I am inside but they don't want to see. You didn't want to see either. You wanted only my body."

Nicholas felt a sharp pang. What she said was true. He had been so captivated with the challenge she presented, he had disregarded everything else. "Well, I want to see now. Did you like it at Mrs. Alford's?"

"No, I hated it. They thought me savage, and I thought them stupid. Even the lessons were stupid. Finger-painting and needlepoint and how to curtsy. Rising Star taught me much more from her books than any of those girls learned at the academy." Her face lit with a reminiscent smile. "Rising Star knew so much, she had many books and she was always reading. She was far more clever than Mrs. Alford."

"Her husband must have been very proud of her."

Her smile faded. "Joshua? Joshua was ashamed because she was an Apache." Her lips tightened. "He killed her."

Nicholas's gaze rose swiftly to her face. "Murder?"

"She was with child and he told her he did not wish it. She rode away from Killara and died when her child was born." Her voice lowered fiercely. "She was *strong*. If she had wanted to live . . ." Her gray eyes were suddenly glittering with tears. "She was gentle and kind but it made no difference. Her skin was not white and they killed her for it. She told me once that the way to live in a white man's world was to take on his ways and and become what he wished you to be. She was wrong. No matter what she did, the Delaneys would not accept her as one of them."

The pain was naked in her face and he was experiencing a reflection of her agony within himself. He tried to think of something to distract her from that poignant memory. He lifted his wine goblet to his lips. "Did you like nothing about your schooling?"

She didn't answer immediately, and it was evident she was trying to gather her composure. "I learned to play the piano. I love music." She made a face. "When I was first learning I was terrible, and Mrs. Alford would come in and try to make me stop. She said the noise was disturbing the other students."

"But you wouldn't do it," Nicholas guessed.

"I knew I would get better and I needed it."

Nicholas could understand how she needed something of her own to shelter her from the loneliness and prejudice surrounding her, even if it were only music.

"What type of music do you prefer?"

She smiled eagerly. "Everything. I like everything from folk songs to Beethoven. It's wonderful how music makes everything take on beauty and sparkle. Do you like music?"

"Very much. I'd like to hear you play sometime."

He should have known Silver would take delight in music. Anyone so sensual would naturally be attuned to the pleasures of sound. "We have some fine young composers in Russia now. I think you'd enjoy hearing their music. There's a young man named Rimsky-Korsakoff who shows great promise." He looked down into the ruby-red depths of his wineglass. "St. Petersburg can be very gay. Concerts, ballets, balls—"

"You're trying to persuade me to go to Russia," Silver said bluntly. "I told you I wouldn't go. I leave Mrs. Alford's shortly and I intend to continue my studies."

"What studies?" Nicholas asked impatiently. "You've already said you know more than the other women at the academy. Perhaps you wish to perfect your skill at needlepoint?"

"I'm going to go to a university and study medicine."

"You intend to be a nurse?"

She stiffened. "I'm going to be a doctor."

"Women do not become doctors," Nicholas said flatly.

"They do now." Silver set her plate aside and reached for the crystal dessert bowl in which the raspberries were swimming in rich cream. "Why should I be a nurse when I can be a better doctor than most I've seen in the profession. It's not reasonable."

"They won't accept you at a university," Nicholas said gently.

"I'll find a way." Silver dipped her spoon into the raspberries and met his gaze across the table. "Because I'm not Rising Star, Nicholas. I won't pretend to be what I am not and I'll let no one rob me of anything I choose to keep."

There was no challenge in her expression, and Nicholas realized that she was speaking with absolute sincerity. He experienced a sudden thrust of pity mixed with respect and admiration. Poor little fire-bird, she didn't realize what a difficult task she'd set for herself. Or perhaps she did and was so accustomed to the struggle for acceptance that she could perceive nothing different in this battle from the ones that had gone before. "I could help you."

She laughed with genuine amusement. "Instead of a house and jewels, you're going to buy me with an entry to a university?" She shook her head. "I wouldn't take it from you. I want the victory to be mine."

He hadn't thought of using his influence as a carte blanche. He had wanted to help her and had made the offer impulsively. My God, what was he thinking? He wanted Silver in his bed, under his protection, not struggling in a university thousands of miles away from him. Silver's plan was all foolishness anyway. She would be hurt and snubbed beyond anything in her present experience. No, she'd be much better off under his protection, where he could guard her from both the outside world and herself. "Then it looks as if I'll have to find a more tempting prize to dangle before you," he said lightly. "Would you consider a fine piano?"

"No, thank you."

"Pity. Have you finished your dessert?"

She ate the last berry and set down her spoon. "Yes, why?"

"Because I'm about to seduce you and I wouldn't dare interfere with one of your primary pleasures." He stood up and came around the table, pulling her to her feet and into his arms. "Before offering one in its place." His head came down and his lips hovered over her mouth. "Open your lips, love. I want to taste you."

She opened her lips and his tongue entered, caressed, and explored. He could feel her heart pounding against his chest and she seemed to be holding her breath. He caught her tongue in his mouth and sucked it gently, tasting the textures. His body was hardening and he knew he couldn't wait much longer. He lifted his head. "You taste of raspberries and sugar. So sweet." He was unbuttoning her shirtwaist. "Come to bed, Silver. There are things I want to show you, things I want to do to you."

She leaned against him, gazing up into his eyes. Such beautiful eyes, she though dreamily. Dark with mystery and hinting at wonderful secrets. "What do you want to show me?"

He pulled off her blouse and threw it aside. He found he was too impatient to bother with anything more. Lord, he had scarcely touched her and he was ready. He lifted her swiftly in his arms and carried her to the bed.

"Do you remember that picture I showed you?"

Silver felt her heart suddenly jerk with excitement. "Are you going to do that to me?"

"Among other pleasurable things." He laid her on the bed and began to strip off his clothes quickly.

"Will I like it?"

"Oh, yes, love." He looked down at her and smiled. "First we'll have the main course, and then we'll have a lagniappe."

"Lagniappe?"

He came to her, all supple bronze muscle and golden mane. "It's a word I learned in New Orleans," he whispered. "It's a word I like very much."

"What does it mean?"

He pulled her camisole down to bare her breasts. He drew a shaky breath, his golden head bending forward until his warm breath was feathering a nipple. "Something extra," he said thickly. "Lagniappe means a little something extra."

Silver gazed out the window at the bustling wharf below. Since they were taking on only fuel and not passengers here in Memphis, Nicholas had said they would be on their way in a matter of hours. She would probably have no opportunity to escape again before they reached New Orleans, she thought absently. Then the placidity of the thought suddenly sent a shock through her.

But there was no chance of escape now, she assured herself quickly. Nicholas had carefully locked both doors before he had left the stateroom to join Robert, Mikhail, and Valentin in the pilot house. She was merely being sensible not to be upset over a circumstance she couldn't change.

One hand clenched on the peach-colored velvet of the curtains. She was lying to herself. She had been captivated, seduced by the hot, dark hours in Nicholas's bed last night and this morning. She wanted to let herself be brought once more under that sensual pleasure spell. But it was even worse than that. She wanted to *stay* with Nicholas. He was the magnet that drew her and caused her to cling to captivity. He was the reason she was giving up so tamely.

Yet she mustn't give up. Etaine needed her and Silver must not let lust keep her from returning to her.

The sound of a key turning in the door that led to the deck startled her. Nicholas? But he had just left. . . .

"Good morning, Miss Delaney." Lee Bassinger stood in the doorway, a faint smile on his lips. "I'm glad you're dressed. We won't have much time."

"Where did you get a key to this stateroom?" she asked, surprised and wary.

"I have keys to every stateroom on the *Rose*, and you'll remember this particular stateroom used to be mine." He pocketed the key. "And will be again. Come along. I saw Nicholas disappear into the pilot house, but we can't count on him staying there long." His gaze ran over her. "Not with a pretty lady like you waiting for him."

"I'd rather stay here than go with you," Silver said bluntly.

"But you're not going with me," Bassinger said.

"I'm staying on the *Rose* and you're going to escape. That is what you want, isn't it?"

"Yes," she said cautiously. "But why would you want to help me?"

"I don't want to help you. But I do want to deprive Savron of something he values. Now, do you want to get away from him or not?"

"Of course." Naturally she wanted to get away from him, she told herself. There was nothing for her here, and she could accomplish a great deal if she returned to the circus and Etaine. The reluctance she felt was evidence only of the dangerous sway Nicholas was beginning to have over her feelings. She started forward briskly, passing Bassinger as she went out on deck. "How do I get off the boat without being seen by Nicholas? The gangplank is in clear view from the pilot house."

"It's all arranged. I took the precaution of going ashore and contacting a few of my employees. They'll give you any assistance you need." He drew a file out of his pocket and deliberately broke the lock from the inside before shutting the door. "Go down to the boiler deck by the rear stairs. There will be two men in a rowboat off the stern. They'll row you upstream, around the bend and out of sight. I've given them some money for you to facilitate your flight." He bowed. "Good-bye, Miss Delaney. I was hoping to become much better acquainted with you, but one must accept these little disappointments in life."

Silver hesitated uneasily. Bassinger was gazing at her with that tight, empty smile, his cold eyes reptilian, and he was far too pleased with himself. There was something that wasn't right. Yet it was perfectly in character for Bassinger to want to hurt Nicholas in any way he could. Perhaps she was being too suspicious.

She turned away. "Good-bye."

"No thank-you?" Bassinger asked silkily.

She glanced back over her shoulder and slowly shook her head. "I believe I'll wait to see if there's something to be thankful for."

Then she was gone, hurrying toward the back stairs which led to the boiler deck.

"Face it, Nicky, there's no sign of her," Valentin said quietly. "We've queried everyone on the wharfs, searched the streets, inquired at the livery stables. You even rode twenty miles north to see if she had taken off on foot." He leaned against the rail and looked out at the moonlit river. "If she's still in Memphis, she's found a damned good hiding place."

"I don't think she is in Memphis," Nicholas said tersely. "She's more accustomed to wild country than cities. She grew up in a hell of a lot more dangerous land than this. The farther away from the *Rose* she traveled, the more secure she'd feel."

"Then you think she's somewhere in the forest or on the road?"

"I don't know," Nicholas said wearily. "I can only guess what Silver would do. I'm going to ride out and try the main road going south to make sure she didn't go that way. Mikhail is making a round of the taverns, on the wharf to see if he can pick up any information."

"You need to rest, Nicky." Valentin gazed at him worriedly. Nicholas had not slept for nearly forty-eight hours, and he looked it. His skin was drawn tightly over the broad bones of his cheeks, and dark circles were imprinted beneath his eyes. "Wouldn't tomorrow do as well? It's after midnight."

"I must find her tonight. The *Rose* is leaving Memphis at dawn tomorrow."

Valentin's eyes widened. "You're giving up the search?"

"Don't be a fool. Of course I'm not giving up." Nicholas paused. "God, I'm sorry, Valentin. I guess I am tired." He rubbed the bunched muscles at the back of his neck to relieve the tension. "Since I can't find her, I'll have to try to guess her destination, then reach it before she does. We'll take the boat back upriver to St. Louis."

"Mrs. Alford's Academy?"

Nicholas shook his head. "The circus. When we first took her, she appeared to be most worried that she couldn't get back to the circus. She told me later that she has friends there. It would be natural for her to go to them for help."

"It's over three hundred miles back to St. Louis. That's a terrible trip for a woman alone. Do you think she'll be able to make it safely?"

Nicholas's hands tightened on the rail. That was the question he'd been asking himself. "She'll make it."

Valentin looked away from Nicholas to gaze at the

glowing lanterns hanging by the gangplank. "You could forget about trying to find her. She's not going to tell you where Dominic Delaney is, Nicky."

Nicholas didn't answer.

"But then, that's not the reason you tore Memphis apart looking for her, is it?" Valentin asked softly. "Delaney might have started all this, but he's not the crux of the matter now."

"I'll find Silver and then go after her uncle," Nicholas said grimly. "I'll have them both."

"But if you have to kill Delaney, you may find that Silver will object to your plans for her. Perhaps to the extent of sticking her little knife in you." Valentin paused. "You're going to have to decide which is most important to you."

"First I have to find her." Nicholas turned away. "I'm going to get something to eat and then ride out. I've told Mikhail if he learns anything to come to your cabin with the information. I'll check with you when I come back."

"Very well." Valentin gazed after him until he disappeared into the saloon. Slowly he turned and rested his arms on the rail, staring thoughtfully into the dark water. The situation in which Nicholas was embroiled was no longer amusing, and Valentin was beginning to feel uneasy. Nicholas's passion for Silver was rapidly becoming an obsession and seemed to contain the seeds of tragedy.

He knew Nicholas had little trust in women. Who could blame him with a bitch like Natalya for a mother? And Silver was even more wary than

Nicholas and every bit as wild. Perhaps it would be better if Nicholas searched in vain for her.

"Good evening, Count Marinov, no news of Miss Delaney?"

Valentin turned to see Lee Bassinger strolling toward him. "Not yet."

Bassinger smiled. "Nicholas must be truly worried by now. I feel called upon to render assistance."

"Assistance?"

"I'm well known in this city. I'm going ashore to see if I can obtain information from my manager here on the wharf. He has his ear to the ground and perhaps he'll know someone who has seen her."

"I'm sure Nicholas will appreciate your concern," Valentin said dryly. What was the bastard up to? Bassinger had lounged around the *Rose* for the last two days observing all their efforts with that meaningless smile. Now, out of nowhere, he had decided to help. "But he thinks Silver may have left Memphis and gone back north. The *Rose* leaves for St. Louis at dawn."

Bassinger's smile stayed in place. "Perhaps Nicholas is wrong. I'll endeavor to find out for him." He put on his high silk hat, pulled on his kidskin gloves, and turned toward the gangplank. "I'll be back shortly."

"What do you mean, she's not here?" Bassinger's light green eyes were narrowed with rage. "I told you to hold her here in this warehouse until I came."

The two men standing before him exchanged uneasy glances. Then the taller of the two took a deep breath and burst out, "She got away from us."

"What!" A flush of rage mantled Bassinger's cheeks. "You fools! How could she get away? There were two of you."

"She damn near killed me," the shorter one, who had a scraggly beard, said testily. "She kicked me in the balls and pushed Steve here into the river. Then she took off running and was gone before we knew it."

Bassinger's palm cracked against the bearded cheek of the man called Landon. "I may kill you myself." Bassinger's eyes were blazing with fury. "How long ago, Landon?"

Landon's hand went to his cheek and his face turned ugly. If the crazy son of a bitch didn't pay so good, he'd—

"How long?" Bassinger demanded impatiently.

"Only an hour or so after we took her," admitted the taller man, called Steve by Landon. "We went ashore upriver just like you said and told her we'd take her someplace safe to hide. She didn't want to come with us, so we tried to scare her a little." He went on defensively. "It's not our fault. She was suspicious from the time she got into the rowboat."

"Not your fault?" Bassinger began to curse viciously. "Why didn't you come to me with this information?"

"You told us to stay away from the *Rose* and from you," Landon said quickly.

"That was because I didn't want suspicion to fall on me, you idiot." And because he'd wanted to linger and savor Savron's frustration and worry for as long as possible before he revealed that he was in possession of what Savron wanted. He'd enjoyed these last two days enormously, thinking he held a secret power over that damn Russian, and now to find he had nothing. Nothing! "Did you search for her?"

Both men nodded quickly.

Of course they had searched, Bassinger realized with fury. So had Savron and his friends. The damn bitch had escaped from all of them. He whirled and strode toward the door. "I'll make damn sure you never find work on this wharf again." He slammed the door behind him and strode down the street.

She was gone. The key was gone. Those stupid sons of bitches had let her get away. He had to get control of himself. He was so enraged, he couldn't think, and he needed to plan his next move.

Silver Delaney was gone, but Savron suspected she had returned to St. Louis, Bassinger thought. Perhaps he was right. But even if Savron didn't find the woman, Bassinger's best move would be to stay close to him. If one key had been lost, perhaps another could be found.

He could see the lanterns of the *Rose* in the distance and quickened his steps. He would be on the *Rose* when it sailed for St. Louis at dawn.

9

"**G**od, you look tired." Khadil's pink eyes were concerned as her gaze ran over Silver's sweat-stained, dusty and torn shirtwaist and skirt. "And those clothes look as if they've been dragged through bramble bushes."

"They have." Silver sat down on Khadil's brass-studded leather trunk, trying to ignore the weariness that plagued every muscle. "Among other shrubbery. I've been traveling for nearly two weeks, most of it on foot. How is Etaine?"

"Well." Khadil's expression was reproachful. "But she was worried when you didn't come. Sebastien even went to your school but they would tell him nothing except that you had gone on a short trip."

So Mrs. Alford had believed the note Nicholas had sent, Silver thought. Well, it should have come as no surprise. The woman had always regarded Indian women only one step above prostitutes. No, it wasn't surprise she was feeling, but the same depression that had been nagging at her since the moment she had been released from the stateroom by Bassinger. It had followed her like an annoying shadow on the long, hard trip from Memphis and was still with her now. But it had nothing to do with her leaving Nicholas, she assured herself quickly. She had her life to live and she must not be beguiled by Nicholas Savron. She moved her shoulders, unconsciously trying to shrug off the thought of him. Why did memories of Nicholas persist when she would probably never see him again?

"It was impossible for me to leave a message when I suddenly had to leave the academy," Silver explained. "Where is Etaine now?"

"Performing. She should be through soon. I will go and tell her you are here." Khadil stood up. "You will need a bath and a change of clothes. I'll get Sebastien to bring you some hot water and you'll find my hairbrush in that chest. I don't think my clothes would fit you, you're much taller than I am. I'll see if Fatima has something that will do." She smiled shyly. "It is good that you have come back to us, Silver. We have missed you."

Silver's throat tightened. "I've missed you too."

The albino's smile was wide with pleasure as she left the tent.

Silver gazed at the flame flickering in the lantern on the crude table a few feet away. They had missed her. They cared about her. This was where she belonged, not as the woman of a man who cared nothing for her once she had left his bed. She had been right to leave Nicholas and come back to the people who found worth in her.

She rose quickly, lifted the lid of Khadil's chest, and located the hairbrush. She would keep herself busy repairing the ravages of the trail until Etaine was free to come to her, and would not give one more thought to Nicholas. She began to run the bristles of the brush slowly through her long hair, her gaze once more on the golden flames of the lantern. How beautifully it shimmered in the darkness of the tent, like a burst of golden sunlight, like Nicholas's hair beneath the chandeliers in the Grand Saloon. . . .

Etaine's laughter pealed out as soon as she caught sight of Silver. "You look like one of the caliph's dancing daughters in Fatima's act." She clapped her hands in delight. "I like this costume much better than that ugly uniform. You should wear it all the time."

"I'm afraid Fatima wouldn't appreciate my appropriating her costume on a permanent basis," Silver said dryly, glancing down at herself. The filmy scarlet skirt and matching short-sleeve velvet jacket were very comfortable and she was beginning to think Eastern women must be more sensible than she had dreamed if they had eliminated the wearing of undergarments. Still, the extremely low square neck of the jacket was far from practical and seemed purposely designed to lift and frame a woman's breasts for the delectation of the onlooker. "She made it clear she wanted it back."

Etaine laughed again and ran across the tent into Silver's arms, hugging her with all her strength. "You look better in it than she does. You look beautiful. Oh, Silver, I've missed you so."

Silver's arms tightened around the child's slight body. Etaine didn't seem any thinner, and her color was good. "Well, I'm here now. You haven't had any more attacks?"

Etaine shook her head. "I've been fine. Maybe I'm growing out of it, as you said I might." She sat down on Khadil's pallet beside Silver and nestled into the curve of her arm, her short white-gold curls shimmering against Silver's flame-colored bodice. "I was worried about you. I thought perhaps my father—" She broke off and was silent a moment before continuing haltingly. "I wondered if you'd had an accident."

What the child meant was that she had been afraid that Monteith had found a way of getting rid of Silver.

"No, I had to go away for a while, but I'm back now and everything is going to be better."

"Is it?" Etaine's voice was wistful. "I hope so." She brightened. "Anyway, I'm glad you came back before we left St. Louis."

Silver stiffened. "You're leaving?"

"I think so. For the last week my father has been talking about it. He says the Americans don't appreciate the circus as Europeans do and—"

"He's taking the circus to Europe?" Silver interrupted, startled. "When?"

Etaine shrugged. "He didn't say. I can't ask; it wouldn't do any good." She was silent a moment before whispering, "I don't want to leave you, Silver. Sometimes I think of being far away from you and I

get so scared. While you're here I always believe
everything will turn out fine, that I'll get well."

"You *will* get well," Silver said fiercely. "And you
won't leave me. I'll find a way to keep you here in
America."

Etaine tilted her head and looked at Silver, and for
a moment the child's eyes had the weary sadness of a
woman in her twilight years. "I don't believe he'll let
me stay, no matter what you do. I've been thinking a
lot lately and I know now what he wants of me."

Silver frowned. "What?"

"Death," Etaine said simply. "He wants me to die."

Silver shivered and her arm tightened convulsively
around Etaine's thin shoulders. "You could be
wrong."

"No." Etaine's clear gaze met her own. "He hates
me. I don't know why, but he does. Sometimes when
he looks at me I know he's thinking that he wishes I
were already dead."

Silver did not try to dissuade or convince her that a
father would not harm his child. Monteith was capable of anything in her opinion, and Etaine's instincts
were probably correct. The child possessed a wisdom
far beyond her years and suffering had honed that
wisdom. If it were true that Monteith's neglect and
cruelty toward Etaine was more malevolent than
merely callous, then it would be safer for her to be on
guard. She could only offer comfort at this juncture.
"I've never lied to you, have I, Etaine?"

"No."

"Then listen carefully to me. I promise you I'll take

you away from him to a place where you'll be safe and well," Silver said softly. "I vow it on the grave of Rising Star. Do you believe me?"

"I believe you will try." Etaine smiled gravely. "You mustn't feel sad if you can't help me, Silver. I've been very happy. I have wonderful friends and my life has been good."

Dear God, the child was speaking as if her death were inevitable, Silver realized with a thrill of panic. She forced herself to smile. "It will be better." She gave Etaine an affectionate hug. "Now run along and let me sleep. I'm very tired. We'll talk more in the morning."

"Yes, Etaine, it's time you went to bed." The deep voice was smooth and mellow as dark honey in spite of its clipped British accent. "Bid your friend good-night and go to our tent."

Monteith. Silver drew a deep breath and braced herself. Then she turned and gazed at the man standing in the doorway of the tent.

Monteith was as beautiful in his own way as his daughter. He possessed the same white-gold hair, fine-boned grace, and handsome features. Of only medium height, his royal carriage made every inch impressive. He must have been in his early forties, but his smooth, fair skin was unlined and he appeared curiously ageless.

Silver had never seen him wear anything but gray, and tonight was no exception. His pearl-gray trousers, darker gray frock coat, and silk waistcoat gave him a curiously phantomlike elegance in the nimbus of light cast by the lantern. "Good evening, Monteith."

"You look charming, my dear," Monteith said. "Perhaps I should offer you a position in my circus. I'm sure the gentlemen would flock to see you." His voice lowered silkily. "And you appear to be so comfortable among us. May I ask if you intend to be here long this time?"

"Only a few days." Silver glanced down at Etaine. "Khadil said it would be all right if I shared her tent and there are a few arrangements I wish to make before I leave."

"Nonsense. When I heard you were here, I told Khadil to move in with one of the other freaks for the night and let you have exclusive use of her tent. A young lady must have her privacy." His gaze flicked to Etaine and his smile glittered in the lantern light. "I believe I told you to go to bed," he said softly. "You're not usually so stupid, Etaine. I don't wish to tell you again." He snapped his fingers.

Two bright spots of color appeared in the child's ivory cheeks and she scrambled quickly to her feet. "I'm going. Good night, Silver." She ran toward the door, carefully avoiding brushing her father. "I'll see you in the morning."

Monteith turned to watch her leave and then his gaze returned to Silver. "Children can be terribly disobedient, can't they, Silver? I must remember to do something about that in the near future."

Silver felt a ripple of fear. Monteith's physical presence seemed to encompass and smother her. He was being far too polite and charming to her. Monteith maintained a pleasant façade only for his audiences and had never been hesitant about displaying his displeasure for both her presence at his circus and her association with Etaine. "You don't seem unhappy to see me here. If I remember correctly, you weren't this cordial the last time I saw you."

"I can afford to be generous. We won't be here much longer, so your interference with Etaine will cease to be a problem."

"I help Etaine. Surely no one could call that a problem."

"No?" His brow rose. "But then, we all have our own viewpoints." He turned to leave. "And our individual purposes in life."

"The reason I came back was to talk to you about Etaine."

"Really? How interesting. Tomorrow we must make time for that conversation." He glanced back over his shoulder, his dark blue eyes glittering coldly. "Sleep well, Silver."

Silver gazed after him. Monteith's presence always held a strange fascination for her. She supposed it was his resemblance to Etaine that bothered her so greatly. Being with him was like peering into a broken looking glass and seeing a beloved friend's reflection twisted and fragmented. Etaine's zest and warmth, her loving nature and joy in life were the precise opposites of her father's traits. His cold beauty and mocking cruelty were repulsive, and the aura of power he emanated disturbed Silver even more.

She got up and blew out the lantern, then settled down on Khadil's pallet and closed her eyes. She was so tired, and seeing Monteith had made her realize how many problems confronted her; Etaine, Monteith, her own plans for the future.

And the other possibility that she had been afraid even to think about.

She swallowed, fighting down the panic that persisted in rising within her. It was foolish to worry, when she would probably have her monthly flux any day. If not, then it meant she would have to see Nicholas only one last time. She would certainly not lie here sleepless, thinking about possibilities that might never come to pass. She would need all her strength and control tomorrow, when she would try to persuade Monteith to give up Etaine.

"Don't move!" A hand clamped down over Silver's mouth, smothering her outcry as she was jarred out of a sound sleep into half waking. "And if you sink your teeth into me, by God, I'll gag you. I'm not at all pleased with you, Silver."

Nicholas!

Even in the darkness she could never fail to recognize him. That musky scent, the deep vibrance of his voice . . . Joy cascaded through her in a blinding tide. Something lost was found. A bond that had been broken was now newly forged.

He was astride her, she could feel the iron-hard strength of his thighs through the layers of clothes that separated them. That was wrong, she thought hazily. There should be nothing separating them. Not time, nor distance, not even the flimsy barriers of fabrics.

"Silver?" There was a sudden note of concern in Nicholas's voice. "Are you all right? Dammit, Monteith said you were only tired. I should have—"

"Monteith?" She was abruptly wide awake and began to struggle beneath Nicholas's weight.

"That's better," Nicholas said dryly. "It's not like you to be so meek. For a minute I was afraid you were ill. I was sure— Ouch!" He jerked his hand away from her teeth. "Get your fangs out of me. I told you I'd—"

"Let me go!" Silver said fiercely. "Not again, Nicholas!"

"Oh, yes," Nicholas said softly. "Again and again and again. It may never stop. If you run away, I'll only follow. Haven't you realized that yet, Silver?"

The darkness of the tent was soft as ebony velvet and vibrant with the essence of Nicholas, reaching out, enfolding her. She could feel his heat, and her heart began to pound harder. "There is nothing to realize."

"You think not?" Grimness threaded Nicholas's voice. "Well then, I'll have to convince you. But not here, you're coming back to the *Rose* with me."

"I'm not leaving here."

"You will. I told Monteith I wanted no one sharing your tent because these people are your friends and I didn't want to chance harming them." His voice hardened. "But I have no intention of leaving without you, Silver. If you fight me, someone will no doubt hear and try to help you. Do you want to risk their being hurt?"

She stopped struggling. Nicholas's tone was unrelenting, and she knew he meant every word he said. She drew a deep breath. "Monteith sent a message to you telling you I was here?"

"He was very well paid to do so. You'll be happy to know you cost me a great deal of money. Monteith is an exceptionally greedy man."

"He's a complete bastard."

"I surmised as much, but it made no difference as long as I could buy what I wanted from him." The muscles of his thighs were hardening and his voice was thick. "And I want you. I believe it will be better if we leave here immediately. Mikhail is waiting outside the circus grounds with a hired carriage." He moved off her, one hand encircling her wrist, and he pulled her to her feet. "Are you going to fight me?"

"No," she said curtly. "Not here. There will be time enough to get away from you without involving my friends."

"Excellent reasoning." He pulled her toward the entrance of the tent. "And extremely convenient for me."

"When did you arrive in St. Louis? I thought perhaps you would give up."

He laughed softly. "No, you didn't."

He was right. She had known he would never give up something he wanted any more than she would have.

"I arrived here nearly a week ago." He was leading

her past the silent darkness of the tents. In the distance she could see the glow of a carriage lantern and Mikhail's huge form on the coachman's seat. "I remembered you said Monteith was no friend of yours, so I went directly to him and struck a bargain. Then all I had to do was wait." His grip suddenly tightened with bruising force on her hand. "God, I could have strangled you for making me sit there and wonder what had happened to you. You could have been raped and thrown into the river and no one would have ever known."

"I know you'd prefer to do any raping yourself."

"I've never raped you," Nicholas said tersely. "And we both know it. You wanted—my God, what are you wearing?"

They had come into the pool of light formed by the lantern on the carriage and Silver glanced down at the flame-colored costume. "It belongs to Fatima, who performs as one of the Caliph's Dancing Daughters." Silver forwned as she remembered something else. "I'm barefoot and now my feet are dusty. You could have given me time to put on my shoes."

"Your feet aren't the only thing that's bare." Nicholas's gaze was on the silken flesh overflowing the low square neckline. "You don't have much more on than you did when you wore that damn bed curtain. For God's sake, what do I have to do to keep you decently covered?" He strode toward the carriage, dragging her along behind him. "This blasted heathen shamelessness has got to—"

"Hello, Silver." Mikhail smiled down at her from

the coachman's seat of the carriage. "That is a pretty costume. We have been very worried about you. I told Nicholas you would not let anything happen to yourself, but he would not listen."

Silver felt a sudden glowing warmth spread through her as she gazed up at his rough-hewn face. She had not realized until this moment how much she had missed the gentle Cossack. "There was nothing to worry about. It was a hard trip but—"

"Later," Nicholas interrupted as he opened the door of the carriage. He lifted her and almost threw her on to the cushions of the seat. "Let's get back to the *Rose*." He climbed into the coach, slammed the door closed, and dropped into the seat opposite her. "You're evidently glad to see Mikhail, at least."

"I like him," Silver said calmly. "And I don't like you."

He flinched. "No, liking has nothing to do with what we feel for each other. I have no use for so tame an emotion anyway."

The moon emerged from behind the clouds and the darkness of the coach was flooded with a pale, pearly half-light. She wished fervently that it had remained dark. She did not want to see how the rays shimmered and frosted Nicholas's golden hair to silver and played upon the supple muscles of his body. How they brought a soft luminence to his white linen shirt and outlined the brawny muscles of his thighs in dark tight-fitted trousers. She had a fleeting memory of how those thighs had felt holding her effortlessly in place while he moved wildly in and out until— No, she mustn't remember. It was over.

She desperately pulled her glance away from him and looked out at the moonlit darkness beyond the window. "How is Valentin?"

"Almost as worried about you as I was." Nicholas leaned back on the seat, his eyes fixed on her with an intensity she could feel even though she was no longer looking at him. "And much more inclined to be charitable. Do you know what I wanted to do with you after I found you?"

"You've already told me. You wanted to strangle me."

"That was the last item on my list. The others were far more lewd in nature. I lay in that bed on the *Rose* and remembered what I'd done with you, and thought about what I still wanted to do." He paused. "A hundred times I wanted to send for a woman but I never did. You seem to have worked some kind of spell over me. It's not a confession that I make with pleasure." His tone hardened. "I will be no woman's puppet ever again."

Again? It seemed impossible that Nicholas had ever yielded to any woman's power, Silver thought with a strange wrenching pang. Who had— No, she would not wonder. "You should have sent for your whore, I wouldn't have cared what you did."

She felt the savage anger vibrate from him in the close confines of the carriage and experienced a sudden tingle of excitement. She heard him draw a deep breath as if struggling for control.

A few minutes passed and she could feel her nerves tighten and the tentative excitement grow. Why didn't he speak?

"Perhaps you weren't so selective," he finally said silkily. "It was an impossibly hard trip for a woman. I'm sure there were men eager to help you for a . . . for compensation."

For a moment she was tempted to lie to him, to tell him he was not the only man who could please her. It would anger him, it would cause that tension she felt in him to explode. The thought excited her. Then she realized what she was doing and was disgusted with herself. She would not lie. "I needed no help and took none."

She could feel a little of the tension flow out of him as he relaxed. "That was very wise. I would have been quite incensed with you if you'd given your favors to any other man. So incensed I would probably have put you over my knee and spanked your bottom until you couldn't sit down for a month." He paused. "Afterward."

Her gaze flew back to his face. "Afterward?" Her voice sounded strange, breathless. The excitement was blossoming, growing. Her breasts were lifting and falling with the shallowness of her breathing, her sensitive nipples rubbing against the soft velvet of her bodice.

"I'm not such a fool that I don't realize what's of first importance to both of us." His voice was thick. "Just as you do. Do you think I don't know what you're trying to do to me? You wanted me angry enough to take you without your consent so that you could have your pleasure and still nurture your resentment." He slowly shook his head. "No, Silver, you're going to have to admit that you want me as much as I want you, that you can't even wait until we get back to the *Rose* for me to take you, that you want me here and now."

"Here?" She could feel her eyes widen and the color rise to her cheeks.

"Why not? We have a good forty-minute ride until we get to the levee, and I've done without you for almost two weeks. I have no intention of waiting any longer. *Merde*, I almost took you on the pallet in that damn circus tent."

"I have no intention of giving you anything you want."

"Because you're angry with me for taking you away from your friends? But you won't be giving me what I want, you'll be taking what you want. Do you think I don't know you by now?" He suddenly leaned forward and he began swiftly undoing the tiny covered buttons that closed the flame-colored velvet bodice.

"No, I . . ." But he had been too quick and the bodice was pushed aside to reveal the swollen fullness of her breasts. Then he was leaning back in his seat again, his gaze hot and intent upon her. "There. I've been watching those pretty breasts shake and quiver ever since Mikhail started the carriage moving. I thought at times you'd fall out of that little jacket, but unfortunately you never did." Then, as she made a motion to close the jacket, he said sharply, "No, I'm not touching you, I'm only looking at you. We both know how much you like me to look at you." He leaned forward and took her hands in both of his. "I like that costume, it appears to be a singularly convenient garment for our purpose. Tell me, do you have anything on underneath it?"

She didn't answer him.

"No?" He smiled. "How delightful. I'll have a dressmaker fashion several for you and you can wear them for me when I visit you at your house in St. Petersburg."

"I'm not going to St. Petersburg."

"Scarlet is a wonderful color for you," he said, ignoring her reply. "Your nipples are just that color after I've sucked at them for a long time. Do you remember how long I did that the night before you ran away from me? I love your breasts. I love to look at them. I love to touch them. I love to watch them swell and ripen as you become excited." His gaze never left her breasts. "As they're doing now."

She had no need for him to tell her this. She could feel herself blossom, tauten under his gaze. The slight jouncing of the carriage on the cobblestones sent a quiver through every muscle of her body and pulled at her heavy, sensitive breasts like a toying hand. Nicholas's hand.

"Give me your foot."

A ripple of surprise went through her. "Why?"

He reached into his pocket and drew out a pristine white handkerchief. "You accused me of getting your feet dusty. I thought I'd try to make amends." His smile held an entrancing sweetness. "I thought it would please you to see me do so menial a task."

She slowly lifted her leg and stretched out her left foot to rest on his knees. He enfolded it in the handkerchief and ran the soft fine linen over her sole. A little shiver went through her. He looked up. "Did I tickle you?"

"No, I'm not ticklish."

"The other foot." He began running the white cloth over her right foot. "You exaggerated. You're not very dusty at all." His gaze rose to her face as he ran the handkerchief over her sole with deliberate slowness. "And you may not be ticklish, but you're extremely sensitive here. Many women are, you know." He tossed the handkerchief carelessly on the seat beside him and, holding her ankle in one hand, he ran the tips of his fingers lightly from her heel to her instep. She experienced a tingling in her foot that spread up her leg. The muscles of her calf bunched and then hardened. "You see?"

She attempted to draw her foot away from him, but he would not release it. His grip tightened on her ankle. "You have lovely feet. Strong and well shaped." His finger rubbed gently at the curve of her instep. Another shiver ran through her and she felt the muscles of her entire leg tauten. A familiar hot tingle ignited between her thighs.

She suddenly became aware how open and vulnerable was her position. The moonlit intimacy of the carriage, the nakedness of her breasts, Nicholas's strong hand holding her ankle captive, and his fingers moving with teasing delicacy . . . He would stop and wait until the anticipation built and then would start again. His whisper-soft touch came gently, intimately, on her instep.

This time a shudder ran through every muscle of her body. Where had he learned this skillful, subtle manipulation of a woman's body? A flash of resentment came and then was gone as his fingertips once more moved over her instep and the muscles of her stomach contracted as if on command. She moistened her lips with her tongue. "Stop, Nicholas."

He ceased immediately and set her foot on the seat beside him. "Certainly." Then before she could draw her leg away, he was kneeling on the floor of the carriage before her between her thighs, pushing up the filmy scarlet skirt with one hand and gently shifting her other leg to the side with the other. "I think it's time we went on to other pleasures anyway." His head slowly lowered, his gaze on the soft darkness awaiting him. "And this is very pleasurable for you, remember? That night you screamed . . ."

She wanted to scream again as his tongue touched and then began to stroke her with painstaking slowness. She arched helplessly toward him, her fingers reaching out blindly to bury themselves in his golden hair. Searing hunger tore through her as her head fell back against the cushions of the seat. She couldn't get her breath. Heat. Tingling. Clenching.

He lifted his head. "You're so pretty here." He blew gently. She inhaled sharply as she felt his warm breath exploding against her pulsating heart. His hands were lifting, his palms cupping her round buttocks as he slowly lowered his head again. "It's not enough. I'm hungry for you. I want to taste you." His mouth opened, enveloped, sucked.

Her lips opened, the tendons of her throat strained, but she could make no sound. She felt as though she were bathed in fire. The dizzying tempo of the blood running through her veins was almost as painful as the intensity of pleasure she was experiencing.

Nicholas head rose and his hands left her. He fumbled quickly at the front of his trousers and his manhood burst free of restriction. He laid his head on her stomach, his breath coming in harsh rasps. He rubbed his hard cheek against her flesh, luxuriating in the softness of her. "Silver . . ."

Then he was suddenly gone, once again sitting across from her. His fair hair was tousled and his ebony eyes blazed as he reached out and lifted her onto his lap. "Come to me." His voice was soft, urgent, as irresistible as the haunting melody of Pan's flute.

His hands cupped her hips as he slid her slowly down the rigid stalk of his manhood. Her knees braced on the cushions of the seat on either side of him. His hands left her and gently began to rub at her insteps as he let her feel every bold inch of his dimension within her.

She bit her lower lip to keep her delirious jolt of pleasure unknown to him. But it was to no avail; he did know, Nicholas always knew.

Her hands clutched his shoulders as he began a fiery rhythm that turned her mindless with a fever of ecstasy. She couldn't repress the low moan that trembled deep in her throat.

"Let go." Nicholas's voice was a silkening crooning in her ear. "This is where you belong. This is what you want. Say it, Silver."

"No!" Her fingers went up to tangle in his hair. "No."

"Say it!"

"Yes!" Her fingers clenched again in his hair. She was panting, her breath coming in little sobs. "But it doesn't matter, it means nothing. Do you hear me? It doesn't mean anything!"

He went still. Then, slowly, his hands cupped her cheeks in his two hands and tilted her head back to look into her eyes. She had expected to see lust, perhaps triumph, but there was something else in his glittering eyes that bewildered her. Sadness. "I know," he said softly. "But that's all you'll give me." His lips brushed her own with exquisite tenderness. "Firebird." He closed his eyes and for a moment she thought she saw a flicker of pain on his face. Then his eyes opened and he smiled crookedly. "So I'll take what gifts I'm allowed as I've always done before. Perhaps you'll find it to be a fair exchange."

Then he was clearly done with conversation as he began to thrust with a force and power that held an odd element of desperation.

She was still lost in a haze of delight and lethargy when he moved her to the seat opposite him again. He swiftly put his clothes in order and then leaned forward to carefully fasten the buttons on her velvet bodice and arrange her filmy skirts around her. His features were set and curiously grave in the moon-light streaming through the window into the carriage. "I have some questions to ask you about Dominic Delaney."

She gazed at him in disbelief. "Why do you think I would tell you anything now when I wouldn't before?"

"Because they aren't the same questions. Valentin thinks I've made a mistake, but I have to *know*, dammit. You're becoming too—" He broke off, search-ing for words. "He may be right; the Randall Agency was wrong about your having a lover. They could be wrong about what happened at Hell's Bluff."

"I don't know what you're talking about. I haven't been back to Hell's Bluff in four years."

"It happened four years ago," Nicholas said tightly. "You were there with Dominic Delaney and Elspeth MacGregor. You—"

The carriage came to a halt as Mikhail reined in the team. He called, "We are here."

"Damn," Nicholas muttered, and opened the door of the carriage. He stepped down on the cobblestone street overlooking the levee and walked quickly to-ward the hitching post where Mikhail was tying the horses.

Mikhail turned. "I will go tell Robert we are ready to leave. You will want to carry Silver down to the *Rose*. She might cut her feet on these rough stones."

Nicholas's frown faded and a smile of amusement curved his lips. "I'll see that her delicate toes never come in contact with these coarse stones. Trust me."

"I trust you," Mikhail said gravely. "But I know you and she does not. You have not been kind to her. It is no wonder she ran away from you."

Nicholas expression became shuttered. "I kept my promise to you."

Mikhail nodded. "But you have made none to her. She is a woman who has no one, a woman who belongs nowhere. Such a woman needs promises." He paused. "Though she may never tell you she does." He turned away. "She has great pride." He didn't wait for an answer but started down the slanting levee, his bootheels clicking loudly on the cobblestones.

Nicholas gazed after him, then turned and crossed the few paces back to the door of the carriage. He opened the door and stood looking at her. Sensual Scheherazade. Fierce warrior. Lonely waif. Silver.

She frowned in puzzlement. "Why are looking at me like that?"

"No reason." He held out his arms. "Come. Mikhail is worried about you cutting your feet. I promised him I'd—"

Pain.

His head exploded with white-hot agony. "What . . ."

The pain struck again!

Darkness.

"Nicholas!" Silver frantically slid across the seat. He was falling to the ground!

"Good evening, Miss Delaney." Lee Bassinger

stepped forward, a coil of rope in one hand and a pistol in the other. "I can't tell you how glad I am to see you. I've been waiting here on the wharf a long time for Nicholas to bring you back to us. Now, stretch out your hands so that I can tie your wrists. I have no intention of letting you get away again."

"No," she said. Nicholas was lying still and white on the cobblestones. "Is he dead?" Her voice was faraway, only a wisp of sound. "Have you killed him?"

"He's alive." His shrewd gaze searched her face. "You seem uncommonly concerned for a lady who has done nothing but try to escape from the man. It's foolish of you to reveal such a weakness for Savron. It makes things too easy for me." He leaned down and pressed the barrel of the pistol to Nicholas's temple. "Give me your hands or I'll blow a neat little hole in his highness's handsome head."

She drew a deep, quivering breath and then, slowly, she held out her hands to be bound.

10

"Where is she?" Nicholas whispered, gazing up at Valentin and Mikhail. He sat up on the bed, ignoring the blinding pain that jagged through his head and threatened to fling him back into the darkness. "Were we followed from that damn circus?"

"We don't know. When you didn't follow him to the boat, Mikhail came back up the levee. He found you unconscious with two lumps as big as ostrich eggs on your head." Valentin paused. "The carriage was gone and so was Silver. We thought perhaps she might have demonstrated her opposition to your plans for her."

"No!" Nicholas swung his feet to the floor. Christ, he was dizzy. "It must have been one of her friends from the circus. I have to get back there."

"It wouldn't do any good." Lee Bassinger stood in the doorway of the stateroom, the omnipresent smile on his lips. "Miss Delaney is accepting my hospitality at the moment." He strolled into the room. "I do hope you're feeling better, Savron. I really hated to hit you

202

on the head, as I wanted you to be able to think clearly when I offered my terms."

"Terms?" Nicholas asked coldly. "The only terms I may accede to involve the precise manner in which you meet your end, Bassinger."

"So arrogant." Bassinger's tone was almost approving. "Do you know that's what drew me to you that night at Madam LaRue's? You wore your damn arrogance like an ermine-trimmed cloak and everyone was fawning all over you. The great Russian prince with the whole world at his fingertips. You were just like those fancy Natchez planter folk up on the hill." His green eyes were glittering in the lamplight. "I was scum and I came from scum, but I showed them. I'm richer than all of them now."

"Where's Silver, Bassinger?" Nicholas's words were measured as he tried to control his temper. "Tell me now and I may let you live. It's not likely, but there is a possibility."

"Your little pullet? She must be good if you still want her after all the trouble she's caused you. Perhaps I may try her myself."

"I've changed my mind. There's no possibility at all that you'll survive."

"I will break his bones," Mikhail offered mildly. "He will tell you after the second bone is snapped." He studied Bassinger. "Perhaps after only the first one is broken. I think he has no courage."

"Keep him away from me." Bassinger took a step back. "If anything happens to me, I've given orders that your little whore's throat be cut. My men are loyal to me; they know I don't tolerate disobedience."

"Wait, Mikhail." Nicholas experienced a surge of frustration liberally laced with cold panic. "We'll listen to him."

"How kind," Bassinger said caustically. "You don't seem to realize that I'm in charge here now. It's my choice what will happen to your whore and what will happen to you."

"And what do you propose to do to us?" Nicholas asked without expression. "I'm sure you have a plan in mind."

"Oh, yes." Bassinger nodded with satisfaction. "I'm going to rid you of a little of that arrogance. I'm going to get the *Rose* back and I'm going to enjoy having your little schoolgirl do a number of pleasurable tricks for me."

Nicholas hands clenched into fists at his side. "I do believe I may draw and quarter you."

"Excellent idea," Valentin murmured, his light eyes icy cold. "I'd be delighted to assist."

Bassinger moistened his lips with his tongue. "This isn't Russia, your highness. You don't have any power here, while I have judges bought and paid for all along the Mississippi. I'm the one who's prince here. I can do whatever I want."

"You can have the *Rose*," Nicholas said crisply. "Return the woman and I'll sign over the papers."

"That's not enough, it's too easy for you. You treated me like a stray pup nibbling at your heels." Bassinger's fair skin was suddenly flushed with color. "Well, now you can trail at my heels for a while. If I feel generous, I may let you return the *Rose* to me when we reach New Orleans." He laughed excitedly. "Don't you think that's only fair, your highness?"

It was more than vengeance driving him, Nicholas realized, the man was not quite sane. The knowledge caused terror to sleet through him. There was no way to either reason or bargain with a madman. "And how do you intend to accomplish this?"

"Why, we're going to have a race," Bassinger said. "That should amuse your highness, you being a gambling man. I have your woman on the *Mary L*, one of my other boats docked just down the levee. The *Mary L* is smaller and lighter than the *Rose* and she's carrying no cargo and only about twenty-five passengers. When I return to the boat, I'll order that we set out for New Orleans. You will naturally follow." He smiled. "If you arrive first in New Orleans, I'll allow you to return the *Rose* and give you the bitch you apparently hold in such esteem. If I win, you'll still return the *Rose* and I'll keep the Delaney woman until I tire of her." His smile deepened benevolently. "Don't worry, I seldom keep women for long after I've broken them. Though your half-breed seems more spirited than most, I'm sure it will take only a little longer." He turned toward the door. "I think I'm being most generous under the circumstances. I'll even allow you glimpses of your strumpet from time to time if you keep close enough on my heels. I'll bring her up to the Texas deck when she's not entertaining me in my cabin." He opened the door and glanced back at them, fierce satisfaction on his face. "You understand, of course, that since I've made the rules and the stakes, I can also change them at any time. You might remember that, your highness."

The door closed behind him.

Valentin gave a low whistle. "Nicky, he's not—"

"Sane," Nicholas finished grimly. "And it wouldn't surprise me if he were capable of the same sorts of vicious little tricks made notorious by our good tsar Ivan."

"What do we do?" Mikhail asked.

"We follow him." Nicholas stood up, swaying as waves of pain pounded his temples. "Yapping at the bastard's heels."

"I don't like it," Valentin said, frowning. "Why don't we go after him now and—"

"He'd kill her," Nicholas said harshly. "Do you think I wouldn't prefer that too? I can't risk it. It's my fault Silver is being used as Bassinger's pawn. If I hadn't brought her on board the *Rose*, he would never have known she existed. The blame for anything he does lies on my shoulders."

"He will not keep his bargain," Mikhail said flatly.

Nicholas didn't answer for a moment. "I know that." His lips tightened into a thin line. He moved toward the door. "We'll give Bassinger what he wants and watch for a chance to get Silver away from him."

Valentin nodded. "And then?"

"Then I'll kill him as slowly and as painfully as possible." Nicholas opened the door. "I'm going up to the pilot house to talk to Robert. Put ashore our

passengers with enough money to buy them passage
back to New Orleans on another riverboat and get rid
of any cargo in the hold. I want the *Rose* as light as
possible. If what Bassinger claims about the *Mary L* is
true, it won't help much, but we have to try everything we can. I want to be right behind him from the
moment the *Mary L* leaves the levee." He glanced over
his shoulder. "And make sure there's a rifle on board.
The *Rose* may not be able to catch the *Mary L* but a
bullet might."

"Come along, sweet bitch." Bassinger jerked Silver
to her feet. "We're under way, and though I'd like to
linger here in my cabin with you, I have an even
greater pleasure in mind. We're going to put on a
show for your lover." He checked the bonds around
her wrists in front of her. "It's a spectacle I've been
planning since you poured that bottle of wine on my
head."

"You looked very funny," Silver said calmly.
"Everyone thought so. Do you remember how they
laughed at you? They'll laugh again when I—" She
broke off, her head snapping back as Bassinger struck
her viciously on the cheek. Then she shook her head to
clear it of the stinging pain and smiled. "I will
remember that when my hands aren't tied."

"You'll remember a good deal more than that." He
shoved her out onto the deck and then in the direction
of the stairs leading to the Texas deck. "And so will
Savron. He's right behind us and he'll be able to view
our little tableau very clearly." He half lifted, half

pushed her up the stairs. "You're quite helpless, you
know. No one will interfere. Most of the passengers
are asleep, but I've ordered their staterooms locked as
a precaution. As for the crew, they value their jobs
and will discreetly attend to their duties. A few of
them will even enjoy watching." He flung his arms
wide as they reached the deck. "You see, I've already
prepared the stage. We want our audience to be able
to see every detail."

A multitude of lanterns lit this end of the Texas
deck. They hung on the rails and sat on the deck and
on the stairs leading to the pilot house. The entire
area was as brilliantly lit as the stage to which
Bassinger was comparing it. A roughly clad young
man with a scarred cheek was lighting another
lantern, and looked up to smile at Bassinger. "All set,
sir. Almost as bright as day up here."

"Good. Oh, how rude I'm being. This is one of my
employees, Henry Bracken," Bassinger said smoothly
as he pushed Silver toward the rail at the rear of the
boat. "Henry has tastes similar to my own, and I often
allow him to watch as I chastise my little girls for
their wickedness." He stood beside her at the rail and
pointed to the white riverboat gleaming in the darkness a few hundred yards distant. "There's the *Rose*.
It's too far away for you to see if your lover is in the
pilot house watching us, but I assure you he'll be
there." His gaze didn't leave her face as he held out his
hand. "The rawhide, Henry."

Henry Bracken hurried forward and placed the long
leather strap in Bassinger's hand. Bassinger quickly

knotted the rawhide over the ropes binding Silver's wrists and then bound her to the rail. "And he can see you very clearly. How fortunate that you're wearing red. That costume should be quite visible from a distance." He stepped behind her, out of her line of vision. "The whip, Henry."

"Right away, sir."

Silver inhaled sharply. He was going to beat her. She should have expected this. She braced herself.

"Ah, you're getting ready for the first blow. What a beautiful sight that is. But it never does any good to prepare yourself, the pain is just as bad as if you don't. Thank you, Henry." A whistling sound snaked through the air. "It's a fine whip. It will leave lovely crimson weals, but won't scar your permanently. That will come later."

"There won't be a later," Silver said, tugging futilely at the rawhide strap. "I'll kill you, Bassinger."

"They all say that, don't they, Henry?" Bassinger's laugh was high and excited. "First there's anger, then the pain, and then the screaming." His voice lowered. "And then the pleading. I'm going to enjoy that most of all. When you're down on your knees offering to do anything I want if I'll only stop the pain."

"I'll never go down on my knees to you."

"Yes, you will, but first I want to make you scream very loudly so Nicholas can hear you." The whip whistled again. "I have a fancy to let his highness know how much I'm hurting you. Scream high and sweetly, bitch."

The whip struck her back, slicing through the velvet

as if it were only mist. The sudden pain caused her to gasp and reach out blindly to grab the rail and hold on tight as waves of agony rolled over her. She would not fall. She would not scream. It was the only victory she could wrest from her helplessness. She would not give Bassinger that triumph.

"Scream!" The whip struck again.

She gritted her teeth and looked blindly out at the river as the hot agony scalded through her.

"Scream!"

The lash struck again.

"I've told them to keep the boilers going full blast." Valentin rushed into the pilot house, skidding to a stop as he reached Nicholas. "I think we're drawing closer but—" He stopped as he gazed at Nicholas's face. "What's wrong?"

Nicholas didn't reply, his agonized gaze riveted on the riverboat ahead of them.

Robert finally answered for him. "Bassinger has tied Silver to the rail," he said hoarsely. "He's using a whip on her."

Valentin's gaze followed that of Nicholas and Robert to the brightly lit Texas deck of the *Mary L.* He swallowed. "Christ, how long has it been going on?"

"Five minutes, maybe a little more." Robert looked away, his hands tightening on the wheel. "It can't go on much longer. She's a woman, for God's sake. She'll collapse and that will be the end of it."

"She won't collapse." Nicholas's eyes were glittering in the lantern light. "I wish she would. She won't give in to the pain until he kills her." He turned to Robert with barely leashed violence. "He'll *kill* her, dammit. We can't let that happen. Get me closer so that I can use this rifle on him."

"I'm trying." Robert's face was taut with strain. "I can only go as fast as the boilers will let me. The *Rose* is heavier than the *Mary L.* We're edging up on her and I should have you within range in another few minutes."

"A few minutes!" Nicholas looked at him incredulously. "He's beating her to death with that whip."

"Nicholas," Valentin's voice was very gentle. "He can't do any more than he's doing right now."

Nicholas began to curse beneath his breath, his dark eyes wild in his pale face. He strode across the room and jerked open the door. "I've *got* to do something. Do you know what it's like to have that lash flaying your back? We may not be in range, but we're close enough so that a few shots may gain his attention. Maybe he'll decide to postpone his demonstration until another time." He ran down the steps to the Texas deck and then to the rail at the front of the riverboat. He knelt, steadying the rifle on the rail. Dear God, what if Bassinger ignored the shots? He swallowed as the bile rose to his throat at the thought. His hands were shaking and he tried to steady them on the rifle, his gaze on Silver's straight, rigid figure at the rail of the *Rose*.

He could hear Bassinger yelling something over and over as the whip cracked on Silver's slender back. What kind of whip was it? Igor had used a knout on him. Ten lashes with a knout were supposed to kill a man, but thirty hadn't killed Nicholas. She had taken more than ten lashes now. Pray God, it was another kind of whip Bassinger was using on Silver.

God, why did she stand there so proudly? The silent defiance of her stance was all that crazy bastard needed to keep that lash ripping at her. There was a blurring before Nicholas's eyes and then he felt two tears run slowly down his cheeks. He wiped his eyes with his sleeve before he took aim with the rifle.

The shot startled Bassinger enough to cause him to freeze and peer out into the darkness. He turned to Henry. "How close are they?"

"Not close enough," Bracken said. "That shot couldn't have come within fifty yards of the *Mary L.*"

"But they're growing nearer." Bassinger hesitated. "Tell the pilot to put on more steam."

"They're going at almost full steam now," Bracken said. "I don't know—"

"Put on more steam," Bassinger said between his teeth. "I know you're enjoying this pretty little slut's punishment but she'll still be here when you get back."

She might at that, Bracken thought. Silver's spine was still as ramrod straight as when Bassinger had started, though the scarlet velvet was now almost completely cut away and her golden back crisscrossed with angry red weals. "I wanna be here when she breaks."

"Then hurry." Bassinger turned back to Silver. "She can't last much longer."

Bracken gave a last reluctant glance at Silver and then hurried down the deck toward the staircase leading to the pilot house.

A second shot echoed over the river.

"Nicholas must be very perturbed to try anything so futile," Bassinger drawled. "It has to be annoying for him to feel so helpless. But you're not helping me, my dear. One shrill, agonized scream would increase his pain tremendously." He drew back his arm. "I'm done toying with you." The lash came down with his full strength behind it, breaking the skin and causing a tiny river of blood to run down her back. "Scream, you strumpet!"

A shudder of agony wracked Silver's body.

She did not scream.

"We're not gaining on them." Nicholas ran up the stairs to the pilot house. "We're supposed to be gaining on them. What the hell is wrong?"

"They're putting on more steam." Robert's gaze was fixed in horror on the *Mary L* and his voice was only a level above a whisper. "My God, they were going at almost full steam and they're still feeding those boilers."

"Then they'll pull away from us," Nicholas said hoarsely.

The pilot numbly shook his head. "No, I don't think so."

Hope leapt within Nicholas. "Why not?"

"Lord." Robert closed his eyes. "The *Sultana*." His eyes flicked open and he swerved the wheel violently to the left.

"What the devil are you doing?" Nicholas shouted.

"I'm getting out of the way." Robert didn't look at him as he veered toward the eastern bank of the river. "And hoping to God I'm in time."

"Out of the way of what?"

"Those boilers are going to blow. The *Mary L* can't take that much steam with those faulty boilers. They're going to blow up and take the *Mary L* with her."

"Blow up?" Nicholas could only stare at him. "Silver is on the *Mary L*. It can't—"

The Mary L *exploded.*

11

Who was screaming? Silver wondered dazedly. She knew it wasn't herself; she had kept all the screaming inside, where it could give Bassinger no pleasure. Yet these screams held all the pain and desperation she had refused to release.

She opened her eyes. Smoke. Black smoke. A red glare. Fire? She struggled up on one elbow. She was still tethered to the rail, but now a section of the rail was on top of her, torn from its moorings by the explosion.

Explosion! The memory brought her sitting bolt upright and she gasped with pain as she once again became conscious of the fiery throbbing of her lacerated back.

Bassinger? She forced herself to turn and look around the deck, though every movement was an agony. No Bassinger. The deck was littered with shattered glass blown from the windows of the pilot house, and there were little fires licking at the wooden planks of the deck from the broken, overturned lanterns. Her gaze lifted and shock plummeted through her. "Oh, my God."

The pilot house that had formerly perched on the Texas deck had vanished, one of the tall smokestacks was gone entirely, and the other was broken and spewing a thick cloud of scalding steam. The railing at the front of the boat was aflame and she could hear a crackling roar from the hurricane deck that denoted a larger fire raging below. The boilers, she thought. Robert had said something about the faulty boilers on the *Mary L*, she remembered vaguely. They must have exploded when Bassinger had ordered the added steam.

The rail was pressing heavily on her lower body and she tried to push it off her before she realized it was impossible. She would have to cut the rawhide strap before she would be able to move the railing.

The riverboat suddenly gave a lurch that sent a thrill of fear through her. The *Mary L* was taking on water. It wouldn't be long before it began to sink and she was bound helplessly to the rail.

The broken glass!

She carefully edged sideways until she could reach a pointed sliver of glass and pick it up with her thumb and forefinger. The glass sliced through her flesh and blood spurted. She dropped the glass. Blast it! She tried again and managed to keep her grip on the sliver this time. Carefully she began to saw through the rawhide thong binding her to the rail.

Who *was* that screaming? It was a chorus of voices, men, women, and children in an agony of terror.

There was something she should remember, but she couldn't seem to think. The frayed rawhide thong snapped and she pushed the heavy railing off her legs. Now for the ropes binding her wrists. She would need a larger piece of glass.

The passengers! Bassinger had said he had locked the doors of the staterooms. They were prisoners caught in the fire and death below. She had no time to saw through the ropes.

The fires from the lanterns . . . The flames could burn through the ropes far quicker than she could cut through them with pieces of glass.

Faster but more painful. There were several burns on her wrists and forearms before she managed to rid herself of the ropes. She wouldn't think about it; the burns hurt no more than the stripes on her back.

Then she was on her feet, running toward the stairs. A thicker haze of smoke lay over the deck below and she could barely make out the door to the grand saloon as she made her way toward it. She stumbled. There was something in her way . . .

Bracken. His eyes were open and staring, a two-foot jagged sword of glass penetrating his breast. Silver took a deep breath and swallowed hard. She mustn't be squeamish. He was in the way. She grabbed Bracken's legs, tugging and pulling until he was clear of the door.

The riverboat was now listing heavily to the starboard and she had difficulty keeping her balance as she ran into the grand saloon. The *Mary L* was structured much like the *Rose*, the doors of the passenger cabins opening on either side of the common room, she noticed with relief. But thank God, it was much, much smaller and the shouts and pounding appeared to be coming entirely from behind the ten doors on this side of the saloon. "I'm coming," she called desperately. "It's all right, I'll get you out."

But how? She had no key and no tool to open those locked doors.

Well, there were plenty of tools on the boiler deck.

If there was still a boiler deck.

Still, it was her only chance. She turned and ran from the saloon and then down the steps to the boiler deck.

There were no fires on this deck; the entire deck was flooded with at least three feet of muddy river water.

Nothing was left of the boilers but jagged fangs of metal . . .

Bodies floated like garish bits of flotsam . . .

Horribly scalded bodies . . .

Silver closed her eyes for a moment, unable to bear the sight. Men should not look like this in death. There should be dignity.

She opened her eyes and forced herself to look around. Her sick horror would not save the people locked in those cabins. It was river water not water from the burst boilers that was now flooding the deck. It should be safe to go down and look around. She jumped down onto the deck and waded through the water, averting her gaze from the gruesome carnage around her. A moment later she had located a crowbar, grabbed it, and was hurriedly wading back toward the stairs.

Then she was running up the steps, down the deck, and into the saloon. She inserted the crowbar into the doorjamb of the first door. "It will only be a moment. I have something now."

It took so long, she thought in despair. Why wasn't she stronger? The wood finally splintered and the door swung open. A young woman wearing a flowered pink peignoir and carrying a small child ran out into the saloon as tears ran down her cheeks. "We're all going to die!" she sobbed, clutching the child desperately.

"No." Silver was already working on the next door. "Help me!"

"But we're going to die."

"You may be stupid enough to die here, but I intend to live," Silver said impatiently. "Now, help—"

"Silver!" Nicholas's voice!

Relief surged through Silver. Nicholas was strong. Nicholas would help her. "Here! In the saloon, Nicholas."

Then he was beside her, his face blackened by smoke, his white shirt grimy and stained. "You're very dirty," she said vaguely. "Help me, Nicholas, there's not much time."

He stood there, looking at her, an odd radiance shining beneath the grime. "You're dirty too." His index finger reached out to gently touch her sooty cheek. "I thought you were dead."

"I will be if you don't help me get these poor people

out of their cabins." She pried desperately with the
crowbar. "Bassinger locked them all in and this damn
boat is sinking . . ."

"Stand back." He took the crowbar and broke the
lock with one slicing blow. "Valentin is in a rowboat
tied to the stern of the hurricane deck and Mikhail is
picking up survivors in another boat." He was going
from door to door swiftly breaking the locks. Passengers were streaming from the cabins into the saloon;
the smoke was thickening. "Get to the boat at the
stern and off the *Mary L*," he shouted.

There were cries of relief and a rush toward the
door of the saloon as the freed passengers dashed
toward safety.

Silver stood and watched as the saloon emptied.
Two more doors.

"Dammit, Silver, get out of here," Nicholas said
harshly, glancing over his shoulder.

She shook her head.

He broke the lock and moved to the last door.
"You've done your part. You can't help here. Why the
hell don't you get off the boat?"

Two men dressed only in their long underwear
rushed by her and out of the saloon.

"I can't leave," she said simply. "Not while you're
still here." It all seemed very clear, even through the
haze of pain and exhaustion enveloping her. She
could not leave when Nicholas stayed. She could not
live if Nicholas died.

Then the last door was open and Nicholas was
running toward her, grabbing her by the arm and

pushing her from the saloon. A towheaded boy of thirteen years or so rushed by them toward the small boat at the rear of the deck.

It was difficult to walk, she thought dimly. Her legs felt as heavy as if she were still wading through the water on the boiler deck. But there was no water here. How puzzling.

"Are you all right?" Nicholas asked quietly. "I'd carry you, but I don't want to touch your back."

Her back. Oh, yes, Bassinger had been whipping her. It all seemed like such a long time ago. The pain was now coursing not only in her back but in every muscle of her body. "I . . . can . . . walk." She was almost to the rail. Only a few more steps. "I . . . didn't scream."

Nicholas's hand tightened on her arm. "I know you didn't."

"He wanted me to scream. He kept saying it over and over."

"Lord." Nicholas's voice was hoarse, ragged. "For God's sake, Silver, shut up. You're killing me."

"I'm sorry . . . I didn't . . ." What had she been going to say?

Then Valentin was reaching out to help her into the boat, seating her beside the towheaded young boy who had passed them on the deck.

Cork life preservers floated on the surface of the river, and she could see several men clutching them and swimming toward the *Rose*.

Nicholas untied the rope, jumped into the boat, and sat down beside Valentin. "Let's go. The *Mary L* can't

stay afloat much longer taking on this much water."
He grabbed an oar and he and Valentin began to row
with powerful steady strokes away from the riverboat.

The *Mary L* was listing and, except for the hissing of
the escaping steam from the broken smokestack and
the harsh whoosh of flames, was ominously silent.
Tears began to flow down Silver's cheeks as she gazed
at the wreckage. How many lives had been lost? How
many might still be lost in this river tonight?

"It won't be long now," Nicholas said gently. "You'll
be back on the *Rose* in a few minutes."

"Some of those men in the water will have burns."
She spoke haltingly, trying to think clearly through
the pain and horror clouding her comprehension. "I'll
have to use linseed oil and wrap them in raw cotton."

"You won't do anything but go to bed," Nicholas
said grimly. "We're heading back to St. Louis and
they'll get plenty of medical help there."

"No, I can—"

"Savron!"

The cry was a shriek of terror and Nicholas turned
in his seat to look back at the *Mary L*. The red glare of
the fire on the hurricane deck was mirrored on the
waters. A dark head was bobbing on the wavelets
spread by the slowly sinking riverboat. "Savron, help
me!"

Bassinger!

Bassinger was clinging to one of the supports
separating the hurricane deck from the boiler deck, a

rivulet of blood running down his face from a cut on the temple. "Come back! I can't swim!"

Nicholas gazed at him, his face as hard and stone cold as the men who had died on the *Mary L* this night. He turned and looked at Silver sitting ramrod straight, bearing her pain and exhaustion in silence.

He started to row again.

"Savron, come back." Bassinger's voice rose to a panicky screech. *"You can't leave me!"*

"Can't I?" Nicholas took another long pull at the oar. "Watch me." Then he remembered Silver's words.

His voice was savage as he called back over his shoulder. *"Scream,* you son of a bitch!"

Bassinger screamed, a piercing wail of terror in the night.

A moment later the *Mary L* slid slowly, sluggishly, beneath the waters of the Mississippi.

Nicholas was sitting in the tufted olive wing chair beside the bed, the soft glow of the lamplight casting an aura of radiance about his golden head. He was wearing dark blue trousers and his white linen shirt was immaculate. *He* was immaculate, Silver thought with resentment. It was unfair that he look this faultlessly elegant when she felt so unkempt. She found she was on her stomach and tried to roll over and voice her displeasure.

"No." His hands were immediately on her shoulders, keeping her from moving. "The doctor said there would be less pain if you don't rest on your back for a while."

"You're not dirty any longer."

He smiled. "Neither are you. Your nurse cleaned you up quite nicely." He straightened the sheet over her. "She thought you quite a docile patient until the doctor told her he was keeping you that way with morphine."

"Morphine? I've been asleep?"

"For almost three days. We've been docked in St. Louis since the night the *Mary L* went down."

"The *Mary L*," she whispered. She closed her eyes and then quickly opened them again as the horrifying visions of that night came back to her. "How many were lost?"

"We don't know exactly. At least four passengers and ten crew members. Robert says it's a miracle more didn't perish. Quite a few of the crew suffered bad burns." His face clouded. "A few died after we docked here in St. Louis. We weren't able to move all the survivors to the hospital immediately so the parish priest has been coming daily to hear confession and give last rites."

Silver swallowed. What a tragic loss of life Bassinger had brought about. So much suffering. "I can help." She struggled to a sitting position and started to toss the covers aside.

He stopped her again. "They don't need your help. There are any number of volunteer nurses watching over the victims, and they'll be moving the last of them to the hospital this afternoon. You stay where you are."

He stood up and poured a small quantity of water into a goblet from a pitcher on the nightstand. He knelt beside her and held the glass to her lips. "Drink. I've been moistening your lips with water while you slept, but you have to be thirsty."

She *was* thirsty. She took a careful sip and then another. "You've stayed here with me?"

He nodded. "Since we arrived in St. Louis and had ample help for the survivors."

She looked at him wonderingly. "Why?"

He deliberately gave her almost the same answer she had given him in the saloon of the *Mary L.* "How could I leave? You were still here."

She could only stare at him as the silence resonated with his words. She could feel her heart start to pound and she moistened her lips with her tongue. His dark eyes were gentle, deep, holding her gaze effortlessly. "I don't understand you."

"And I don't understand you," he said softly. "But I think it's time we started. We've been strangers too long." He set the goblet back on the nightstand but remained kneeling by her side. "Tell me about Hell's Bluff."

She frowned in puzzlement. He had started to ask her something about Hell's Bluff in the carriage the night Bassinger had forced her on board the *Mary L.* "Hell's Bluff is a mining town near Killara."

"I know that," Nicholas said impatiently. "I want to know about what happened there. You told Valentin you had never met a count before, but that couldn't have been true. You had to have known André Marzonoff."

"André Marzonoff? Well, I didn't actually know him," she said slowly. "And I forgot he was a count. It was a long time ago."

Nicholas looked away from her. "What do you mean, you didn't know him? You watched him die."

"No, we were too late. Elspeth was there and tried to stop it, but Dominic and I came too late. He was already dead when we got to the hanging tree."

"The hanging tree?"

"It's a huge oak tree on the edge of Hell's Bluff. Elspeth found out that the vigilantes were going to lynch Marzonoff and she was very upset. She told me they had become friends and, if he had stolen a horse, it was because he didn't understand that it was wrong." Silver shook her head. "He must have been very stupid."

"He wasn't particularly clever." Nicholas stopped to clear his throat. "What connection did Dominic Delaney have with the lynching?"

"He didn't know anything about it. He was at Rina's."

"The madam?"

Silver nodded. "I ran to get him because I knew he could stop the lynching if anyone could. I was afraid Elspeth would get hurt and—" She stopped. "You knew this Marzonoff?"

"He was my cousin."

"Then I'm sorry I called him stupid. I didn't really

know him, but anyone who would steal a horse in a town like Hell's Bluff must have been." She gazed at him, thinking hard. "It was so long ago, but Elspeth said something. . . ."

His gaze flew back to meet her own. "What?"

She bit her lower lip. "I just don't remember. It wasn't important at the time. I think she said Marzonoff said something about a Nicholas right before he died. I guess you'll have to ask her."

"But I can't ask her," he said dryly. "She's in the company of your elusive uncle."

Her expression became wary. "And I won't tell you where he is."

"That has been established." A corner of his lips curved in a crooked smile. "It may no longer be necessary if you can tell me why Charles Durbin would send me a letter telling me Dominic Delaney was responsible for my cousin's death."

"Durbin!" Silver's eyes widened in surprise and then glittered with anger. "Why, that yellow bastard."

"You know the gentleman?"

"Dominic shot his son. It was a fair fight, but Durbin put a price on his head anyway. When Elspeth told him she'd blow his head off if he didn't leave Dominic alone, he backed off but—"

"The women of your family seem to be of a singularly violent temperament."

"He deserved it," Silver said fiercely. "He was probably afraid to send any more bounty hunters after Dominic, so he snooped around until he found out about your cousin and then tried to get you to go after him. You couldn't have been stupid enough to believe anything that weasel told you?"

"If you recall, I had no acquaintance with Durbin or any of you. I had to rely on the Randall Investigative Agency and they—"

"Are fools," Silver said flatly.

"Exactly."

"But you're a fool, too, for not asking me before this. I could have told you what happened."

"I believe you swore you wouldn't tell me anything," Nicholas said wearily. "And I would scarcely have trusted any story you'd seen fit to regale me with when I first met you. You told me yourself you would only lie to me."

He was right, Silver thought. "But you believe me now?" she whispered.

"Yes," he said quietly. "Because you also said you would be honest with someone who had your respect. Whatever else we feel, I think there's no doubt that we've fought our way through to respect for each other."

There was silence in the room.

"Dominic didn't want your cousin to die," she finally said haltingly. "He would have saved him if he could have. Do you understand?"

Nicholas gazed at her without answering.

"You can ask Elspeth." She hesitated, the ingrained distrust of a lifetime struggling with instinct and the desire to ease his troubled mind. Then she rushed on, "You can find her and Dominic in Tyre. They're going on one final expedition before they go home to Killara."

A sudden brilliant smile lit Nicholas's face. "Thank you, but I don't think it will be necessary to see them. I know what I came here to find out." His hand reached out and gently stroked the dark hair at her temple. "Poor Silver, it wasn't easy to tell me this, was it? Neither one of us is very good at trust." His smile became bittersweet. "I suppose we've both learned it's safer not to let anyone too close."

He was trying to tell her something beyond what his words were conveying, but she couldn't grasp what it was. They were too far apart, she thought in despair. Strangers. She looked away. "I can't stay here. I have to get back to the circus."

He frowned impatiently. "You can wait until you heal."

"No." She clutched the sheet to her breasts. The burns on her wrists were bandaged, she noticed absently. She had forgotten about holding her wrists over the lantern flame to free them. "I have to leave. I've been here too long as it is. Etaine needs me."

"Etaine?"

"Monteith's daughter. She's only a child and can't fight Monteith alone." She brushed her hair from her face, wincing as the muscles rippled beneath the flesh of her lacerated back. "She thinks he wants her dead and she may be right. Monteith is capable of anything. Where are my clothes?"

"That bit of scarlet gauze you were wearing is in rags and I haven't procured any replacements yet."

Nicholas's eyes twinkled. "You could always try the bed curtains again."

"This isn't funny. Etaine needs me." Silver's hand tightened on the sheet. "She has a lung affliction and—"

He placed his fingers on her lips to silence her. "I'm not laughing," he said softly. "You say the child is in danger? That's not reasonable if the man is her father, Silver."

"Just because he's capable of begetting a child doesn't stop him from being a monster. He makes her go into a cage with three lions every day of her life. Does that sound like a loving, fatherly thing to do?" she asked fiercely. "I promised her I'd take her away from Monteith. I was going to wire Patrick and ask him to send me a draft on a local bank. I thought Monteith would give her up if I gave him enough money."

"I don't know. Monteith impressed me as being something of a puzzle. Still, money might be the key." He stood up. "You want the child?"

"Of course I want her. I just told you that I've made her a promise. Now, get me something to wear."

He shook his head. "You stay where you are. The doctor said you should spend at least another week in bed. I have to oversee the moving of more burned patients to the hospital, but I'll send Valentin to get your Etaine." He turned toward the door. "Don't worry, I'll give Monteith enough money to be sure he releases the girl to you."

Silver gazed at him suspiciously. "Why should you

do that? Etaine is my problem." She paused. "I still won't go to St. Petersburg with you."

He flinched. "I'm not without compassion for a helpless child. I don't demand my pound of flesh in every instance."

She gazed at him, the frown still wrinkling her brow.

He laughed harshly. "My God, what do I have to do to convince you? You want the child. I'm giving her to you. I'll give you any damn thing you want. As soon as you're well you can leave me and I won't reach out a hand to stop you."

"Why?"

"Why?" he echoed incredulously. "I stood there and watched Bassinger try to beat you to death, knowing I couldn't do a damn thing to stop him." His hands slowly closed into fists at his sides. "I was helpless. I stood there muttering curses and prayers." He paused. "And promises. One of those promises was that if you lived, I'd release you and let you go your own way."

Silver experienced a strange throb of pain. He was giving her what she had fought for so fiercely. How foolish to feel this aching emptiness. "Guilt?"

He nodded, his lips twisting in a mirthless smile. "Oh, yes, I'm capable of feeling guilt . . . and compassion . . . and many other emotions besides lust and anger and a desire for revenge. It's unfortunate our association will end before I'm able to demonstrate any of my more virtuous qualities." He opened the door. "Though you would probably only suspect me of pretending to lure you into my bed again."

"No," she said impulsively. Then when he looked at her in surprise, she hesitated before continuing slowly. "You wouldn't pretend. I think you're an honest man."

He bowed mockingly. "Many thanks. I suppose I should be grateful to be granted your trust in one area at least." He gazed at her for a long moment, a multitude of expressions flickering over his face. "I'll send Valentin and the child to you as soon as he returns."

The door swung shut behind him.

Silver stared at the mahogany panels of the door for a long time before she slowly turned to lie on her stomach, her cheek nestled against the pillow. Her captivity was over. Soon she would be free to take Etaine to Killara, where the child would be safe. She should be wildly happy. She *was* happy. Naturally her body would miss Nicholas, who had awakened it to pleasure, but her heart would not miss him and she would surely forget him in a few months.

Forget Nicholas? Forget his seductive golden beauty and sorcerer's smile? Forget the moments when she had glimpsed tenderness behind that cynical façade?

Of course she would forget him. The tears running down her cheeks were due only to temporary physical weakness, not sadness. She must get on with her life, for there was no place in Nicholas's for her that she would accept.

She wiped her damp cheeks against the pillow. She

must plan her future, for she thought it quite possible that she would have Nicholas's child. If this was true, she must take measures to protect that child. She had taken her pleasure, but the baby must not be allowed to suffer for her recklessness. She must leave the *Rose* as soon as Valentin returned with Etaine, but there was something she had to do first.

But she would not worry about that now. She would rest and gather strength and perhaps remember Nicholas's face when he had smiled at her. It could do no harm to indulge herself when she would be leaving him so soon. Yes, she would lie here and think of Nicholas. . . .

12

"The circus is gone?" Silver gazed at Valentin blankly. "But it couldn't be gone. I was there only three nights ago."

"They packed up and left the next morning." Valentin said gently. "Monteith arranged passage for his troupe and animals on the *Jefferson Davis* to New Orleans. According to the shipping agent, he was planning on taking another ship when he reached New Orleans."

"He's going to Europe," Silver said numbly. "Etaine said—"

"Not Europe. At least, not immediately," Valentin said. "Russia."

Silver's eyes widened. "Russia!"

Valentin nodded ruefully. "He was evidently very impressed by Nicholas's affluence. He told the shipping agent he was sure Russia would have rich pickings."

"Which port?"

"The agent wasn't sure. Monteith said he would

decide when he got to New Orleans and found what ships were available."

Silver drew a deep quivering breath. Oh, Lord, she didn't even know where Monteith had taken Etaine. Well, she had to find out and quickly. "Where's Nicholas?"

"He's gone ashore to telegraph Randall's in New Orleans and try to have them intercept Monteith."

"Those idiots will never—" She broke off and her hands tightened on the sheet until her knuckles turned white. She must not become upset. She had to think . . . and act. "Valentin, I need clothes. Would you buy a gown, shoes, and cloak from one of the volunteers nursing the survivors?"

He gazed at her warily. "Nicholas won't like it. You're not well enough to get up yet."

"Would he like it better if I walked down that gangplank wearing no gown at all?"

"*Touché.*" He grimaced. "It seems I have no choice. Anything else?"

"Money. I have to go ashore and purchase something."

"I don't suppose you'd be willing to tell me the nature of the purchase?"

"No."

"Nor let me accompany you?"

"No."

Valentin shook his head gravely. "I can't let you go unless you promise to come back. Nicky would have me skewered and roasted over slow flames if I let you run away again."

"I promise. I have every intention of returning to the *Rose*."

Valentin hesitated before slowly reaching into his pocket and pulling out a fat roll of bills and tossing it on the bed. "I know you're upset, Silver, but don't do anything foolish."

"I won't." Silver felt a sudden stinging behind her eyes as she looked up into his worried face. This might be the last time she'd see Valentin, and she realized she would truly miss his wry humor and droll pretense at fopishness. "Thank you, Valentin."

"It's Nicky's money." He made a face. "But my head, if you don't keep your word."

"I'll come back."

Valentin studied her. "I believe you." He turned away. "So I'll use my considerable charm to talk one of the good ladies out of her clothes. You won't be pleased. They all dress with the depressing drabness of most virtuous women." He lifted his brow as he glanced back over his shoulder. "You won't change your mind?"

Silver shook her head.

Valentin sighed. "I didn't think so." He shut the door quietly behind him.

"Hurry," Silver said impatiently. "I told you there wasn't much time, Father."

The plump, white-haired priest's breath was coming in little pants as he followed Silver up the gangplank of the *Rose*. "I am hurrying, young lady," he said indignantly. "It will do that poor dying soul no good if I expire before I can give him the last rites."

Silver caught sight of Mikhail watching them at the top of the gangplank. "Is Nicholas back?"

Mikhail nodded, puzzled. "He's in his cabin."

"Good." Silver turned briskly and started toward the stairs leading to the hurricane deck. "Come along, Father Jason."

The priest scurried after her.

Mikhail gazed after them thoughtfully for a moment. Then he walked slowly toward the stairs and began climbing the steps.

Silver threw open the door to Nicholas's cabin and strode into the stateroom.

Nicholas jumped to his feet. "It's about time you saw fit to come back. Valentin says you left long before dark. If you ever—" He broke off as he caught sight of the priest behind her. "What are you doing here, Father Jason?"

The priest leaned against the doorjamb attempting to catch his breath. "This young lady said it was urgent that I come. I assume another one of the seamen is near death, your highness."

"I didn't say that. Only that the matter was urgent." Silver came forward to stand before Nicholas. "And it is." She drew a small derringer from beneath her cloak and pointed it at Nicholas. "He has to marry us."

Nicholas's froze, his expression stunned. "I beg your pardon?"

"You heard me. He's going to marry us." She

paused and moistened her lips with her tongue. "Or I'll shoot you."

"Indeed?" Nicholas lifted his brow. "How blood-thirsty of you. May I ask where you got that pistol?"

"I bought it in a shop on the wharf." She added reluctantly, "With your money." She hurried on. "But I'll pay you back."

His lips twitched. "I should hope so."

Father Jason straightened away from the door-jamb. "This is outrageous," he said incredulously. "Young lady, I will perform no marriage rites between you and his highness while he's under duress." He moved forward to stand beside Silver. "You should be ashamed, threatening a man such as he. Do you realize this gentleman is looked upon as a hero by the citizens of St. Louis for his selfless charity toward those poor survivors of the tragedy of the *Mary L*?"

"No." She kept the pistol trained on Nicholas. "I only realize I must have a legal father for my child."

Nicholas went still. "Your child?"

"I'm over two weeks late for my flux and this is not usual for me. I have to go after Etaine and I can't risk leaving without protecting my child." She met his eyes. "I will not bring shame to any child I bear. It will be enough that he will have Apache blood." She paused. "Don't worry, I realize the blame lies also with me. I want only your name for my child. When I leave here, you will never see me again. I'm sure you'll have no problem dissolving the bond when you return to your own country."

"That's a comforting thought." Nicholas's eyes were

narrowed on her face. "You've obviously thought a great deal about this."

"Not a great deal." She smiled shakily. "If I didn't tend to act impulsively, this situation would never have occurred." She lifted her chin. "But I will make it come right."

Father Jason was frowning uncertainly. "You have known this woman in the carnal sense, my son?"

Nicholas's gaze did not leave Silver's face. "Oh, yes, Father, it couldn't have been more carnal."

"It is possible that the child is not of your seed. . . ." Father Jason suggested tentatively. "Perhaps the young woman has engaged in similar activities with other gentlemen."

"If there is a child, it is mine," Nicholas said unequivocally.

"Have you no shame that you admit to disgracing this woman?"

"He didn't disgrace me." Silver said indignantly. "I was the one who chose to—"

"Anyone in St. Petersburg will tell you what a base scoundrel I am," Nicholas interrupted quickly. "No woman is safe from my lust."

"But you obviously repent your past. Perhaps if you vow not to transgress again, a penance or two would be sufficient—" Father Jason broke off as his gaze alighted on the mural on the wall facing him. Stunned, his gaze shifted from perversity to perversity. "Dear sweet Mary, I seem to have been mistaken in you. This is the chamber of a debaucher and his whore."

"I don't have much time," Silver said impatiently. "I have passage on a riverboat that leaves here in forty minutes. Marry us, Father."

"You seem to have no choice," Nicholas told the priest solemnly. He glanced down at the derringer in Silver's hand. "And I most certainly do not. Perhaps we'd better accede graciously to—" He broke off as his gaze traveled over Silver's head to the open doorway. Something flickered in his eyes and his head made a negative motion that was almost imperceptible. "Best proceed with the ceremony, Father."

"Quickly," Silver urged.

Father Jason gave her an exasperated glance. "You're a most demanding female. I'm not so sure his highness is completely to blame for—" His glance again happened on the murals. He quickly drew out a black book and began reciting the words of the marriage rite.

The ceremony was over in an amazingly short time, and Silver understood very few of the Latin phrases. She watched suspiciously as the priest closed the book. "It's done?"

"It's done," the priest said.

"I want a paper," Silver said firmly. "Something to prove that a marriage has taken place."

Nicholas gestured to the small elegant desk across the room. "There's pen, paper, and ink, Father."

The priest hurried over to the desk and scrawled a few lines on a piece of paper he found in the desk drawer.

Silver followed him, glanced hurriedly at the paper, and nodded. "That should be sufficient. Thank you."

"May I go now?" Father Jason asked caustically. "This has all been most irregular."

Silver nodded absently, her gaze turned back to Nicholas as the priest hurried from the stateroom. "It was necessary," she whispered. "I couldn't take a chance. I had to protect my child. You don't know the pain of belonging nowhere."

"Don't I?" he asked "How can you be sure?"

"Perhaps I can't be sure." She drew a deep shaky breath. "You said we knew very little about each other." Her hand tightened on the pistol. "Well, it's over and you're free to do anything you wish now."

His lips curved in a curious smile. "I fully intend to do just that."

She nodded and then folded the document the priest had given her and slipped it into the pocket of her cloak. "Good-bye, Nicholas."

He didn't speak but continued to look at her with that faint smile.

"It really *was* necessary that I—" She broke off, looking at him helplessly. "Truly." She turned and ran from the stateroom.

Mikhail's huge form was blocking the gangplank when she reached the boiler deck.

"Good-bye, Mikhail." Her voice was husky and she had to clear it. "Perhaps we'll meet again."

She tried to slip around him but he deliberately stepped into her path again.

She frowned. "You don't understand, I have to leave now. I have to catch a boat to New Orleans within the hour."

He silently shook his head.

Her lips tightened. "Get out of my way, Mikhail."

"You could always point your little pistol at him," Nicholas said from behind her. "But I doubt if he'd be as easily intimidated as I was."

Silver drew the derringer from beneath her cloak. "Let me pass, Mikhail."

Mikhail smiled gently at her and again shook his head.

"Mikhail, I'll shoot you." Silver said, trying to make her voice convincing. It was very difficult when the big bull was gazing at her with such cheerful affection. "Truly. You know I—Nicholas!"

He had picked her up and slung her over his shoulder. "Let me down!" Her hair was cascading over her eyes and she could see nothing as he turned and strode toward the staircase. "What are you doing? I'll—"

"Hush, I'm tired of threats." He was climbing the steps. "And stop wriggling. This is the only way I can hold you without hurting your back."

"Where are you taking me?"

"Back to bed. I told you the doctor said you weren't to get up. I should have known as soon as I turned my back you'd be running around as if that bastard had been stroking you with a feather instead of a whip."

"Etaine—"

"I told you I'd take care of delivering your little waif to you. Why didn't you trust me?"

"She's my responsibility. I can't expect you to—"

"You don't expect anything of anyone and you don't trust anyone but yourself." The crimson carpet of the saloon suddenly came into her line of vision. "I keep my word, dammit."

"Let me down. I have a boat to catch."

"In case it escaped your notice, you're on a boat now." He shifted his hold on her to open a door. "And its destination just happens to be New Orleans."

"I have to leave right away. I don't know how long Monteith will be in New Orleans." Her tone was anguished. "He may be gone when I get there."

"I've given orders to Robert that we're to leave as soon as we finish taking on more fuel." He set her on her feet, carefully avoiding touching her back, and turned to light the kerosene lamp on the rosewood table beside the door. "Which should be no longer than thirty minutes."

She brushed the hair out of her eyes, noticing absently that Nicholas had not brought her to the master stateroom, but to a much smaller one. Perhaps it had been the first door he had passed. "But I have to—"

"I do wish you'd stop arguing, Silver. I've had a very eventful day and I find I'm quite weary. May I have this now? You obviously have no intention of using it at the moment." He took the derringer she was still clutching and set it on the rosewood table. "I think I'm taking all this quite well, don't you? After all, it's not every day a man is forced at the point of a gun into the holy nuptials."

"I told you I had to do it."

"But why did you have to do it?" The amusement and mockery faded from his expression. "Wouldn't it have been easier for you to come to me and tell me there was a possibility of a child?"

She shook her head emphatically. "I needed marriage. I know you probably would have offered your protection, but that wouldn't make the child less a bastard. I knew you wouldn't marry me."

"Did you?" His dark eyes narrowed on her face. "You seem very certain."

She shrugged. "I'm not such a fool that I don't know that princes don't wed with half-breeds born on the wrong side of the blanket. Even Father Jason did everything he could to persuade you that marriage wasn't necessary with a woman like me."

"There are no women like you," Nicholas said softly. "There's only one Silver Delaney."

Her gaze lifted to meet his own and she suddenly caught her breath. She felt as if she were spinning, drowning in a dark golden pool of sensation. Drowning. For a fleeting instant she remembered that moment when she had sunk beneath the waters of the river, fighting for her life, knowing there was something wonderful waiting for her if she could just stay alive long enough to grasp it. Something wonderful. Not lust, but something deeper, more mystical . . . It was coming closer. It was just beyond the horizon. Soon she would be able to see it.

"You could have let me go," she said haltingly. "After I had my paper from the priest, I would never have bothered you again. Why did you follow me?"

"Because I knew you'd let no feather drift to earth for me to seize so that I might summon you back to me." His hand reached out and gently brushed a swath of silky dark hair from her face. "What a very wary firebird you are, Silver."

She looked away from him. "That's no answer."

"You don't trust me enough for me to give you any other . . . as yet."

"And you have little trust in me."

"But I'm learning, Silver. I was taught a very bitter lesson a long time ago." He smiled. "But now we have time to learn each other. Marriage is forever."

"No!" she said, distressed. "I never meant to trap you in that fashion. You can have it dissolved."

"There is no divorce in my family," he said flatly. "You should have taken time to query me on the subject. Now you're just as much a captive as you were when I first brought you aboard the *Rose*."

"And so are you," Silver said, frowning. "Truly, I never meant—"

"It's done." He made an imperious gesture with his left hand. "There is no use talking about it." He took a step forward, took off her cloak, and began unbuttoning the shiny black buttons on the bodice of her gray gown. "It's time you went back to bed. Wherever did you get this ugly gown? You seem to have an affinity for acquiring hideous garments."

"Valentin bought it from one of the nurses," she

said absently, her thoughts on his words. "You don't seem overly upset about the marriage."

His eyes were twinkling as he stripped the gown off her. "One of the things you must learn about me is that I seldom do anything I don't wish to do."

"But I forced you." She frowned. "Didn't I?"

"You certainly pointed a gun at me," he agreed placidly. "You're a very dangerous lady, Silver."

He stripped her shoes and undergarments from her and crossed to the double bed across the room and pulled back the pale green satin spread. "Now, come and lie down so that I can cover you up." His voice had thickened a trifle. "I'm trying to forget about my recently acquired conjugal privileges and remember you're not well."

She obediently crossed the room and slipped under the sheets and turned on her stomach, her cheek cradled on the pillow as she turned to look at him. "*Did* I force you?"

"Perhaps." He stood looking down at her. "Or perhaps I saw a way I could have what I wanted, what I was too guilt-ridden to take for myself."

"Which one?" She couldn't breathe. It was so close, shimmering beyond the dark mystery of his eyes. Something wonderful.

"Someday I'll tell you," he said. "But not until you have no need for me to do so."

"How maddening you are." She scowled. "I don't think I like Russians."

He laughed. "Then you're definitely going to the wrong country, aren't you?"

"I might not have to go to Russia. I might find Etaine before they leave New Orleans."

"Possibly." His hand moved over her hair, stroking the heavy fall that tumbled over her shoulder and off the side of the bed. "I love the texture of your hair. It's like midnight silk." He drew his hand reluctantly away and slowly straightened. "I'll leave you to nap now. I'll order our dinner served here in the stateroom in a few hours."

"But you don't think Monteith will still be in New Orleans, do you? You think I'll have to go to Russia."

"I have no idea, but I do believe it's your destiny to go to Russia at some time." He smiled mischievously. "We Russians are great fatalists, you know. We believe our every step is guided by destiny."

"And what is your destiny, Nicholas?"

His smile faded and his dark eyes became grave. "Who knows? Perhaps it's to follow the firebird until she lets me mount her and soar to the sun. I have a great fondness for firebirds. I followed one once and she led me from hell to purgatory. I'm willing to try my luck again and aim for a more celestial destination."

"Fairy tales again." Silver laughed uncertainly. He was all golden beauty and entrancing enigma, more bewildering now than she had ever known him to be.

He bent swiftly and kissed her with slow warmth and exquisite tenderness. "I hope not." Then he straightened and was walking toward the door.

He turned to look at her as his hand grasped the

china doorknob. "Do you find this stateroom suitable? We can choose another one if you like."

"This is quite nice." She gazed at him in puzzlement. "But why didn't you take me back to the master stateroom?"

"Because Father Jason was right, that stateroom was for a debaucher and his whore. Not for her highness, Princess Silver Savron." He bowed, his expression half mocking, half grave. "And certainly not for my wife."

Silver felt a surge of wild unreasoning happiness out of all proportion to his words. "I see. I didn't know you made distinctions of that nature."

"Then you've already learned something new about me." Suddenly a frown darkened his brow. "Which reminds me that we have a few things to discuss."

"Yes?"

"You're my wife now and there are a few things I will not tolerate."

"Indeed?"

"You will not run wild as you have done since I've known you. My country is different from your own; there are dangers of which you have no knowledge. You're not even familiar with the language."

Silver's lashes lowered to veil her eyes.

"You will not go out without a groom or accompanied by Valentin, Mikhail, or myself." Nicholas cast her a wary glance, but she seemed to be taking the strictures very meekly.

"You will leave the locating of Monteith and his circus to me."

Silver smothered a yawn with her hand.

"You will be guided by me in all matters concerning—"

"I'm very tired, Nicholas."

He gazed at her suspiciously. "That's all you have to say?"

Silver's eyes closed. "That's all I have to say."

Doubtful, he stared at her for a long moment, then he shrugged and turned to extinguish the kerosene lamp on the table by the door. Perhaps it wouldn't be too difficult a task to tame a firebird after all. "I'm glad you're being sensible." He opened the door. "Rest well, Silver."

The door closed behind him.

At once Silver's lids flickered open to reveal crystal-gray eyes shimmering with excitement, anticipation, and a secret amusement.

She smiled in the darkness.

Don't miss the enthralling sequel to this book, *Satin Ice*, also by Iris Johansen and part of the concluding trinity of THE DELANEYS, THE UNTAMED YEARS.

THE DELANEY DYNASTY

Three of Bantam's bestselling romance authors, Kay Hooper, Iris Johansen and Fayrene Preston, have established a unique event in romance publishing—the creation of the Delaney Dynasty—a family filled with fascinating male and female characters whose love stories are deeply sensual and unforgettable. Each author's work stands alone, but read with the other books is part of a panoramic picture of a colorful, exciting, and heartwarming family.

The stories of the members of the Delaney Dynasty began with the publication of THE SHAMROCK TRINITY, the first trio of contemporary love stories of the Delaney brothers—*Rafe, The Maverick* by Kay Hooper; *York, The Renegade* by Iris Johansen; and *Burke, The Kingpin* by Fayrene Preston. These three romances received such wide acclaim and generated such a clamor for more stories of the Delaneys that our authors soon gave us the next three contemporaries—THE DELANEYS OF KILLAROO: *Adelaide, The Enchantress* by Kay Hooper; *Matilda, The Adventuress* by Iris Johansen; and *Sydney, The Temptress* by Fayrene Preston.

The authors' fascination with the Delaneys grew and, particularly, they were captivated by the daring and romantic ancestors who started it all. Thus, the Delaney historicals were created, one of which you have just read.

Setting the stage for the trilogy THE DELANEYS, THE UNTAMED YEARS, though, was THIS FIERCE SPLENDOR by Iris Johansen. In the pages that follow we are giving you excerpts of THE DELANEYS OF KILLAROO, THIS FIERCE SPLENDOR, and two of the other books of the trilogy THE DELANEYS, THE UNTAMED YEARS. We hope these excerpts will tempt you to get any of the books you may have missed . . . as well as to look forward to the second and last set of historical novels that will follow up THE UNTAMED YEARS and be published in the late fall of 1988.

ASK FOR THE BOOKS OF THE DELANEY DYNASTY SERIES AT YOUR LOCAL BOOKSTORE OR GET THEM THROUGH THE MAIL BY USING THE COUPON AT THE BACK OF THIS BOOK.

The Delaneys of Killaroo:

Adelaide, The Enchantress

by Kay Hooper

He probably wouldn't have noticed them except for the koala. It wasn't, after all, unusual to see a horse at a racetrack, or even a girl walking beside a horse. And it wasn't that unusual to see a koala in Australia.

But he'd never seen one with four leather gloves covering its paws and riding a horse.

He didn't know much about koalas, but this one seemed a fair example of the species. It looked absurdly cuddly, with tufts of ears and a round little body, button eyes, and a large black nose.

Shane Marston turned his astonished eyes from the koala to the horse that walked quietly, obediently, beside the girl holding his lead rope. He wore no blanket or leg bandages, and seemed not to mind the koala clinging to his back.

The girl stopped just inside the wide barn hall and dropped the lead rope, and while the horse stood calmly she held out her arm toward the koala, calling, "Sebastian."

The little creature reached a gloved paw toward her, not completely releasing the horse's mane until he could grasp her arm. Then he left the horse in a smooth transfer to the girl's back, his limbs firmly around her neck.

Shane stood very still, gazing at the girl and feeling the shock of her voice still echoing in his mind. It was the sweetest, most gentle voice he had ever heard, and it touched something inside him, something that had never been touched before. His throat felt tight and his heart pounded, and he was bewildered because suddenly he couldn't breathe very well.

She was not thin, but she was small and looked amazingly fragile. Her skin was very fair, almost translucent. The only color she could boast of was the vibrant red of her short hair; and though that hair was a badge of passion and temper, in her face was reflected only gentleness and calm.

She was not, he realized on some uncaring level of himself, a beautiful young woman. Her mouth was too wide for beauty, her eyes too large. Yet that tender mouth would always draw the gaze of a man, and those dark eyes would haunt his dreams.

"You want to meet her?"

Shane started at the sound of Tate Justin's voice. Tate didn't wait for an answer, but started walking forward.

Shane fell into step beside him, eager to meet the girl with the soft, gentle voice and the fiery hair.

"Addie." Tate smiled rather sardonically. "A guest of ours wants to meet you; he's an American horse breeder. Adelaide Delaney, Shane Marston."

Shane, peculiarly sensitive to undercurrents, saw something flash between them, something genuinely humorous on Tate's part and somewhat pained on hers.

She turned to Shane, looking up at him. "Mr. Marston."

Shane held the small hand, instinctively gentle, his fingers tingling again while a faint shock registered at the back of his mind. Her name . . . Was it possible? No . . . half a world away . . . "A pleasure, Miss Delaney," he said, releasing her hand when it occurred to him that he had held it too long.

"I'll leave you two to get acquainted," Tate said, and then walked away.

She gazed after him for a moment, then gave Shane an easy, friendly half smile. "You're interested in Australian horses, Mr. Marston?"

"Shane. And yes, I am."

"Breeding stock, or racers?"

"Primarily breeding stock." Shane reached out to pass a hand down Resolute's sloping shoulders. "He's a fine animal."

"Yes, he is." Her voice gentled even more with the words.

Shane chuckled suddenly and gestured to the koala asleep with his chin on her shoulder. "And unusual, since he allows the koala to ride him."

"Sebastian's the unusual one." She reached up to trail a finger along the koala's foreleg, and a tufted ear twitched sleepily. "He was orphaned young, and instead of climbing trees he took to people and horses. Some people, mind you, and some horses. He's a bit temperamental—but then, so is Resolute." She smiled. "I believe American racehorses sometimes choose odd stable companions?"

"They certainly do," Shane said, remembering the moth-eaten cockatoo at his stable.

Shane looked down at her lustrous coppery curls and felt his heart turn over. He was conscious of an abrupt sense of urgency, a fiery prodding along his nerve endings.

Addie frowned a little and touched his arm in a seemingly instinctive gesture. "Are you all right?"

He looked down at her, feeling her touch clear through to his bones. "Yes. I suppose I haven't recovered from jet lag yet, that's all."

The dark eyes searched his briefly, but she nodded and dropped her hand. "It was nice meeting you—" she began.

Shane smiled broadly. "Oh, I'll be around for a while," he said. "In Australia—and on the tracks. You're riding this afternoon?"

Addie nodded. "Yes, and tomorrow." She didn't seem surprised that he knew she rode. "Then up to Sydney with Resolute for the weekend races."

Shane bit back what he wanted to say. "I see. Well, I believe I'll watch you ride today." He grinned. "Should I bet on you?"

Seriously, she said, "I intend to win."

"Then I'll bet my kingdom."

She laughed a little, the sound once again running through Shane like a haunting song, then waved casually and walked away. He stood stock still for several minutes, gazing after her. Suddenly aware of the increasing noise that heralded the beginning of the afternoon races, he headed toward the track.

Addie had just won the last race on a horse improbably named Catch Me If You Can. She went through the routine of unsaddling, weighing out, and speaking to a delighted owner and a somewhat stunned trainer. Then, tiredly, she headed back for the changing room. She showered and changed into jeans and a light blouse.

Shane was outside, waiting for her.

"I won some money," he said, smiling at her. "And I was hoping you'd go out with me somewhere to celebrate."

"I'd like that." Addie was a little surprised by her instant acceptance, and frowned briefly. "Let me check on Resolute first, all right?"

"Where would you like to have dinner?"

Addie started a little. "Oh, wherever you like. Somewhere casual, please; I travel light on the circuit, so I never pack dressy things."

"Fine. We can go in my rental car, and pick up your Jeep later."

"All right then, and thanks."

"My pleasure." He watched her lock up the Jeep and pocket her keys, then took her arm courteously as they headed toward the parking area near the stables.

Shane didn't try to fool himself into believing that manners had compelled him to take her arm; he was, in fact, very well mannered. That had little to do with it, however. He had taken her arm because he knew he'd go out of his mind if he couldn't touch her even in a polite and casual way. And though it might have seemed just that outwardly, he was very conscious that there was nothing casual in his reaction to the touch.

He felt a sizzling jolt when he touched her, his breath catching oddly and his head becoming curiously light. The strength of his own feelings distrubed him, not in the least because she seemed almost too frail to withstand the powerful force of such vital desire. And it did no good at all to remind himself that she was quite obviously a strong woman; her soft voice, her shimmering halo of silky red hair, small size, and magical gift with animals made her appear ethereal, and all his male instincts urged him to believe in frailty rather than strength.

Shane had always taken his attraction to women lightly in the past; he enjoyed their company, whether casual or intimate. He had a great many female friends, and the lovers in his past tended to remain firm friends after the affairs had ended. Though in a position of comfortable wealth and gifted with blond hair and green eyes that caused the American tabloids to persist in referring to him as "the sleekest, sexiest Thoroughbred in racing circles," Shane had never cared much for casual sex.

Not since his experimental teens had he taken a woman to bed without first having genuinely liked her—and if those invited declined, they never lost Shane as a friend.

What he had seen and heard of Addie, he certainly liked. He liked the frank gaze of her dark eyes, her quick smile and fluid grace. Her voice held a strange power to move him; and her gift with animals and—apparently—people fascinated him.

Yet, for all that, he knew almost nothing about her. Nothing to explain why his very bones seemed to dissolve when she looked at him or spoke to him. Nothing to explain the rabid fear he only just had managed to control while watching her race. Nothing to explain this urgent, driving need to touch her.

Shane knew what desire felt like, and he had even known the feeling to occur spontaneously when first meeting a woman—but that was like comparing the rumble of thunder to the violence of a hurricane.

You'll frighten her to death, he told himself fiercely. If he let go. If he gave in to desires urging him to tumble them both into the nearest bed and violently explore these feelings he had never felt before . . .

She was too gentle and frail, he told himself, to respond to that kind of savagery. Too magically ethereal to want anything but tenderness and gentleness. She was sheer enchantment.

Shane knew dimly that he was already placing her on a pedestal, already setting her like some Greek goddess on an Olympus where an earthy hand could never mark her.

And he hardly heard the inner voice reminding him that the ancient gods and goddesses, for all their divinity, had been remarkably human at heart and quite definitely earthy in their passions.

Beneath the magic.

The Delaneys ouf Killaroo:

Matilda, The Adventuress

by Iris Johansen

"What the hell! There's a woman standing in the middle of the road!" Roman's foot stomped on the brakes of the Jeep. The vehicle swerved and then skidded to the side of the road. He could hear the screech of brakes from the long column of trucks and trailers he was leading. The sound was immediately followed by the blistering curses of the drivers.

"Well, there goes tomorrow's shooting." Brent gingerly touched the bruise he'd just acquired on his forehead from banging his head on the dashboard of the Jeep. "Unless you'd care to write in a barroom brawl. I'm going to have a devil of a bruise on my matchless profile."

"Are you all right?"

The breathless question came from the woman who had run up to the Jeep as soon as it had come to a halt. Her tousled cinnamon-colored hair, sparkling as though touched by a golden hand, shimmered in the headlights; Roman was fascinated for a fleeting instant by that brilliant halo of color. He shifted his gaze to her face. "What the hell did you think you were doing? I almost ran over you."

"Lord, I'm sorry. I didn't realize you were going so fast. I just wanted to . . ." Her eyes widened in amazement. "You're Roman Gallagher. How wonderful. I've always wanted to meet you."

"Yes." Hell, not another would-be starlet, he thought. He'd had his fill of actresses throwing themselves into his path in the hopes of getting a part in one of his films. As his gaze touched her he was startled to feel a swift and incredible desire for her. It didn't make a damn bit of sense to him. She wasn't even sexy. Yet his reaction had been undeniable. A tingle of annoyance went through him.

She smiled, and he inhaled sharply. Warmth. Lord, her

smile illuminated her thin face like the Southern Cross illuminated the night sky.

"I love your films," she said. "I thought *Fulfillment* was terrific, and I've seen all your documentaries. My favorite was the one you did on the Barrier Reef."

He tried to mask his surprise. She had clearly done her homework. He hadn't made a documentary in seven years, and at that time his audience had been extremely small. "Thank you. I enjoyed filming it, even though the subject of the reefs had been done a hundred or so times before."

"But not like you did it. The underwater scenes were . . ." She took an eager step closer, her brown eyes shining in the reflected beam of the headlights. She met his gaze and suddenly her eyes widened in curious surprise, and she forgot what she wanted to say. Then she shook her head as if to clear it and laughed uncertainly. "There aren't any words to describe that film. I wanted to hop on the next boat to the reef."

"I'm surprised you didn't."

She whirled to her left, and faced the man who had just stepped down from the truck directly behind the Jeep. She squinted into the shadows as she tried to match a face with the familiar voice. "Dennis?" Then, as the man came into the perimeter of the headlights, his gray-flecked sandy brown hair and rough-hewn features became clearer. She flew across the road and into his arms, and gave him an enthusiastic hug. "Dennis Billet, what on earth are you doing here?"

"I could ask you the same thing." His hazel eyes were twinkling down at her. "Except I've given up being surprised at the places you turn up. Nowadays I just accept the fact that if there's excitement or trouble or danger around, sooner or later you'll be there."

"I hate to interrupt this reunion, but I have a location to set up." Roman's tone was caustic. For some irrational reason he was displeased at the sight of the golden-haired woman in Billet's arms. "You know this woman, Dennis?"

Dennis nodded. "We go back a long way." He placed his arm companionably around her waist as he turned to face Roman. "Manda Delaney, this is my boss, Roman Gallagher."

Manda was frowning. "Location? You're going to set up a movie location here? But you can't do that!"

"I have a drawerful of permits back in Sydney that says the opposite." Roman's lips tightened. "I'd damn well better be able to do it. Are you saying you have a prior claim?"

"No, not exactly." She ran her fingers through her shining hair. "I tried to get one, but the authorities said the entire area had already been leased. I thought it was a mistake. No one comes to Deadman's Ridge anymore. There haven't been any opals found in this field for over twenty-five years."

"Which is why I had no trouble obtaining a three-month lease on the ridge."

"You're going to be here for three months?" The dismay on her face was unmistakable. "Look, can't you go somewhere else? I know I don't have a legal permit, but I was here first, and my business is very important."

He was staring at her in disbelief. "Do you realize how much money I'd lose per day looking for another location?"

She made a face. "No chance?"

"No chance." His eyes narrowed. "May I assume you're not an actress then?"

"Me?" She was astonished. "Why would you think I was an actress?"

He stiffened. "What's your business here? Are you a newspaper reporter?"

"What is this? Twenty questions?"

His lips twisted. "I know you people consider questions the prerogative of the press, but you should have thought of that before you decided to trespass on my land. Lord, I thought I'd gotten away from vultures like you."

"I'm *not* a reporter."

"Then just what is your business here, Miss Delaney?"

"Manda." She smiled and again he felt warmth radiate through him. "I'm afraid my business is of a private nature. However, I assure you it's most urgent. I promise I won't get in your way if you let me stay." Her voice dropped to wheedling softness. "I know you'll understand."

Dennis Billet suddenly burst into laughter. "Manda,

you never change. Be careful, Roman, she'll be talking you out of your mobile home in another minute."

She had come very close to getting what she wanted from him. Roman felt a flare of anger when he realized that if he hadn't been jarred by Dennis's obvious amusement, he would probably have let her stay. "I can't help you. I've made it a rule to close my set to outsiders." Roman got back into the Jeep and started the ignition. He noticed Dennis's arm still held the woman in a casual embrace, and he found his pilot's familiarity with Manda Delaney oddly annoying. The woman was obviously an accomplished charmer and accustomed to getting her own way with men. Well, she would find he distinctly disliked being used by anyone, women in particular. "I'll give you one day to pack up and get off the property."

"But you don't understand. I can't—" The rest of her sentence was lost as he revved the engine of the Jeep. "I *have* to stay here. There are reasons. . . ."

The Jeep jumped forward as he pressed the accelerator. A few seconds later he'd driven several yards down the road.

"You weren't very polite," Brent drawled. "You didn't introduce me, and I got the distinct impression that something about the lady annoyed the hell out of you. Pity. She could have been very entertaining to have around. You could have thought about *my* convenience, Roman. You drag me out here in the wilds with an all-male cast, forbid me to seduce any of the women on your production crew, and then send packing the only alluring woman who crosses our path. How inconsiderate can you be?"

"I'm sure you'll survive. Besides, she wasn't all that pretty."

"You don't think so? Personally, I prefer the unconventional type."

"Too thin."

"But she really fills out a T-shirt."

"I didn't notice," Roman said.

Brent glanced sidewise at him, and then smiled. "Oh, yes, you noticed all right. Is it okay if I go after her and offer her my sympathy, my gorgeous body, and anything else she'll accept?"

"Why should I care? She's nothing to me." Roman's hands tightened unconsciously on the steering wheel. "Though I don't think it's worth your while. She'll be gone tomorrow."

"Long enough. Haven't you heard I'm irresistible? All my press clippings say so." The amusement was abruptly gone from Brent's expression. "If you want her yourself, I'll back away, Roman. My role in your film means too much to me to jeopardize our professional relationship over a woman."

For the briefest instant Roman was tempted to tell him to back off, to keep away from her. The instinct was brutally primitive. Lord, what had gotten into him tonight? There was no way he was going to involve himself with Manda Delaney. Her appearance in his life had been entirely too coincidental, and her reluctance to tell him the purpose of her business in the opal field was distinctly suspicious. She could be anything from a con artist on the make, to one of the paparazzi out to get an exclusive interview. This was sheer madness. He forced himself to relax and the moment of insanity passed. He shrugged. "Do what you like. She doesn't appeal to me."

Manda laughed softly as she stood in the middle of the road watching the receding taillights of the vehicles of the caravan. The desert was no longer tranquil, and the entire situation was fraught with complications. Yet she was still feeling a familiar shiver of excitement. Change. Things were changing, events were going to occur, people would act and react. How she loved adventure and change and this time the potential was more exciting than ever before.

Because a difficult, sensual man named Roman Gallagher was leading that caravan and she had suddenly realized he just might be the greatest adventure of all.

The Delaneys of Killaroo:

Sydney, The Temptress

by Fayrene Preston

One floor above the casino, from behind the one-way glass, Nicholas Charron watched her, as he had every night for the past three nights.

Her name was Sydney Delaney. He had gotten this information from the registration card she had filled out when she had arrived on the island three days ago. Alone.

With each night that passed his curiosity about her grew. She seemed intensely interested in the games, but she had yet to place a bet. And he had seen several men approach her, but with scarcely a look she had sent them on their way.

From his remote observation post he had a complete view of the entire casino. Men and women dressed in their evening finery milled below him in a rhythm of bright color and swirling motion, uncaring that just beyond the casino's wide expanse of windowed walls lay the wonder and the glory of the Great Barrier Reef. Their disregard of the natural beauty of the reef and the star-brilliant night above it amused him. While most casinos were windowless, his was not. He deliberately had had the windows included in the design as his own private joke—just as he had giant seawater aquariums set in the long wall that ran across the back of the casino. Although the aquariums featured the vividly patterned fish that swam in the waters of the reef, he knew that to the majority of the people in the casino, the fish provided little more than an exotic backdrop for the real reason they had come to the island—the gaming.

He understood people, their vices, their greed. Soon, Nicholas promised himself, he would understand Sydney Delaney.

He turned away from the window and walked to the long row of monitors that provided coverage of the entire casino. With a quick flick of a series of switches, four screens glowed simultaneously with her image.

Sydney Delaney was clearly beautiful, but there were many women in his casino tonight who were as beautiful, if not more so. Yet there was something about her that had drawn his attention to her and had kept it there. Unprecedented for him.

Once, a long time ago, he had seen a figurine of a young girl in a Chicago store window, so fine and delicate, she appeared translucent, so fragile and expensive, a glass dome had protected her. He had wanted the figurine. The woman below reminded him of that figurine.

He looked closer, trying to decipher, to take apart, and thus explain, the pull she was exerting on him. Her hair seemed a dark burgundy and hung in a lustrous mass to below her shoulders. He frowned, for the color seemed to contain a depth that the screen of the monitor couldn't satisfactorily register.

In the monitor that caught her profile he saw a straight nose and a clean sweep of jaw. Another monitor showed him finely shaped brows arched over wide, light-colored eyes of an undiscernable shade and a disconcerting mouth, full and perfectly formed to fit under a man's lips.

A third monitor revealed a full-length picture of her. The long dress she wore was of cream-colored slipper satin. The neckline was high, but the back dipped to the waist, exposing skin that, on the monitor at least, appeared flawless. In involuntary anticipation of the time when he would touch that flawless skin, his fingers curled one by one, into his palm.

Experience told him that most of the gowns on the women in the casino revealed more and cost more than the one she wore, but it didn't matter. Any clothing would look marvelous on her, he concluded.

There was an elegance about her and a grace, even as she remained still, and motion and noise swirled around her—like the sea that surrounded the island . . . his island, the Isle of Charron.

Did she have that much command over her emotions and nerves? he wondered. The question intrigued him.

His mind returned briefly to the glass dome that had surrounded the fragile figurine years before. Glass could be broken.

* * *

If a panther could live on a tropical island, his name would surely be Nicholas Charron, Sydney decided. She had never seen him, but she could *feel* him—like a violent disturbance in the atmosphere.

Strangely, she never questioned why she felt he was there above her, watching. She just did. She knew that he paced in his control room above the casino, and she sensed his eyes on her, like a warm breath across her skin.

The fact that he was observing her from behind a one-way mirror made her feel exposed, unprotected, and it was a feeling she hated above all else. But she dealt with the vulnerability he was opening up in her as she always did—with absolute control over her body and her mind.

As was her way, she never went into any situation blind if she could help it. Before she had come to the Isle of Charron, she had researched the island, the casino, and the man who owned both. She had learned a great deal, but not all.

Nicholas Charron was a mysterious man. It was known that he was an American expatriate, but exactly what he had done from the time he left America to the time he bought the Isle of Charron was shrouded in mystery. However, over the last five years he had developed an island resort and casino like nothing Australia had seen before, especially on the Great Barrier Reef. They called his casino and hotel complex Charron's Glass Palace—like everything else on the island, his name was attached, whether he intended it to be or not. As a result, the Isle of Charron had gained an international reputation among jet setters and high rollers. They came to spend money, to have a good time, and if possible to see Nicholas Charron.

Speculation ran high, and extraordinary things were whispered about him. He had an aura that was as dark as the night, and to the thrill-seeking gamblers, his mystique was as big a draw as his casino.

But he never came down onto the casino floor, and only rarely did he invite anyone to his apartment at the top of the resort complex. Unless . . .

People talked and word spread. She hadn't been on the island more than a day, when an excited lady she had encountered on the beach had told her that sometimes Nicholas Charron would stand in his control room above the casino floor and scan the action below him to choose a woman for the night.

Sydney had watched women do things she knew were calculated to attract the attention of the dark man everyone talked about but very few ever saw. Somehow she had known the women wouldn't be successful. Somehow she had known it was *she* he watched.

She was being pursued by someone who couldn't be seen, only felt, but Sydney refused to give in to the agitation that ran through her veins with a singing excitement. She had to keep her mind on her purpose for being in the casino. Since she had been on the island, she had carefully studied the action of each of the games, and tonight she had chosen craps to observe. It was a fast-paced game, and the chances of winning large amounts of money seemed good. Wondering about the odds, she opened her purse and pulled out a small calculator.

Within the space of a few seconds two men stood on either side of her.

And watching from the control room, Nicholas Charron reached for the phone.

One man was big and muscular and had a face so grooved and pitted, it looked as if it had been pulled straight off the side of Ayers Rock. The other man, an Oriental, was short and wiry with flat black eyes that stared at her without expression.

It was the larger of the two men who spoke. "I'm sorry, miss, you'll have to come with us."

"Where exactly is it that you're taking me?" she asked as they halted before a set of black stainless steel doors.

"To Mr. Charron's apartment."

The doors swished open, and they stepped into a lift. The doors closed, sealing her and the strange men by her side off from the comfort and familiarity of the crowd in the casino.

Three floors above ground level, the lift glided to a stop, the doors opened, and Sydney was facing the silent sanctuary of the owner of the Isle of Charron. Slowly she began to walk forward.

She was truly lovely, Nicholas thought, watching her.

Exquisite. Instinct had told him that she wasn't like the women he usually summoned to him, and he had been proved right. When she had first looked up and seen his men on either side of her, his theory had been confirmed. Her expression had changed from composure to fear. For an instant she had looked so defenseless, that something like pain had twisted inside of him. To his mind, it hadn't seemed right that the first strong emotion he saw on her face should be fear. On a beautifully carved table a crystal swan swam on a mirror lake.

"Good evening."

She started at the deep voice. She hadn't even seen him, yet there he was! He was standing on a level above her, in front of a window, and for a moment she couldn't separate him from the night. They seemed as one.

As she had trained herself to do, she waited a beat before answering him. "Good evening."

Three long strides brought him down to her. "Thank you for coming."

"Did I have any choice?"

His mouth curved with humor. "Not really, but I won't apologize. I never apologize."

THIS FIERCE SPLENDOR

by Iris Johansen

It is 1870 and the Scottish beauty and scholar Elspeth MacGregor has traveled to Hell's Bluff in the Arizona Territory to hire Dominic Delaney to lead her to the magical lost city of Kantalan. Elspeth assumes her business with Dominic will be simple—but learns quickly that nothing is simple about this magnetic man-on-the-run who is the only person who knows the location of the fabulous city of dark mysteries and magnificent treasures. He refuses to guide her. He refuses even to speak with her again. But his nephew Patrick, a mischievous young man, is Elspeth's ally and has hatched a plan to create a confrontation between her and his uncle.

"Firecrackers?" Elspeth eyed with alarm the stack of slender sticks linked with long fuses. She had been curious about the large blanket-wrapped bundle since Patrick had picked it up from Sam Li's shack, but she had never imagined it contained anything as exotic as firecrackers. "What are we going to do with firecrackers?" she asked again.

Patrick was busy tying the fuses together. "You said you wanted to get Dom's attention and make a statement of your determination." He looked up and grinned at her. "This will make a very resounding statement, I guarantee."

"I'm sure it will," she said faintly. She glanced at the large whitewashed house across the street. "But I had a more sedate statement in mind."

"You want Dom jerked from his lair and forced to confront you in the fastest possible way." His nimble fingers moved to the second string of firecrackers. "This is the only way I could think for you to do it."

"The only way or the most interesting way?" she asked dryly. "I think you're planning on enjoying this."

"Sure, I always did like a good show."

Elspeth wished she could think of something else. She had an idea Patrick's plan had elements more explosive than the firecrackers. "Your uncle is going to be very angry."

"Yep."

"But he'd probably be angry at my coming here anyway."

"Uh-huh."

"And it's really his own fault for being so narrow-minded and uncooperative. This is a very important undertaking; it can add greatly to our fund of knowl—"

She was interrupted by his low chuckle. "I think you're trying to talk yourself into something."

She grinned back at him. "I think I've done it." She knelt beside him. "Let me help you."

"Very well. You take these two packets and run them from the front door down the steps and into the street. I'll take the rest inside and string them along the hall on the second floor and down the stairs to the front door."

"No."

He lifted his head. "What?"

"I said no. This is my responsibility. I'll be the one to set the firecrackers inside the house and light them. You're clearly trying to spare me the risk of being discovered."

"What I'm trying to do is spare you a sight that might shock the bejiggers out of you. I think you'd better wait outside until I call you."

"No." She took the larger stack of firecrackers from him. "Do I light each one as I put it in place?"

He sighed with resignation. "All you have to do is to light the long fuse on the first packet. Place that one at the end of the corridor on the second floor. The fuse will allow you enough time to trail the firecrackers down the stairs to the front hall."

His enthusiasm was contagious. A tiny flare of excitement began to smolder beneath Elspeth's apprehension. "Is the front door left unlocked?"

Patrick nodded. "Rina wouldn't think of discouraging business, be it day or night."

"Then I guess I won't have any problem." She hesitated, then squared her shoulders and started across the street.

"You might have one problem," Patrick called out.

Elspeth stopped and turned to face him with swift alarm. "What?"

"Matches." He took a box from his pocket and grinned. "Catch." He tossed the box across the few feet separating them. "It's hard to light a fuse without them."

Ten minutes later she was standing in the foyer laying the last of the strings of firecrackers on the bottom step. The house was still in half darkness.

She wished there was more light. She would have liked to have seen if the furnishings of a bordello were as exotic as she had imagined. Perhaps when the firecrackers went off she would be able to see more.

The front door opened quietly to reveal Patrick's thick hair outlined against a pearl-gray wedge of sky. "All set?"

"Yes," she whispered. "I lit the first fuse just as you told me. Shouldn't it have gone off by now?"

"Any second." He closed the door behind him.

"What do we do now?"

"We get out of the line of fire." He drew her to the corner of the foyer farthest from the staircase. "And then we wait."

They didn't have to wait long. Patrick had scarcely gotten the words out when there was an explosion!

"Here we go," Patrick murmured over the barrage of explosions. "How's this for a statement, Elspeth?"

The first explosion jerked Dominic from sleep. Gunfire. In the hall outside. He moved with the sure instinct that had guided him for the last ten years. By the time of the second explosion, he was on his feet reaching for his gunbelt. When the third explosion rocked the hall, he was at the door.

"Dominic," Rina said sleepily. She sat up and brushed a shining brown lock of hair from her cheek. "What the hell—" She broke off as another explosion jarred her fully awake. "No, Dom, don't go out there." She jumped out of bed, reaching hurriedly for her lacy peignoir.

Dominic wasn't listening. All his senses were strained toward the danger in the hall. God, he was tired of this. Tired of never going to sleep without worrying if he'd face gunfire when he woke. He yanked open the door, stepping quickly to the side to avoid a possible spate of gunshots. The explosions continued, but there were no bullets sailing through the air, impacting floors and woodwork. He cautiously looked around the doorframe. The hall was filled with smoke and the explosions weren't coming from a gun. He stared blankly at the string of explosives on the floor going off one after the other. "Firecrackers!"

"What?" Rina was beside him. "Who would do a thing like this?"

He didn't have to consider the possibilities for more than a minute. He had been in the Nugget when Patrick and his friends had ridden through the doors on horseback throwing firecrackers right and left. "For Patrick, every day is a day for celebration," he said dryly. "I imagine this was his way of bidding us a fond good-bye until next week. But, if I know my nephew, he wouldn't be able to resist staying and watching the fun." He was striding down the hall following the exploding string of firecrackers. "And when I catch up with him, I'm going to tie a string of firecrackers to *his* tail." The explosions had reached the head of the stairs and so had he. He called down into the dimness at the foot of the stairwell. "Patrick, I'm about to lift your scalp."

He thought he heard a shout of laughter amid the explosions sparking down the stairs. It didn't improve his temper. He started down but was forced to move slowly to keep behind the exploding firecrackers. "Did you consider the possibility you might have set the house on fire? Or that someone could have started shooting before they realized it was a tom-fool trick?"

"It wasn't Patrick's fault, Mr. Delaney." Elspeth moved out of the shadowed hallway to the foot of the stairs. She stood very straight, her eyes fixed on him as if mesmerized. "This was entirely my idea."

She could barely get the words past her dry throat. She had never seen a real live man naked, and Dominic Delaney was boldly and unashamedly naked. "I've come to ask you to reconsider."

The expression of stunned surprise on his face was superceded by a fierce look. "The hell you have." He started down the steps toward her, each word punctuated by the explosion of the firecrackers. "I don't like women who use their sex as a shield to invade a man's privacy and put him at a disadvantage. I don't like it one bit."

"You said you wouldn't see me. I had to do something to change the state of things."

In case you didn't hear me the first time, the answer is *no*." His blue-gray eyes glinted fiercely through the smoke. "But you knew it would be no, didn't you, Miss Elspeth MacGregor?"

"Yes, but it appeared to be the only way to get you to take my offer seriously."

"Dom, what's going on?" asked a lovely brown-haired woman clad in a blue lace peignoir from the top of the steps. Her gaze fell on Elspeth's prim, black-gowned figure at the bottom of the stairs. "Jesus, what's happened?"

"Nothing to concern you, Rina. Go on back to bed." Dominic Delaney's gaze never wavered from Elspeth. "I'll take care of this."

There were other faces peering over the banisters now, but Elspeth was scarcely aware of them. All her attention was focused on the naked man coming down the stairs toward her. She was exquisitely conscious of everything about him. The sleek ripple of the muscles of his thighs, the way his chest moved in and out with each breath. His strange eyes gazing at her with insolence and anger and something else.

The Delaneys, The Untamed Years:

GOLDEN FLAMES

by Kay Hooper

Victoria was waiting for him in the lobby of her hotel, and Falcon paused for a moment just inside the doors to gaze at her before she saw him. The black velvet cloak she wore hid a part of her gown from him, but he saw with a feeling of triumph that she had indeed worn red, as he'd asked her to do. The gown was obviously tulle, and the red was a deep, rich color which, along with the black cloak, set off her fair beauty strikingly. Her hair was up in an intricate style, made curiously fragile by a black satin ribbon woven in among the gleaming strands. She had fastened the cloak at her throat, which prevented him from seeing if the rubies dangling from her delicate ears were matched by a necklace, lending fire to her creamy breasts. Fortunately, his imagination where she was concerned was vivid.

He approached her on cat feet. "Beautiful. Just beautiful."

She looked up at him, startled by his silent approach, and a faint color swept up her cheeks. But there was something new in her eyes, something half shy and half excited, and he knew his seductive efforts had borne fruit. He offered his arm with a slight bow, and amusement rose in him when she accepted the arm, her sidelong glance showing a rueful appreciation of his gentlemanly manners.

The lady was no fool; plainly, she found his publicly donned courtesy quite definitely suspect.

"Why do I feel I'm being led into the lion's den?" she murmured as he guided her out to the waiting carriage.

Falcon laughed softly. "I can't imagine. Are you afraid of me, Victoria?"

She didn't answer until they were inside the closed carriage and moving. "Afraid of you?" She seemed to consider the matter, gazing at him in the shadowed interior. "I think it would be unwise of me to pretend you aren't a dangerous man."

"Not dangerous to you, surely," he said in a silky tone.

Her green eyes were serious. "Western men are a peculiar breed, a law unto themselves. Sometimes their gallant manners would make a European nobleman cringe in shame at his own lack, and at other times they're as rough and raw as the land that bred them. Dangerous to me? To any woman, I should think."

After a moment, he smiled. "I was born in Ireland."

"Were you? But you're a Western man nonetheless. A Texas Ranger, didn't you say?"

"Yes, for several years."

"And a Union soldier before that." Her tone was thoughtful. "And before that—a scout, perhaps? An Indian fighter?"

"Both," he confessed, oddly pleased by her perception.

"And the scar?"

He lifted a hand to finger the crescent mark on his cheekbone. "This? When I was a boy, my brothers and I often rode through Apache camps near our ranch, borrowing the Indian custom of counting coup."

"Trying to touch as many braves as possible? I've heard of it. Is that how you were hurt?"

He smiled. "In a way. My half-broke mustang took exception to a raid one night and threw me. I landed on a sharp stone. A battle scar, of sorts."

She smiled in return, thinking of a young boy cursing his temperamental mount.

"Did I tell you how beautiful you are?" he said suddenly, huskily.

Her smile faded slightly, leaving only the curve of delicate lips. "Yes. Yes, you did. Thank you."

Falcon reached out to touch her cheek gently, and then his hand dropped to toy with the fastening of her cloak. "Is this to keep out the cold? Or me?"

Her gloved fingers tightened around each other in her lap, and Victoria felt her breath grow short. "The dictates of fashion," she said finally.

He unfastened the cloak slowly, holding her eyes with his, very aware that her breath, like his, was shallow and quick. And some distant part of him marveled at these incredible feelings. She felt it too, this aching fire, and he was delighted by her swift response to him. "Fashion can go to hell," he muttered.

Victoria made no move to stop him, though she knew she should be ashamed of her wanton desire to have him see her, touch her, kiss her. What she felt was excitement.

He opened the cloak completely, pushing it back over her shoulders, and caught his breath at what he saw. The gown was cut low, baring her luscious breasts almost to the nipples, and against the creamy flesh a ruby necklace gleamed with dark fire. The lanterns hung outside the carriage sent a part of their light into the shadowed interior, playing over her exposed flesh with the loving glow of pale gold. Her breasts rose and fell quickly, each motion suggesting that the gown couldn't possibly hold the full mounds captive a moment longer.

"God, you're so beautiful," he said hoarsely, and his hands were on her bare shoulders, turning her toward him. He was inflamed even more by her instant, pliant response.

Victoria didn't even try to resist him. She had invited this, she realized dimly, invited this by agreeing to accompany him tonight, by wearing the provocative gown. And why couldn't she feel ashamed of that? Why did she feel only achingly, vibrantly alive and incredibly excited? Why did she want to feel his hands on her, his lips . . .

One of his hands slid down her back, finding the swell of her buttocks and pulling her as close as possible, even as his other arm surrounded her, crushing her upper body against him. He could feel the firm pillow of her bosom pressed to his chest, feel as well as hear her soft gasp, and an urgent sound escaped him just before his lips captured hers.

She was prepared for the shocking possession of his tongue this time—as well as she could be prepared for a sensation so devastating—and her body responded feverishly. Against his hard chest her breasts swelled and ached, and her arms slid up around his neck of their own volition. He was easing her back into the corner, and she could feel his arousal against her hip, bold and demanding.

When he released her lips at last she could only gasp, and her head fell back instinctively as he plundered the soft, vulnerable flesh of her throat. Her fingers twined in his thick, silky hair, and she wanted suddenly to remove her gloves so that she could feel his hair, his skin. And then his lips moved lower to brush hotly against her straining breasts, and she forgot everything except sheer pleasure.

"So sweet," he whispered thickly. Her low moan sorely tested his control. "Victoria . . ."

She had never known such pleasure existed, and the only coherent thought in her mind was the desire to feel more. She was hot, cold, shaking, her body a prisoner of the sensations sweeping over it with the relentless rhythm of an ocean's waves. The hot, wet caress of his tongue seared her skin, and his hand gently squeezed her breast until she thought she'd go out of her mind, until the stiffened nipple thrust free of confining silk and his mouth closed hotly around it.

All her senses were centered there, drawn by his pleasuring mouth, burning with a hunger she had never known. Something inside her, some dimly perceived barrier, melted in the heat of his caress, and she couldn't even find the breath to cry out her astonished delight.

She was hardly aware of his hand sliding down over her quivering belly, but a sudden touch at the vulnerable apex of her thighs jerked an instinctive, shocked protest from her lips. "No! Falcon, don't!"

"Shhh," he murmured against her skin, his hand rubbing gently through the layers of clothing while his mind vividly imagined the soft, damp warmth too much material hid from him. He wanted to draw her skirt up, find his way through the delicate feminine underthings until he could touch that heat, caress the womanly core of her. His entire body ached with the need to feel her naked and passionate against him. His tongue teased her nipple delicately with tiny, fiery, hungry licks. "Don't stop me, sweet. So sweet. You taste so good."

Victoria wanted to protest again, but the heat at her breast had sent a part of its fire lower, deeper into her body, and the hot clamoring inside her became a hollow, bittersweet need. "Falcon . . . you shouldn't . . . I can't . . ."

He lifted his head slowly, his darkened eyes intent on her flushed face. She looked thoroughly kissed, heartbreakingly beautiful in her innocent awareness. Her lips were red and swollen, her eyes sleepy with desire and dimly shocked. He slid his hand back up over her belly, cupping her breast gently and briefly before easing the silk upward until she was decently covered again. Then he surrounded her flushed face softly in one large hand and kissed her, vaguely surprised at the surge of tenderness he felt.

He brought them both upright, drawing the cloak back over her shoulders as she slowly lowered her arms, and fastening it again. And when she was sitting demurely, gazing at him with huge eyes, he leaned back into his own corner and sighed softly. "No one at the party will doubt that I want you," he murmured. "A man can never hide what a woman does to him."

Her eyes flicked downward to the straining evidence of his arousal, and then skittered hastily back to his face in confusion. Between the plantation of her childhood and Morgan's thriving ranch, she could hardly have avoided learning of the physical evidence of male sexuality, but his soft, bold reference to his body's response to her was both shocking and—in some part of herself she didn't want to acknowledge—exciting.

He chuckled softly. "Making love in a carriage is an awkward business," he offered. "If there had been a bed nearby, sweet, a loaded gun wouldn't have stopped me."

The Delaneys, The Untamed Years:

COPPER FIRE

by Fayrene Preston

Minutes later Brianne closed the door to her room, then leaned back against it. Across the room, Sloan sat. He was so still he might have been dead—except for his eyes. They were blazing with a fiery, golden life. She should say something, she mused, but for the life of her, she couldn't think of anything. So she waited.

"Did you get your gentleman friend settled?" he asked in a voice that was very low and quite calm.

"I don't know him well enough to call him a friend. And yes, he's in his room."

"No doubt in one of Mrs. Potter's finest."

"He's on this floor," she admitted, thinking that she had never known anyone who could manage to convey so much displeasure without using a trace of emotion in his voice. "But he's at the other end of the hall."

"I must confess, I'm surprised."

"Oh?" She pushed away from the door and walked to the edge of the bed. "At what?"

"That you can still manage to stand upright with the problems of so many people weighing on your shoulders."

"Henrietta and Phineas are no burden."

He came up out of his chair and was standing in front of her before she had a chance to blink. "You little fool! Don't you know the jeopardy you put yourself in by stopping to help a strange man?"

"I couldn't just pass him by!"

Gripping her shoulders, he spoke from between clenched teeth. "Not only should you have passed him by, you should have ridden so wide a circle around him, he wouldn't have even known you were in the area!"

She wrenched out of his hold. "I wasn't going to leave someone alone out there who needed help!"

"No, of course you wouldn't! That would have been the sensible thing to do, wouldn't it?"

"Sloan! I was raised to take care of myself. I can put a bullet in the center of an ace of spades at a hundred paces."

"But can you put a bullet in a man's heart?"

"If I have to."

"I don't believe you."

Swiftly, Brianne moved to where her gear was piled and jerked up her rifle. Pointing it straight at his heart, she asked, "Do you want me to prove it?"

He smiled, and his voice softened. "You wouldn't even get that rifle cocked, redhead."

She believed him, and tossed the rifle down. "Get out, Sloan."

"When I'm good and ready."

Brianne exploded. "I don't understand you!"

Sloan didn't understand himself either. And he didn't understand her. She was standing within arm's reach of him, her hair streaming in wild glory down her back, her skin giving off the sweetly seducing fragrance he had first smelled when he had seen her rising from her bath. Only a thin sash held her robe around her, and delicate satin ribbons closed her gown over her breasts.

Angry at her for putting herself in danger, and angry at himself for being angry, he reached for her.

She didn't come to him easily. She pushed against him, fighting with all her might. But his strength was the greater, and so was his need.

His mouth crushed down on hers, his powerful arms pulled her tightly against him. Reason wasn't entirely lost, but what was left was fogged by a pounding desire. He stripped off her robe, then fell with her onto the bed.

Brianne felt the impact of the mattress against her back and was furious. She didn't want to feel the weight of his leg as it lay over hers. She didn't want to experience the rub of his tongue against her own. She didn't want to feel his hand covering her breast. She didn't! She didn't!

Sloan's fingers grasped a ribboned bow and pulled. So easy. He untied another, and another, until he could lay the edges of the gown back, baring her breasts. He tore his mouth away from her lips so that he could see her, and what he saw nearly took his breath away. No woman could be so perfectly formed, he thought. It had to be an illusion.

Brianne raised her fist and hit against Sloan's chest, but the blow had all the force of a puff of wind. When had she become so weak? she wondered. When had she become so hot?

"Stop," she said, in a voice that sounded more like an entreaty than an order. "Please . . ."

Gazing into her emerald-green eyes, Sloan saw that they had softened. He liked that look. "I don't want to stop, Brianne." A soft breath escaped her lips, and he tried to capture it with his mouth. "Say please again," he whispered against her lips.

Desire was a new sensation to Brianne. How easy it would be to give in to it; heat was exploding everywhere in her. Yet she couldn't surrender. It wasn't in her makeup.

She tried to twist away, but with one strong arm he brought her back. She rolled her head, trying to escape his mouth. "Stop it, Sloan. Now!" Her words were whispered, but he heard.

He raised his head again to look at her, but he kept his hand on her breast, as if he had no intention of letting her go. "I want you, Brianne."

"But I don't want you!"

He smiled. "I can make you want me, and I won't even have to work at it." To prove his point, he caressed her slowly, teasingly. She moaned. "See?" he murmured.

Brianne looked up at him and was immediately confused. How could Sloan's face remain so hard, even while he was seducing her, *even while he was smiling?*

Then, as if a flash of light had suddenly sought out and revealed the darkest place in her mind, she remembered why his smile seemed so familiar to her. She had seen that same smile on the only living thing that had ever hurt her—a wolf. He had looked at her with pale gold eyes and a teeth-baring smile right before he sank his teeth into her arm, tearing at her flesh.

The memory gave her back her strength. In the space of two heartbeats she rolled off the bed, lunged for the rifle, aimed it right at his heart, and thumbed back the hammer. "This is a Model 1873 Winchester .44/40," she said, "and it is now cocked, with a bullet in the chamber and fifteen more behind it." A forceful and cool assurance filled her voice.

With her face flushed with anger, her gown gaping open and exposing heaving breasts tipped by rigid nipples, Sloan thought he had never seen a more beautiful woman in his life. God, but he wanted her!

"Mrs. Porter is going to be awfully upset if she finds blood splattered all over this room," he said calmly.

"I'll buy this damn hotel if it comes to that! Now, get up, Sloan, and get out of here."

He sat up, slid to the edge of the bed, and stood up. Slowly, he walked toward her, stopping only when the barrel of the rifle was touching his chest. "You're an interesting lady, redhead. You're wealthy enough to buy a hotel, you have guts enough to shoot me, and you're beautiful enough to make me want you like I've never wanted another woman. I'll leave for now, but I'll be back. We're not through, you and I. Not nearly."

OFFICIAL DELANEYS, THE UNTAMED YEARS
MISSISSIPPI QUEEN' RIVERBOAT CRUISE
SWEEPSTAKES RULES

1. NO PURCHASE NECESSARY. Enter by completing the Official Entry Form below (or print your name, address, date of birth and telephone number on a plain 3″ x 5″ card) and send to:

> Bantam Books
> Delaneys, THE UNTAMED YEARS Sweepstakes
> Dept. HBG
> 666 Fifth Avenue
> New York, NY 10103

2. One Grand Prize will be awarded. There will be no prize substitutions or cash equivalents permitted. Grand Prize is a 7-night riverboat cruise for two on the luxury steamboat, The Mississippi Queen. Double occupancy accommodations, meals and on-board entertainment included. Round trip airfare provided by Reliable Travel International, Inc. (Estimated retail value $5,500.00. Exact value depends on actual point of departure.)

3. All entries must be postmarked and received by Bantam Books no later than August 1, 1988. The winner, chosen by random drawing, will be announced and notified by November 30, 1988. Trip must be completed by December 31, 1989, and is subject to space availability determined by Delta Queen Steamboat Company, and airline space availability determined by Reliable Travel International. If the Grand Prize winner is under 21 years of age on August 1, 1988, he/she must be accompanied by a parent or guardian. Taxes on the prize are the sole responsibility of the winner. Odds of winning depend on the number of completed entries received. Enter as often as you wish, but each entry must be mailed separately. Bantam Books is not responsible for lost, misdirected or incomplete entries.

4. The sweepstakes is open to residents of the U.S. and Canada, except the Province of Quebec, and is void where prohibited by law. If the winner is a Canadian he/she will be required to correctly answer a skill question in order to receive the prize. All federal, state and local regulations apply. Employees of Reliable Travel International, The Delta Queen Steamboat Co., and Bantam, Doubleday, Dell Publishing Group, Inc., their subsidiary and affiliates, and their immediate ramilies are ineligible to enter.

5. The winner may be required to submit an Affidavit of Eligibility and Promotional Release supplied by Bantam Books. The winner's name and likeness may be used for publicity purposes without additional compensation.

6. For an extra copy of the Official Rules and Entry Form, send a self-addressed stamped envelope (Washington and Vermont Residents need not affix postage) by June 15, 1988 to:

> Bantam Books
> Delaneys, THE UNTAMED YEARS Sweepstakes
> Dept. HBG
> 666 Fifth Avenue
> New York, NY 10103

- -

OFFICIAL ENTRY FORM
DELANEYS, THE UNTAMED YEARS
MISSISSIPPI QUEEN' RIVERBOAT CRUISE SWEEPSTAKES

Name _____

Address _____

City _____ State _____ Zip Code _____

SW'10